T0171499

NO END OF
GUILTYCREATURES

Also by David P. Simmons, MD

The Sum of Her Parts

NO END OF GUILTY CREATURES

DAVID P. SIMMONS

iUniverse, Inc.
Bloomington

No End of Guilty Creatures

iUniverse books may be ordered through booksellers or by contacting:

iUniverse
1663 Liberty Drive
Bloomington, IN 47403
www.iuniverse.com
1-800-Authors (1-800-288-4677)

ISBN: 978-1-4620-0519-2 (sc)
ISBN: 978-1-4502-9677-9 (dj)
ISBN: 978-1-4502-9675-5 (ebook)

Library of Congress Control Number: 2011904973

Printed in the United States of America

iUniverse rev. date: 05/10/2011

. . . guilty creatures sitting at a play
Have by the very cunning of the scene
Been struck so to the soul, that presently
They have proclaim'd their malefactions;
For murder, though it have no tongue, will speak
With most miraculous organ.

—William Shakespeare

Hamlet, Act II, Scene 2

BENJAMIN BEACH

Wrapped in a heavy wool blanket and surrounded by light bird chatter, I tapped my feet in the sunbeams streaming onto the porch. Spring was busy chasing winter away, so Molly and I were cuddling in my rocker. An English setter, she was too big for my lap, but we loved the togetherness. Her solid frame and my beanpole build made us unlike in appearance. Father had always contended most people looked like their dogs, yet we were like nonidentical twins with matching personalities that made us soul mates.

My dear dog had started it all.

Her barking had broken the news.

Her alarm had propelled me up to the ledge.

Staring up at the tall barn on the flat rock, I could not stop thinking about what had happened there and the story I had to tell about it. When a turkey hen and her chicks started to parade across the back lawn, I tried to focus on the trail their feet swiped in the dew, but my gaze flew back up the hill. The damage to the barn was still there to be seen. The hole in its roof was a yawning mouth. The broken rafter stuck out like a tooth. The stack of shingles clung to one lip. I could not, of course, see the ladder, and the players had all disappeared.

I found Nate facedown on the ledge, skull exploded.

Blood around a lumpy yolk of brain.

Sunny side up on a hot stone skillet.

1

Tears from a rim of rainwater gathered along the eaves were now dropping and exploding on the granite below. The height of the barn always worried me.

Luke was crouching at the edge of the roof.

Dull eyes, black hair, ruddy cheeks.

A scrawny apple tree stood beside the barn. Years ago, as a little girl on a whim, I had packed a seedling into a fissure in that rocky surface, and it had survived.

Harley was lying against the trunk of the tree.

Bleary eyes, brown curls, yellow skin.

Father had built the barn on that stone up the hill because it was the only flat spot close to the house. That way he could keep an eye on us, as he had promised Mother he would.

Myles was standing at the crest of the hill.

Bright eyes, black bangs, ivory brow.

Suddenly an odor rising onto the porch betrayed the first of the day's invaders. A red fox smells a lot like a skunk, just not as overpowering. Nose to ground like a private detective, the villain was tracking the turkeys. The turkey father, who might have protected his family, was elsewhere, gobbling and strutting in front of another mate. Straining against my hand on her collar, Molly watched her hunting rival slink into the woods until her ears cocked to the noise of the next intruder. Slipping off my lap, she padded to the screen door and nosed her way into the house.

The clanging of the brass knocker on the front door jarred me out of my chair. As I limped toward the summons, Molly was growling at the sill, voicing our misgivings. Why had I agreed to this meeting? I owed it to Father. Despite our differences while he was alive, especially when the household was breaking down, I should honor his feelings for his heirs and do whatever it took to preserve the family.

The man standing outside the door had stood out in the courtroom. He had inspected me often, not to undress me, but to read my mind. When the judge had sequestered the jury the other day, I expected I had seen the last of him.

"The door is open." Although forced to receive, I did not have to invite.

An odd mass filled the doorway. Smaller than expected for his trunk, his head was an onion on top of an apple: baldpate and pale face above a chubby red neck.

His features were off-putting, and his glasses made matters worse. The bows pinched his temples like a vise, aggravating the frown squeezing the lenses down onto his nose. The black pupils inside steel rims threatened like a double-barreled shotgun. I would learn the lips below were cocked to shoot off first.

"I'm surprised the welcome mat's not out, for it's Benjamin B. Beach in the flesh."

As his giant belly barged into the hallway, I had to back away or get knocked over. The ghouls seated around this man in the courtroom had hidden his physical boldness. Never having seen him standing on his feet, I did not realize how short he was—surprising for someone who had made such a big impression on the folks in Concord.

"Well, sir, we do not get many visitors this far out of town. What can I do for you?"

"When I called yesterday, Mrs. Brewster, I told you why I was comin' out here. As soon as I heard the verdict, I knew what my next step had to be. You ought to be ready to get down to brass tacks."

"But the jury's decision settled everything."

"Not on your life! I expect to figure out who it was who really put your husband in his grave. You and I need to talk."

"About what? What happens next, and who goes where, I suppose."

"I shouldn't have to explain myself to you of all people, but I will. To begin with, your husband died when that ladder fell from the barn roof with him on it."

"As if you have to tell me how Nate died."

"And your brother-in-law and two nephews have just been tried for his murder."

"I will never understand how the coroner's hearing concluded it was anything but an accident. It forced a trial that turned into a fiasco of justice."

"Your husband squashin' his head on the ledge didn't happen by chance, and it certainly wasn't suicide. Murder charges were inevitable, but the trial result was unbelievable, so here I am, all ready to straighten everything out."

"What happened to Nate was not because of Harley, Myles, or Luke."

Four brutes.

Banging heads.

Locking horns.

Fighting to the finish.

"Well, we know your relatives were involved in a repair of the barn roof, but they were so vague and inconsistent in their stories, murder indictments were logical reactions."

"I do not care what the prosecution claimed. It was not a premeditated execution. That is ridiculous."

"Not at all. What's ridiculous is the fact that once those three took the stand, each changed his story and blamed another in circular fashion. It became a joke when no two of them fingered the same guy. There were three entirely different stories about why that ladder came down with your husband on it."

"The experts were unable to prove the ladder got where it did by means of a deliberate act. That supports my claim it was an accident."

"It's true it was hard to determine what happened. The defendants at first all agreed no one was near the ladder when it fell, but then they started singin' different songs. Yet the jury managed to put it all together and convicted one man."

"Well, I still contend he is innocent, just like the other two. It's a preposterous conclusion."

"You're entitled to your opinion, even if it happens to be wrong. I don't agree with either you or the jury. As far as I'm concerned, this thing's still a whodunit, which is why I'm here today. I plan to dope out who the guilty creature really is—with your help, of course."

"And just how, sir, do you suppose you are going to obtain that? Your manner is far from engaging."

"I'm not worried about that one bit. After we talk about your predicament, I'm sure you'll see the light and cooperate. We can work on this together at the same time the jury works on its next step. The jury determines the punishment for capital murder cases in the State of New Hampshire, don't you know?"

The *Granite State Times* had spelled out the trial sequence ahead of time. There was a lack of objectivity about the expected conclusion, but that was no surprise, particularly for a small-town newspaper with a highfalutin name.

"The first consideration, Mrs. Brewster, is the death penalty. Hangin' has been the required method of execution in this state since 1891, and if you do the math, it has stood the test of time for forty-four years."

Lips crimped together, pupils mere pinpoints, my tutor looked as obnoxious as he sounded.

"If, by some weird chance, the jury doesn't elect the death penalty, that means life imprisonment without parole. As for the other two defendants, the judge will surely reject that crazy prosecutor's last-minute attempt to retain them, too, so they'll go scot-free. At that point, it's my considered judgment your troubles are only gonna get worse."

"Granite Ledge Farm has withstood a lot so far. It is not about to collapse now."

"You're already short a pair of hands out here. What's more, when the others get back, you'll have an unpunished murderer to deal with. That's not likely to be a picnic."

"That is never going to happen, sir. Molly and I will be living here all by ourselves."

"All by yourselves? What on earth do you mean?"

"Not long after the three of them were arrested, I realized none of them would be returning to Granite Ledge."

"Hold on a minute! Since Harley and his two sons lived here with you and Nate for years, it's only logical they would return here, should the trial give them the chance. Even if you could have somehow predicted only one man would weigh out guilty on the scales of justice, how could you have predicted the other two would not come back?"

"The truth dawned on me just before the trial started. Whether or not a conviction happened down the road was going to be immaterial."

"What in the world are you talkin' about?"

"I understand you are a professional examiner, Mr. Beach, so you ought to be able to juggle a few facts. Although jailed together at first, the men ended up in separate facilities while they were awaiting trial. Harley in the State Prison Hospital. Luke in the State School for the Mentally Defective. Myles in the County Jail."

"Okay, you've put three balls into the air. Try to keep them up there."

"Although each facility had a primary function that made them seem different, all three men were imprisoned in similar ways."

"Yes, indeed, they were all safely under lock and key."

"Confined or not, the future for each was decided. It was obvious they were not coming back to Granite Ledge Farm."

"Don't keep me in the dark. Go on!"

"First of all, the doctors indicated Harley was going to die of his liver disease. It might be long and slow, but it was clearly too late for him. Convicted or not, it was not likely he would ever leave the hospital."

"Except in a coffin, if I catch your drift."

"It was going to be similar for Luke. If the jury convicted him, the law does not provide any exclusion for the mentally disabled, so it would punish him as you have outlined. If the jury acquitted him, the State School Board would punish him in a different way. Since there was no treatment for Luke's condition, the small-minded authorities were convinced he could not make it on the outside, so he would be stuck where he was for the rest of his life."

"Well, I'll be damned. Okay, Mrs. Brewster, when special problems for Harley and Luke were identified, I can see how you calculated those two would not make it back. Yet, how you could have read the cards the same way for Myles still escapes me. Clue me in on that one."

"I foresaw several possible paths for Myles. First, if acquitted, he would take off like a rocket to pursue his dreams."

"I can't buy it. He's still just a teenager, so he'd scoot right back home."

"As a total stranger, sir, you have no idea of the power of my nephew's imagination. I had known for a long time he would seize the first chance that came along to pursue his wanderlust. My husband's death was just the ticket."

"I still don't buy it."

"Trust me. Myles would go that way. In the other instance, that is, if the jury convicted him, there were three options: the gallows, the penitentiary, or mercy."

"There are no automatic exclusions for juvenile offenders. I won't blame you for forgettin' that."

"But I did not forget the Governor's right to grant clemency. The

Granite State Times spelled this out clearly before the trial. How could you not remember that?"

"Well, I surely remember the potshot that crummy rag took at me the other day."

"That I have not forgotten, either."

"Your revelations prove just how weird things were out here. Anyway, for the sake of our future discussion, I'll agree now they won't be comin' back." Unhappy about making this concession, Beach punctuated his admission by jabbing one index finger into my face.

Here we go again.

Another man trying to push me around.

Soon I would be leading him around by the nose.

Beach's hands were annoying. They were always in motion, making it impossible to tell if he was left or right-handed. As he talked, both hands skipped and jumped from point to point, from person to person. Neither their pudgy backs nor sausage fingers, bulging like his face and belly, impeded their insistence.

"Now, it's high time to get on to our business together, Mrs. Brewster. The whole thing boils down to clearin' up my personal doubts." The index finger flew back up beside his head.

"Your doubts?"

"Exactly. The claim gets paid only if I decide the facts warrant." The finger dove and poked his chest. "Like I told you over the phone, I represent the Veritable Insurance Company. My job as claims investigator is to determine what happened out here, and you better be sure it's all up to me."

With the finger rising again to menace, evasive action was in order. "I'm sorry. I forgot your name."

A huff and a fist brought a card to my eyes. "Here! So you won't brush me off again. Hearin' you testify in court, I didn't peg you as a scatterbrain."

The man was right, of course. Enough like him had taught me how remembering was critical to survival. Memory of things past prepared me for future attacks. By myself on the farm lately, I hoped my defenses had not rusted. Of course, I had Molly to talk to, but we rarely disagreed, so I got little practice.

The card he handed me, like his jacket and trousers, was rumpled and soiled. The embossed name indicated Benjamin B. Beach had an elevated view of himself.

"Be aware my investigation is independent of the court. The Veritable's a mutual company, therefore solely responsible to its policyholders. They're the owners, don't you know? Discovering an intention to deceive by anyone—dead or alive—would make me very uncomfortable and you very unfortunate."

We were standing uncomfortably in the hallway. Beach had not come out to ask a few questions and be on his way. Since he did not intend to be easy on me, I did not intend to make it easy for him.

"I suggest we move to the porch in the back, Mr. Beach. The day is heating up, so it will be cooler out there." I should have added fresher, for the man's presence was stifling. I also wanted to put the bulk of Father's harvest table between us.

We headed straight through the living room. Although the rest of us shunned it as dark and dank, Father had been fond of its period formality. Calling it the salon, he mentioned Mother only in this room—a tactic that suited me as well since I had shut her out a long time ago. At least this morning, the fragrance of baking bread wafting from the kitchen sweetened the funereal atmosphere.

Crossing the only carpet we had, leaving bedrooms to the left and kitchen to the right, we passed through the screened back door out onto the porch. A true farmer's porch, it ran the entire length of the house, even if Father had appended it, in another of his quirky moves, to the back, not the front. A view of our back forty—a glorification of a bit of grass ringed by flower beds inside a bowl of trees and rocks—was available from anywhere on the porch.

"We are very lucky, Mr. Beach, to have this fine porch."

"It seems too bright to me."

Sunlight blessed the porch most every day, at least those days the tricky northern New England climate allowed us the luxury of sunshine. In the late afternoon, however, the mountain rising up behind the barn robbed us of warmth as the sun declined behind it. Luckily, the mountain was not big enough to prevent pleasant lighting, which persisted until true sunset.

"The house is set so that the valley breezes fan the length of the porch."

Depending on the season, we sniffed the gentle aroma of opening blossoms, the pungent odor of spread manure, the heavy scent of fallen leaves, or the smarting nose of descending cold. No wonder we ate most of our meals outside.

"We can rely on the long sloping roof to shed rain and deflect heat. Black fly season and winter deep-freezes are the only absolute impediments to eating outside."

A large table occupied the northern end of the porch and was close to where a second door led into the kitchen. A wealth of dings, notches, and nicks proved the softness of our trademark eastern white pine.

"That is Father's beloved Windsor chair at the head of the table." The tall bow-back design facilitated scrutiny of his dwindling domain and, toward the end of his life, respiration by his failing lungs. At first a monument to my father's death, the chair became my husband's throne. Having already hijacked control of the household, Nate grabbed the chair right away.

"The shorter low-backs served the rest of us, but they are Windsors, too." Their bows were oak, the spindles hickory, the seats pine, and the legs maple—each native wood selected for a specific function. Shaped, whittled, smoothed, drilled, and assembled by hand, the combination had resisted a hundred or more years of use and abuse.

Before I could offer a seat, Beach imitated Nate and commandeered Father's former spot. Pitching a briefcase onto the table, he flopped down in a strength test the grand old chair had never faced before. I pulled back from the man to study the unknown before me, while Molly poked at his trousers to snuffle out the truth.

"I don't cotton to dumb animals. Their somewhat brighter owners take up all my time." Grumping out his absurd commentary, Beach brushed the dog away and nosed ahead himself. "Your husband's life insurance policy names the Granite Ledge Farm Trust as beneficiary. Seein' how rundown this place is, any monies should come in handy. Still, the payoff doesn't amount to a hill of beans—hardly enough to tempt anyone into murder, I would say."

The all-business agent plucked some items from his briefcase. With a speed indicating familiarity, he arranged a stack of papers and several folders on the table before him. "These little treasures represent my efforts to date in examining the circumstances of your husband's death. The gems I pick up from you will complete my collection. I feel very close to the end."

I sat down in the rocker beyond the other end of the table. My sister, Constance, and I had used this rocker in turn. She had nursed Myles in it, and when she died having Luke, I took it over to feed both boys their bottles. Right up to the triple arrest, I fled to it frequently to put some distance between the men and me. Now, Molly and I enjoyed a new sense of peace when we rocked in it together.

The rocker had a song of its own. A melody of creaks from the loose slats and wobbly arms rose above the bass line the solid rockers played on the floor. Only the tempo was under my control. Settling down in the comfort of its scorped seat and scooped back, I readied myself for Beach, and Molly fortified my position, springing onto my lap.

"First of all, we need to get a few things straight, Mrs. Brewster. Suicide, naturally—though it's really not natural—isn't covered. On the other hand, an accidental death kicks in the double indemnity clause, which makes your assertion very easy to understand. Murder is all well and good, but insurance fraud has to be eliminated, and wrongful death must be exposed."

Murder well and good?

Father, Constance, and Nate dead.

Harley, Myles, and Luke gone.

"What insurance gobbledygook! How can you think like that? You amaze me with your insinuations."

"They are far from insinuations, my dear woman, and I'll be happy to tell you why. Once I uncovered how everyone agreed on your husband's true character, I changed the focus of my concerns appropriately."

"But, my dear Mr. Beach, can you trust your sources?"

"Maybe not the townsfolk, maybe not the newspaper, and words under oath, of course, only sound like the truth. Nevertheless, when I add it all up together, even when I allow for some lies, Nathaniel Brewster comes out lookin' pretty bad. It's crystal clear to me you all had some damn good reasons to want get rid of him. Indeed, it's easy to see how money may have been the least concern."

As he trundled out presumptions, this claims investigator was not talking insurance at all. "And, to simplify my exploration of this little escapade, hereafter the dead man will be Nate, and the widow will be Mrs. B. I trust you won't find that too familiar."

"You may call my husband anything you like, but being impertinent does not entitle you to making disrespectful hypotheses about our family."

"You don't seem to understand. I've studied the case extensively."

"My goodness, man, do you think I have not studied it? I am convinced what happened was an unfortunate accident. It is as simple as that."

"But, Mrs. B, in the wars that went on out here for years, sooner or later, one push or pull was bound to take its toll."

"Life here was, by no means, as unhappy or contentious as the newspaper led everyone to believe. I thank my good neighbor, Cleveland Parsons, for dropping off his old copies of the *Granite State Times*—otherwise I would have stayed in the dark about what that tabloid was claiming."

Paper in the mailbox.

Cleve standing by.

Nate nowhere in sight.

Thank God for little things.

"For someone who gives the impression of a typical New Englander, that Parsons fellow seemed unusually attentive to his next-door neighbor. His attendance record at the trial was perfect. In any case, no matter how you learned about the things bein' said about the situation here on Granite Ledge, the whole town was in agreement on the subject."

"How could they know anything about us?"

"Perhaps they were just guesses—but I doubt it."

"They could not know much at all. Our men did not hang out in Concord."

"Still, the miserable critters that haunted this place were hot topics in town."

"We had to work long and hard to make this farm succeed. That is the only reason our men did not fraternize."

"A little hobnobbin' might've been a good thing for you all."

11

"Obviously, your misguided critics mistook the rarity of our forays into town as a sign of antisocial behavior."

"Pedantic psychological terms like that won't confuse me. To speak plainly, the scuttlebutt sounded like it was right on target."

I was proud of my psychological training, even interrupted as it was. Cutting my educational quest short and coming back to the farm did not mean I had dumped my riches on the roadside. Feeling competent to argue behavioral analysis with Beach, I was confident of my next premise. "Father would have delighted in seeing his descendants put the farm ahead of their own interests the way he had."

"Had your father lived to see this day, he wouldn't have drawn that conclusion—unless, of course, the newspaper was wholly inaccurate, and the court testimony was totally deceitful."

"Did you come here just to sully the reputations of some good men?"

"Whatever the case requires, who better than B. B. Beach to pan for gold—or dig for dirt. To be a successful insurance company, the Veritable has to ensure every detail." The smirk after the pun signaled more than a joke. He was boosting his ego, not benefiting his employer. "I'm just the man for the job."

"My husband is dead. That should be the end of the story."

Crumpled heap.

Wooden ladder.

Woven basket.

Shattered pot.

"I'm not sure I can bear retracing all this again." By pretending to sound helpless, I was tapping my supply of feminine wiles and stoking Beach's sense of masculine superiority. I was confident I could escape all of this snake's attacks, like a mongoose, with speed, agility, and timing. "However, in the hope it might lay this to bed once and for all, I am willing to field your questions."

Beach's first shot was a snap shot. "When did you learn about the policy on Nate?"

"Why, it was only after his death."

"But, as I recall from your testimony, it was before the trial. Isn't that right?"

"Yes. I found out the way everyone else did—when the newspaper reported it."

"A lot of water has gone under the bridge since your father took out the insurance. Hell, though it seems like that Roosevelt fellow was just elected, it's 1935 already. Are you sure you didn't hear about the policy earlier? If not from your father, from your husband?"

"I should not have to say it again. Only Father and Nate knew about the insurance. It could not have motivated any of the rest of us."

"You didn't answer my question, but there is truth in one thing you said. Because the insured always has to pass a physical to get coverage, your husband had to have known about the policy."

"For Nate that would have been like falling off a log."

"Or a roof? I can see Nate keepin' his mouth shut, but the fact that your father did not discuss the policy with you is another matter. I gather you two were pretty thick."

"Daughters and fathers are close by nature. Other men try to break them up."

His inflexible need.

My yielding love.

Neither a subject for discussion.

"Father never, ever breathed a word about insurance to me. Mother never had any. Neither did Constance. Why would anyone expect Nate to have it?"

"Seems weird to me your father didn't tell the person who stood to gain the most."

"I suppose you are referring to me. Since Father did not like us to worry about the future, I assume that is why he never told me."

"And your husband didn't tell you?"

"It was not Nate's style to discuss personal matters with any of us."

After the reading of Father's will, Nate had fumed about all the fuss and nonsense. He declared life after death took care of itself, so red tape was unnecessary. To challenge him for further family documents would only have provoked his wrath. Perhaps I should have looked deeper into the issues, but I was still learning about my husband when my father died.

That Nate's death required exploration was obvious. That the investigation generated a trial was inevitable. The authorities could not have done otherwise. But a minor insurance policy provoking a major inquiry by Beach was unexpected. There had to be more in his prying than simply doing his job.

"Now, Mr. Beach, it is my turn to ask you a question about your almighty policy. Since the only two family members who knew about it were dead, the newspaper's source had to have been you. Is that not correct?"

"I'm askin' the questions here. I determine if the benefit gets paid. Did I not make that clear?"

Perhaps for Beach, people lived to be insured, whereas I simply lived—insurance be damned. Denying that his policy was a carrot for somebody had brought out his whip. I held my tongue.

"Puttin' aside the question of when you learned about the policy, I'm curious to hear if you saw it as a gift from heaven or a ticket to hell?"

"You are quite assertive, sir." A word like "aggressive" would have been more precise. "Is that what the Veritable requires?"

A squawking crow passing overhead pointed the way off this hazardous path. "The wash was hung out long ago. So, please tell me now, Mr. Beach, what exactly do you want from me?"

"I plan but a simple, routine review." The leer confirmed the lie. "I've just a few questions."

"I pray I have the strength for another inquisition."

Ignoring the pastor's warning when he insisted that walking in the ways of the Lord included the aisles of the church, I had abandoned formal religion, although I had not stopped praying. However, since God seemed to have dropped Granite Ledge Farm from his list, I was used to not having my prayers answered.

"Like that pal of yours, Parsons, I was at the trial, too. If you didn't notice, I never missed a single minute." Not satisfied with touting his attendance record, Beach beat his drum some more. "I intend to win the Veritable's Best Agent award this year and expect this little investigation of mine will get it for me." No visible swelling accompanied these boasts.

"But how can you be sure some woman will not best you there, Mr. Beach?"

"There are no female agents in this industry, Mrs. B."

"Well there should be, and they would show you a thing or two, you can be sure."

It was getting hotter by the minute. Beach's white onion face was now apple red. Trickles of sweat looped from temple to cheek to chin. Stretched over his pot, his shirt was see-through wet. Loose within my blouse, I missed my cardigan. In fact, the temperature did not explain his heat or my chill.

"It's high time for me to brew some coffee." A conflict between us as opposites was unavoidable, but some procrastination would at least postpone the clash.

I ignored the halting hand and arresting stare. "It is really hot inside. The stove is like a furnace. You would be much better off waiting out here."

I nailed him to his seat and beat it for my kitchen.

Eleanor Rigby picks up the rice in the church where a wedding has been,
Lives in a dream.
Waits at the window, wearing the face that she keeps in a jar by the door.
Who is it for?

—John Lennon and Paul McCartney
"Eleanor Rigby"

PATIENCE BREWSTER

I felt safe in the kitchen. Always in apple-pie order, it was mine. The only completely feminine location on the farm, it was set up to satisfy my needs and fill the bellies of five men. In case its frilly curtains, lace doilies, and needlepoint cushions were not enough to keep the men out, I had decorated it with pinks, yellows, and violets as amorphous hex signs against males. With the exception of Myles, the men steered clear of my domain. Women's work, they said. The kitchen, therefore, was the one place where I could escape the discord.

After the death of my husband and incarceration of the others, I no longer felt trapped. Calm pervaded the farm. The sun and moon shone brighter. The snow stayed cleaner and whiter, right up to the time spring started nibbling it away to let green come bursting through.

But today, with Beach's arrival, tension had returned to Granite Ledge. This bulldog was going to scratch and dig in hope of unearthing relics to strip bare to the bone. In chasing his own ends, he threatened me. Yet, survival instincts aroused, I would be hard to catch. The red herrings that divert bloodhounds sniffing after foxes could sidetrack bulldogs, too. I could not collar and drag him, but I could surely lure him where he would beg to be let out.

And there was always Molly. Having figured things out in her usual way, she was standing guard in the kitchen doorway. Coat brushed to silk, sweeping tail a paradox in steadiness, Molly watched Beach. Untidy in his careless attire, rivet eyes unblinking, Beach watched Molly.

Leaving the two to stare each other down, I busied myself like a good hostess, drawing water, grinding beans, and perking the pot. Fixing a snack to go with the coffee bought me some extra time. Butter churned yesterday joined bread made today. The man would not reject food, and the dog would clean up the leftovers, if there were any.

Growing curious about the winner of the staring match, I checked through the kitchen window. Hunched over his command post, Beach was now focused on arranging his piles of ammunition. Molly still sat by the door, watching him.

To her disappointment, Molly had little chance to follow her primary instinct—birding. She loved to work coverts in front of a hunter and gun, but Father became winded, and my knees did not tolerate it. None of the others could be bothered. After all, as far as they were concerned, she was just a stupid dog. Proving to be smarter than they were, she focused her hunting passion on table droppings, a rewarding pursuit given how sloppy the men were when they ate.

Molly had enjoyed a lifetime of tidbits falling from table to floor right up to the time the men disappeared from the farm. I had routinely expanded her pleasure by tossing treats off the porch for her to track down. Whenever she wanted me to throw a treat, I required that she ask for it with a spoken request. Father objected to my teaching a dog to beg, especially to ask by barking out loud, but I insisted it was necessary training. While the men did not believe Molly understood a word, and my humming and singing songs to her doubled their criticism, I relished our conversations together.

When I came out the kitchen door, but well before I reached the table, Beach picked up from where I had cut him off. "We'll begin with the cast of characters."

Placing the tray, pewter not silver, down before him, I took up my rocker. The length of the table diminished the strength of his scowl. "Well, Mr. Beach, who interests you the most?"

Beach slathered a slice of bread with more butter than was imaginable. "I've worked the order out. At the time of the great happenin'—maybe better called the big horror—five of you were here on the farm." He stuffed his mouth with bread, the hunk bigger than the hole. "Since you're the oldest in this show, we'll begin with you, even if you are a woman." Cheeks, tongue, and teeth attacked the bread. "Later on we'll take up each man as he appeared on the stage."

"That suits me fine, but I can only tell you what I heard and the little I saw from this porch."

"Well, we won't start with the disaster. That would be skippin' ahead." He stood up, whether to sermonize or swallow, I was not sure. "Here's how I do things in my business. We begin with your early days here on the farm. You describe the years that led up to the grand finale. I pick out the details and, bingo, I explain the crime."

His chewing interrupted by his speaking, Beach recognized the time he had lost. Dropping back onto his behind, he resumed munching and gulping. At last, fingers and jaws still, he tilted the chair back on its rear legs. Father never would have allowed such a thing, but I was used to seeing it because Nate had done it all the time. Beach crossed his arms over his belly, difficult as that was, while his eyes divulged a different hunger. "I'm ready now. From the downbeat, if you will."

"Father bought this farm in the early 1900s." If you begin cautiously, you will not stumble or stub your toes. "I was too young to know the date—or care—but I think it was '01. This wonderful period farmhouse is testament to that."

"It's time for you to accept that we're well into the twentieth century. You really need to modernize out here, Mrs. B."

How I loved things past. The past, even the unpleasant and painful, defined everything. History was predetermined, precise, and therefore placid. There were no surprises—like Benjamin Beach. "Not long after Mother died, Father bought the farm."

"Morton Wimple was a big shot in Concord, accordin' to that Thomas guy who took his place as owner of the general store. Why would he have up and left the store, the town, and presumably his friends?"

"I would not trust whatever Ben Thomas may have told you if I were you. Father did not have a lot to say about why he left, even to me. When I was old enough to think for myself, I deduced he wanted to get away from unpleasant memories. Even dead and gone, Mother had great influence on him."

"But he shouldered an entirely new load."

"Father was a good listener. He paid attention to his customers, whether they were complaining about the losses of bad luck or celebrating the returns on hard work. Since so many of them were farmers, Father built up quite a mental notebook, making him confident he would be a success in farming."

"Wasn't it a little late in life to step into the unknown?"

"Father was resourceful. He figured he could learn what he did not know. He was challenged to make a go of things out here where others had failed."

"Determined, as in headstrong, or foolish, as in headless? Your father was an inexperienced old man hopin' to climb out of a rut, it seems to me."

"No, he was a liberated freethinker. After spending so much time jumping for customers, he wanted to be independent—'being his own boss' was his way of putting it."

"By breakin' his butt?"

Father crouched under our cow.

Powerful hands.

Purposeful pulls.

"You are missing the point. Father loved everything about his new life, including the hard physical work."

The milk let down.

White jets streaming.

Pound after pound in the pail.

"Milking our cow, for example. Father was uplifted by the simplest things."

"How charmin' that sounds. How'd he like bein' weighed down by two little kids?"

Constance did the chickens.

The pigs were mine.

The goats, horse, and cow we shared.

Let them out in the morning.

Led them in at night.

"We did everything we could. Daily chores and Bible lessons were the bricks and mortar of Father's house."

"What your father really needed was a big strong man."

"I was not too young to notice that most men did not stick with things the way Father did. I would now call them gutless." A glance at Beach underscored how gutless did not apply to him.

"It's plain your father made a huge mistake. Calamity was in the cards, saddled with girls as he was."

"Father was not saddled with his daughters at all. We grew up fast and learned quickly. Besides, there were not many distractions this far out of town."

"Imagine that! Weaklin's to do men's work." The deep breath inflating his chest did not make him look bigger or stronger. "Impossible!"

"Father usually found hired hands to help with the really heavy jobs. The problem was they did not last long."

"I imagine two ripenin' young maidens were good reasons to keep 'em on the move."

Constance short and soft.

Full breasts.

Wide hips.

Patience tall and thin.

Long trunk.

Gangly legs.

"People thought we were cute together. Growing up side by side—peas in a pod."

"And helpful hands nearby ready to do the shellin'?" I could just hear old man Thomas blabbing to Beach about that one, too.

"I kept those nasty men at a healthy distance." I looked down to smooth an embarrassingly ruffled skirt.

"I'll wager it was another kettle of fish with that sister of yours." My eyes locked onto his in quick recovery.

"Constance attracted men wherever she went. Even in church they would sit as close as they could. Near her black hair and big curves, they never heard the sermon."

"I hope they waited till after church to make their passes."

The hired hands liked her jokes better than mine.

The bumping and nudging never stopped.

"Father would have beaten anyone he caught fooling around."

"If he caught 'em. I suppose your father expected to kick 'em off the farm before things happened."

The barn door barred escape.
One filthy hand sealed my lips.
Deep hay smothered my moans.
Goat breath fouled my face.
Crushed by his weight.
Split apart.

"Nothing happened! I am confident my sister was chaste right up to her wedding night. You are barking up the wrong tree."

Intimidated by the vestal virgin image, Beach got busy searching his pockets. A tobacco pouch and a handful of matches turned up from one. A tamp and a pipe with a Sherlock Holmes stem showed up from another. Watson would have been my preferred companion. Beach filled and packed the bowl and, after scratching several bull's-eye tip matches on the table leg, he set to puffing like a locomotive, snowing his face in smoke. All this occurred, of course, without asking for permission.

But I liked the hazy shield building up between us, and one whiff of it stirred a rush of bittersweet memories. "My father and I used to sit right here after lunch. That is when he had his first smoke of the day."

Despite chores half done, Father sat tight and sucked his pipe. When he did go back to work, so did the pipe, clamped in his teeth and removed only to dump, fill, and relight. Ever-conscientious Doctor Otis, bless his soul, tried long and hard to interrupt the habit that chased Father to his bed every night and to his grave in the end.

"The other men, who did not smoke, went back to work straight away, but I loved to dawdle and exercise my brain with Father. Listening, discussing, and debating were manna for me."

"Frankly, that sounds like a big bore."

"Those sessions never lasted long enough for me. Just one bowlful and Father shouldered his yoke."

Sometimes, exploring the perplexing world around us, Father confessed his worries to me. Expressing his distress as he watched his family crumble around him helped him cope. For fear of increasing his personal guilt, I did not confirm or deny his concerns. If his openness was also an effort to spare me a similar fate, I was never sure.

Those talks also showcased Father's powers. Despite a small-town background and lack of formal education, he had learned to observe conduct and judge character. In addition, his reading late into the night strengthened his insight into human nature. However, his heart was too soft and his gut too weak for corrective confrontation, which allowed the problem with Nate to escalate.

"After Father died, I was fortunate to have the Concord Municipal Library to stimulate my gray matter, and it was not long before Myles became my sounding board."

"All this intellectual stuff sounds very inspirational. Sort of like a religion for you, it seems."

Religion took Father on the long buggy ride to church every Sunday. As a matter of his faith, the behavior of those he called God's creatures concerned him. As a matter of his heart, the misbehavior of those he considered his responsibilities consumed him. In the later years of our life together on Granite Ledge, as my excuses for not going to church piled up, Father rationalized that God found it more Christian for me to stay at home and keep an eye on the boys.

"I did not leave the farm very much, Mr. Beach. That is something you might understand if you gave this spot a chance. Look at the beauty. Feel the quiet." Lush green stretched out at our feet. "Whenever he could, Father would sit in that same chair and survey his land." The first sensation off the steps was a forgiving softness underfoot. "The back lawn represented work and leisure united. It became his pride and joy. As he was dying, Father entrusted the care of this patch of grass to me." What seemed shallow expressed a deep fertility. "We owe our soil to the river. In the beginning, however long ago, after the glacier carved this valley out, it left a great river to heap sediment high up along its sides. There is only a narrow remnant now, which you cannot see from here, but it does its best to rejuvenate the land along the bottom of the valley."

"This poetic talk bores me. We need to get down to business."

"Bear with me. I am trying to give you a sense of what made this farm and its inhabitants tick. You can hear the river working. We could walk down there and listen to it."

"You can save that for later. I'm a material sort of a guy. I'm more interested in concrete than chatter."

"Well, you could also watch some civil engineers at work. The beavers have deployed a dam this year that is flooding a large part of the lowlands."

Father and I treasured our chance to witness such ingenuity and diligence, whereas the others cursed their leaky boots and wet socks. Studying how the water's flux renewed the land, Father learned to utilize the terrain. Sometimes it was ideal for crops. Other times it was perfect for grazing. Fusing his days of shopkeeper's banter with his nights of private reading, he developed a scheme of crop rotation. This year's cornfield became our Holstein's pasture in a later year.

"No, we've got our own work to do right here on this porch."

"Well, at least take a look at the mountain. In many ways, it determines our life. It is always watching over us."

Mountain was a generous term for the steep palisade of spiky conifers that happened to have the profile of a mountain. Most New Englanders expect exaggeration like this from the rest of the country, but tolerate it poorly among themselves. I did not question this exception out loud for fear of hurting Father's feelings, but I did learn to respect the dominant, if not lofty, position of the landmass in our lives.

"Because of the mountain's height, it controls our sunlight and, therefore, our subsistence. Each day, in the early afternoon, the sun passes behind the mountain, so its stern shadow brings growth to a halt. At that point, its face frowns in dreary black—hence its name, Black Mountain."

"More lousy poetry."

"But I am talking about a concrete effect, which is exactly what you said you were looking for. It tells you a lot about our personalities and our lives."

As the slopes from the riverbank climbed toward the mountain, more and more rocky outcroppings appeared. Up behind the farmhouse was the particularly large, flat protrusion of pure granite where the barn stood. I reflected upon how that ledge had triggered the name of our farm, for it symbolized stone's impediment to farming. Even though Father's blue barn star preached hope, the barn bespoke futility. The barn would tumble down soon—like Nate—but the rock would persist for ages.

"Hello, Mrs. B. I didn't come out here to sit and watch you daydream." As if threatened by natural surroundings, Beach retreated to business

23

matters. "Several people told me you left the family hearth as a very young woman. I understand you caught everybody by surprise when you did that, which means I better hear your version."

"Mercy me, you have that all wrong. I do not think anyone was surprised. Folks assumed someday I would take advantage of my mental powers."

"Are you claimin' your departure was carefully planned—and purely voluntary?" His snicker sent shivers.

"Of course, it was. Although I did everything expected of a woman on a farm, I kept on dreaming about an education and life for myself."

"So you took off for some fancy school?"

The Boston train was crowded and hot.

The cold snap explained my sweater.

Woolly shroud over growing tummy.

"It was not to go to school. I was on my way to college."

"Big deal! Aspirations and all, you left your family flat."

"The truth is I pestered Father nonstop. By the time he consented to my going, the fall semester was fast approaching, and I needed time to get settled."

"The postmaster told me you hightailed it out of here for more than a fling in college. Sounded like you were headin' for the school of hard knocks."

Bloody bedding.

Dead debris.

Whirling room.

Weak and helpless.

You'll live.

Barked the ogress in white.

"Oh, I know all about that gossip." Since Beach had been probing in the general store and post office, I wondered where else he had gone prospecting. "My childless marriage should have convinced them they were wrong."

"Well, you can understand their skepticism, can't you, when you rushed off well before the college opened?"

"I suspect your sources never went to college. I had to show sufficient aptitude before being accepted. The critics still called Radcliffe the Harvard

Annex. Forced to prove its role in educating women, the college did not just take any old body that walked by on the street."

"Well, I'm still not convinced that's why you took your body down there so early. By the way, did you know my office is in Harvard Square? My observations tell me Radcliffe doesn't pay much attention to the bodies of the women they enroll."

"I have given you my explanation for when I left. If you have only snide remarks to make, you would be best to pack up and leave."

"Okay. Okay. If you weren't compelled to leave, I'd like to hear more details about why you chose to go."

Sitting beside the Charles.

Rowers sweeping by.

Rowing for the sake of rowing.

Whether racing or not.

"I was puzzling why I was put on this earth. I wanted to prove myself."

Learning was the same for me.

The library my river.

Pleasure always there.

Reading my reward.

"Once I put a purpose to life, I knew I could be more than a bluestocking—not a *bas bleu* but a complete woman. But you cannot understand any of this, can you, Mr. Beach?"

"If you spoke American, maybe I could."

"A precise vocabulary is more than speaking clearly. It is a harbinger of one's intelligence and the banner of one's education."

With that, the cock commenced to crow. "I suppose next you'll applaud how you ladies got the right to vote. Well, I got some things to be proud of, too. For example, I've always lived in Boston—the Hub of the Universe. Remember? Oliver Wendell Holmes?"

The would-be sophisticate leaped up and strutted along the porch like a peacock. How vanity distorts and deceives.

"If you paid attention to what I am telling you, Mr. Beach, instead of believing what appeals to you, you would realize I did not travel down to the city for a short run of drink and debauchery. I went there for the long haul—to study art and literature, philosophy and psychology."

"Sounds pretty dull to me."

"It was glorious. The knowledge of the classroom professionals. The wisdom of the street poets. All of it rubbing off on me and polishing my intellect."

"We're way off track. I'd like to hear about why you deserted your favorite study hole, the Boston Public Library."

How could Beach know I had used the library across the Charles? He must have gone and badgered the town librarian. Mabel Perkins was the only one in Concord who knew that fact. Perhaps Beach deserved more credit as a sleuth than my first impression allowed.

"I liked Fenway Park, too, which you may already know, but you are quite right about the library. That deep well of knowledge was my favorite watering hole. I researched my paper on the emerging role of women artists in Paris right there in its stacks."

Underwhelmed by my literary endeavor, Beach waxed scientific. "For a new version of old architecture, the library's not too bad. I noticed that when I went there to look up how they erected the Eiffel Tower. Iron sure beats stone. More resistance to collapse and a much smaller footprint. Way more space, air, and light." Sophistication deteriorated into scoff. "Which is all I care to know about the City of Light."

This was not, however, the dead end it seemed to be. The longer we talked, the clearer it was my opponent was not simply an oaf stumbling along the road. He was heading in a certain direction with the navigational skills to get there. I had to be careful.

"Tell me, when you left—voluntarily, of course—were you aware your father was ill?"

Father's lips grabbing for air.
Tongue no longer dancing.
Holding air a little longer.
Weighing life on a new scale.
Rest or die.

"Not really. When I chose to go forward, I did not appreciate how much Father was slipping back. Mother had made him gun-shy, so he was good at covering up and keeping things to himself."

Father sent me alone to the station.
Carrying things was a struggle.

He wanted to hide his gasping.

"Still, I should not have missed what was happening to him. I'm afraid I was caught up in my own good fortune."

"Bein' forthcomin' like this is what I like to hear from you. Keep it up! Tell me, did both of his lovin' daughters miss the signs?"

"We were blossoming together, I am sorry to say, as Father withered on the vine by himself."

"But, once you did find out, you sacrificed your hopes and dreams, which you didn't have to do. You chose to come back to this dismal place and nurse your father."

My mind said no.

My heart said go.

I brought the books I could carry.

"I did not make a choice to come back to help Father. I wanted to do it. I put my studies aside willingly. That was not hard to do."

Dusty tables were manuscripts.

The farmhouse floor my canvas.

Twisted straw my brush.

Songbird music.

Tree frog counterpoint.

"Although I admit, right up to Father's death, I was a bit of a Pollyanna." Puzzled by a sound close to her name, Molly perked up one ear.

"Was your time within those girlish cloisters all that profitable?"

"I was not out for profit."

"It seems to me your life was like fryin' pan to fire. Locked up in a girl's dormitory or stranded on a lonely farm—it's all one and the same."

"My return to the farm was not a sentence of life imprisonment."

"Tell that to the convicted man, Mrs. B." Beach kept on trying to be funny, but he was the only one who laughed at his jokes. "What was your father's condition when you got back?"

"He tried very hard to hide how badly off he was. He would not have fooled Mother—she never missed a thing—and, after all, I am my mother's daughter."

As I grew older, I began to understand how Mother had influenced me, even in the short time we had together. I say understand rather than appreciate, for I believe I had picked up more bad than good from her.

Father's influence had been more positive, but I was not sure if that was because I had lived longer with him or he was a better person.

"Did your sister, who was still back on the farm, inform you of the changin' situation?"

"Constance never wrote. Even though we were close by birth date, it was no secret we drifted apart as we grew up."

"Did the green-eyed monster move in between you?" Maybe the subtle green cast to my eyes had elicited another cliché, but this gibe suggested Murphy's Bar in downtown Concord as another place where Beach had ferreted out information.

"I know people claimed I lorded it over my sister, but that was not accurate. If there was any rift between us, it was genetic in nature."

"Could you explain that one to me?"

"All the time Constance was healthy, she exulted in farm work. She was primitive. She loved to get hot and sweaty."

"Down-to-earth, so to speak?"

"More like born to work with her body. I was fated to achieve with my mind."

"And she certainly followed her destiny, as you did yours."

"Constance was a plain soul. She did not have lofty ambitions."

"But she went places with her beautiful body, I've been led to believe." That would have been from Murphy's again.

"I do not pretend to know what went on while I was away. How can you?"

"After you got back, you both pulled together when you saw the plight of your father, I imagine."

She dropped Father like a stone.

Her blind eyes and deaf ears.

She was gone.

"Constance was as concerned as I was."

I wrapped Father in the knitted baby blanket.

Mother had a pet way to describe it.

The only baby project she completed without him.

"But we approached the problem differently."

"Yet there was an equal commitment to supportin' your father, wasn't there?"

Dreadful climb to the barn.

Frozen fingers.

Swollen udders waiting.

"I took over as many chores as I could."

Constance lying in bed.

Warm fingers.

Caressing erect nipples.

"Constance did other things, but we teamed up as best we could. Not too long after I got back, all my swans turned to geese, and I swallowed any resentment I might have had. More and more, I devoted myself to preserving Father's life and, if I could not accomplish that, his farm."

"Why did he let the farm slide the way he did? It shouldn't have been hard for him to get help. In an economically run-down community like this one, I should think an able-bodied person would've jumped at the job when he saw it."

"For you to presume an able-bodied person must be masculine offends me." Hopping off my lap, Molly proved my point by searching the floor for crumbs. Because she was collecting everything, the male cardinal on the rail was forced to watch.

"According to Father's letters before I came back, he did find plenty of workers. Yet their names changed so frequently it seemed as if he had installed one of those newfangled revolving doors."

"As a country girl, you assume the revolvin' door is new. It was at the end of the last century when the inventor figured out there was a vacuum effect in tall buildin's that made it hard to open a regular door. His invention not only solved the problem, it saved heat, too." Beach did know more about some things than I did, but did he know the things that counted?

"But to get back to the subject, from what I've heard, it sounds like your father was driving the servants away."

"There were no servants here—until after Father's death."

"Okay, let's say his hired hands. I suspect it related to Constance."

"Father was a perfectionist. I imagine the workers tired of that and left of their own free will."

"I know your father was tough on the help. Was he as demandin' of you girls?"

Heavy spring rains.

Blistering summer sun.

Fierce autumn winds.

Deep winter snow.

Delayed chores brought quick complaints.

No cause for late starts.

Early finishes the worst.

"Not at all, Father was a gentle man."

"That's not what they say in town."

"Sometimes, when the chips were down, he did talk tough—but it was all talk."

Now, Father was late.

Now, he quit early.

I forgave him my sleepless nights.

I was confident and no longer afraid.

"All my life, right up to his death, a strong attachment pulled us together."

"I seem to get mixed signals on that subject."

"Well, it is the sort of thing we did not talk about."

"Which was it? The unconscious and forgivin' love of a daughter for a father—or the conscious and uncompromisin' need of a father for a daughter's love?" I could not muster an answer and would not stoop to a reprimand.

Beach was devouring the bread but avoiding the heels. That would have angered Nate, had he been there. "The subject of love reminds me of your husband." Was Beach a mind reader or just plain lucky? "It's time to move on and learn more about the ruler of the roost. As I understand it, as soon as Nate arrived, he started to take over, so that's who I want to hear about next."

Black raven.

Hungry eyes.

Probing beak.

Quick talons.

Without excuse or explanation, I scooped up some scraps and hightailed it to the kitchen.

The creature's at his dirty work again.

—Alexander Pope
Epistle to Dr. Arbuthnot

NATHANIEL BREWSTER

As I stepped back onto the porch, Beach moved across to its edge. The waving of his hands flushed several black-capped chickadees from the rail, and the stomping of his feet scared some gray squirrels from the stairs. A red squirrel complained and held fast. Molly kept on sniffing around, searching for a fallen treat, most likely her favorite, a gob of butter. The sun was burning the porch roof off by now. The backyard was immersed in the paradox of taking a sunbath. It was a bath of sorts: the sunlight's brilliance did wash the green out of the grass. Fortunately, a breeze flowed across the porch and cut through the heat trapped overhead.

Poking his pipe stem over the rail, Beach resumed the grilling. "Where's that alley go?"

"You mean the path leading out past the sugar bush?"

"I don't see any damn bush."

"Sugar bush refers to that grove of trees over there. Those maples bless us with fine sap every year."

"I don't care a bit about sap, sugar maples, or sugar plum fairies, for that matter. Where does the damn path go?"

The footpath that twisted down the hill from the barn hugged the back of the lawn and disappeared into the woods to our right. Running between the legs of this stand, it passed by the shed and ended at the outhouse. Noticeable from the porch, the shed's nearest corner was red and angular, slicing like a bloody hatchet between the tree trunks. Blankets of moss coated the north face of every tree. Colonies of mushrooms and ferns cropped up along the woodland floor. These signs of dampness made the shaded grove gloomier.

"That red swath you can just make out through the trees is the handy little storage box Father put up."

"That's where the cursed ladder came from, isn't it? I can hardly wait to see it." Licking his lips, Beach tasted the future.

When climbing up to the barn started to take Father's breath away, he had roughed out a place down off the ledge to store items used in the fields. His intention was to finish this shed as a structure to be proud of, but he died too soon. When my husband took over, he decided any further work on it was a waste of time, effort, and money. We ended up with a lasting ambiguity: a memorial to Father and a reminder of Nate.

"A little ways down the path from the shed you will find the privy, Mr. Beach."

"Oh, yes, the safe haven for your nephew, Myles. I'm anxious to see it, too."

"You will find it is just a one-holer and really quite modest."

The outhouse was not visible from the porch. It stood deeper in the woods, hidden within a cluster of striped maples, the hardy survivors of a battle with their cousins. The red maples had driven them out of the valley by drinking up most of the water, and the sugar maples had pushed them together on the hillside by stealing most of the light. There, fueled by man's modesty, these lesser maples were thriving.

"What is it about outhouses that interests city folk like you so much?"

"It's not the novelty of the thing, I can tell you. It's how it helped one of the accused men get off the barn roof. I guess whistlin' 'Dixie' all alone in that place was better than hearin' the tirades of a slave driver like Nate."

"You are making a mountain out of a molehill."

"Who knows? Maybe I'll turn it into a gold mine." His laughter fell like lead at my feet. "Too bad I couldn't have come out here with the jury to inspect the crime scene. I had no official role then, but now I've got my chance." I waited for the lip smacking. "No time like the present to study the layout. Think I'll have a look around."

As Beach shot off the porch, a cannonball headed for the target in the woods, I went for the stack of papers on the table.

Brushing crumbs away—a trick I learned from watching Mother keep an eye on Father's tallies—my hand sent the top pages flying. In restoring order to the pile, it was impossible not to sample its contents. The first page introduced the question and predicted its conclusion.

Policy Number: VIC 47928

Insured: Brewster, Nathaniel

In the course of my independent investigation on behalf of the Veritable Insurance Company, I have uncovered many irregularities and identified numerous inconsistencies regarding the circumstances surrounding the demise of the insured. The accompanying folders provide recorded details, including background studies, assorted interviews, character portraits, and testimony analyses. My summation of these observations renders the decision of the Court arguable and, hence, unresolved. As soon as I have finalized this examination, shouldering a collective obligation to my self, employer, society, and justice, I will submit a formal appeal to the court by means of a duly sworn affidavit.

Benjamin B. Beach

Claims Investigator

What I learned skimming a few more pages forced me to sit down. The air was still. The heat was choking. A mockingbird laughed.

These papers were not standard insurance reports at all, not by any stretch of the imagination. This pseudo-insurance man's minor assignment had turned into a major crusade. He had pushed his inquiries outside the mainstream. Having identified some errors and catalogued some problems, he was now anticipating a significant conclusion. I felt a private need to block a public revelation.

Whatever else the archivist's papers might reveal, there was bad news and good news. The bad news was that he had recorded his suspicions in print, and if he reached the right end point, there would be trouble. The good news was that he had not finished his analysis, so if I could lead him astray, there would be no problem. In short, Brewster must sidetrack Beach.

Heavy feet on the porch steps jolted me from concern to composure. "I changed my mind, Mrs. B. I feel I need better handles on the suspects before I case the scene."

"I am sorry, but I seem to have disturbed your papers a bit while cleaning up. Might you be interested in something more to eat before pushing ahead?"

While the body dropping onto his seat at the table said yes, the fingers realigning the papers before him said no. "I'm okay for now. There's lots more to learn, and they say the mind doesn't work well on a full stomach." If so, his paunch had been hampering his brain for years. "We've covered the lead actress. Now it's time for the star of the show."

"Where should I begin?"

"That's easy. How did you two happen to meet?"

Farm animals and wildlife were what I had to talk to.

The rooster's answer was always the same.

The blue jays scolded from a distance.

The cow just chewed.

The rabbits simply froze.

"Although I loved everything around me here, Granite Ledge did not give me enough human interaction and, as I explained earlier, I preferred to use my head rather than my hands. The Congregational Church in Concord provided the solution."

"I can tell this is gonna be unbelievable."

"What you need to understand is I could not survive talking to Father alone. Granted, when we lived in town, I had Mother, too—even if most of what I got from her was criticism. Since Constance and I were like chalk and cheese from the beginning, she was useless. I needed other ears to listen and mouths to respond."

"So you dove into the lair of Bible-wavin' fanatics?"

"We went to church as a family as far back as I can remember. Even after we moved out here, we went in every Sunday. When I came back to the farm from college, I tried to make as many other church functions as I could. There were real people there to talk with, don't you see? I met Nate at one of the socials."

"And your initial impression?"

Tall man in the doorway.

Commotion around.

Clamor within.

"Well, one day I noticed a new fellow moving from group to group. I realize now Nate was studying his options."

"An explorer inspectin' the natives?"

"If you must have a comparison, he was more like a cock in a chicken coop."

"Touché, Mrs. B, touché."

"And I will admit I started clucking right along with the other hens."

"Oh, we are havin' fun, aren't we?" Dueling with Beach would be rewarding. Why not let beating him evolve?

"The women were bemoaning how the run of bad weather had kept the men indoors and underfoot. We were agreeing on the way they disrupted our routines when Nate came up to our little clutch."

"Dominating the flock is what roosters do." My penchant for attaching significance to animals and their actions set me to wondering where Beach had learned this fact. Watching performing roosters at the circus seemed most likely.

"The mood of the group switched from complaint to welcome. Nate had a word for each of us, but I sensed he was singling me out."

"Probably all you girls felt the same way."

Glances at them.

Examination for me.

Naked before him.

Made me warm inside.

"It took some time to warm up to him, stranger and all. He was downright forward, and I was not used to that kind of behavior. Anyway, the others drifted away, leaving us to ourselves."

"What'd you have to say to each other?"

"A few days earlier, when I came into town on errands, I had got wind of the new arrival. I never expected him to show up at church and pick me to talk to, but I was eager to learn where he had lived."

"Why would you care where he came from?"

"You misunderstand. I was not interested in where he came from. I wanted to hear about where he had been—to breathe some fresh air, if you will."

"The way you keep splittin' hairs gives me a pain. I'm more interested in what he was up to."

"In a word, Nate seemed worldly. Although he grew up in Vermont, over in nearby Brattleboro, he left there to go and live in Boston. Why, he had even traveled to New York and Philadelphia."

"A noble pioneer—or a travelin' salesman?"

"We had a lot of places to talk about. Far, far away from Concord, New Hampshire."

"You sound like you discovered Mister Right." The preposition as a conjunction I did not question, and the carping I ignored. Molly gave up on Beach, too. The floor was clean around him, so she lay down at my feet.

It made sense to explain why I had married Nathaniel Brewster. Beach could only have had misconceptions after reading the *Granite State Times* where many had volunteered opinions they had formed on the subject long before Nate died. No wonder he had boasted we were better off without outside influences and cancelled our subscription as soon as Father died.

Still, Nate insisted I check every day for mail in our box way down on the common valley road. At least, with any luck, that meant I might meet up with Cleve checking his box on the stand all the farms shared. Nate would not be able to complain about those contacts because he would be unlikely to discover us.

"I have to admit Nate charmed me off my feet." No man had done that before, but there were not many attempts. Despite what I had witnessed going on around my sister in Concord and many women in Cambridge, I was an easy mark.

"The marriage certificate on file in the Merrimack County archives documents the conquest." I might have felt better if I had an explanation for why I was so vulnerable or an excuse for why I capitulated. At least I drew consolation from my early recognition of how I had been deceived.

"Tell me, Mrs. B, were you lookin' for a man to make things right for you? Or were you the victim of a man lookin' for the right thing for himself?"

"Since the hired hand approach had not been satisfactory, perhaps I was unconsciously looking for some help for Father."

"And you grabbed the first stick that came floatin' down the river."

"I admit Nate's energy, élan, and experience ignited me. Yet you insult me by implying I was out to snare a husband."

"Well, I can see the situation like the nose on your face. You were what's commonly called a sittin' duck."

"And I suppose by that comment you mean to equate my husband with a fox."

Beach's insights abraded me, but my skin was thick. Penetration would require more than guesswork, but as he was probing deeper, I needed to be on guard. In order to deal with his intention to reexamine the guilt or innocence of the convicted and uncover an alternative or two among the exculpated, I analyzed his method.

Did Beach plan to utilize my eyes, ears, and brain to fill the voids he could not close himself? Is that why he had started by prying into my psyche? Was he, in fact, investigating me as well? Did he have a dream of somehow incriminating me?

I would tell my interrogator what I heard and saw, but he would have to interpret the data without my help. How to decipher it was his problem, not mine. "Nate came. He saw. He conquered. What more can I tell you?"

"It seems to me you did it backward in your marriage. It's supposed to be eyes open before, half shut after."

"If you keep on being so rude, I will have to terminate this interview."

Beach did not even blink before threatening me in return. "You better watch your own step." His attacks were exactly like Nate's: they were just part of the masculine routine and more bravado than bravery.

"Like any girl tryin' to make it all alone in a man's world, you've become oversensitive, my dear, and your reaction is understandable. While I don't want to annoy or offend you, I'm sorry but I must get to the facts." Beach was only pretending an apology. "By now you must realize I need the straight facts. For instance, exactly how did your husband hook you?"

"Nate had a certain savvy, which appealed to me, at first. For example, he could extract information from others, roll it up, and store it away. Later he would reintroduce it, restored and rewoven for his own gain."

"And no one would know the difference?"

"An aura of originality prevented recognizing one's own material."

"Sounds like a con man to me."

"More like a chameleon with its ability to change color. Nate could become whatever the situation required."

"I can buy into that. Judgin' from what I've heard, he was not, at all, what he appeared to be."

"Nate fooled a lot of people. He carried me away from the farm. I liked that. I needed that."

"All this by a small-town boy? What exactly had his early life been like?"

He talked sometimes.

Years of churning hunger.

Cold in the holes of his clothes.

"His parents fed and clothed five children. His father worked in the lumber mill. His mother was kitchen maid and dishwasher at the local inn."

His father's flailing belt.

His mother's whipping switch.

"You could say Nate had an ordinary upbringing."

The children's common bed.

His cuddling older sister.

Her clutching ways.

"All in all, it was the usual childhood, Mr. Beach."

"Did Nate finish his schoolin' in the state that has more cows than people?"

"Yes, he did. Although he never faced the challenges of farm life, it was in his home—where dog ate dog—that Nate learned his skills."

Expecting down-to-earth analysis, I faced over-the-top scrutiny instead. "Although I still wonder what you learned cooped up with the turkeys out here, I get the picture your husband learned how to dominate in the zoo he grew up in." The big-city man was working really hard to come up with animal life metaphors.

Nate led his little sister.

Out the attic window.

Up to the peak.

Kitten from his shirt to her hand.

Lessons about flying cats completed.

He left her on the roof.

"Nate tried to help his family because he was the smart one, but those early days were, in many ways, like a course in survival of the fittest."

"I'm not a big fan of Darwinism."

"Really, Mr. Beach? I would think the fact that men should not be considered knuckle-walkers like their chimpanzee cousins would appeal to your scientific predilection." Boosting evolutionary theory now would facilitate undermining Beach's male superiority over time. "Nate left home as soon as it was practical. He wanted to get away and he wanted to get ahead."

"Was more schoolin' his aim? That seemed to be your kick."

"More or less. At that time, with similar needs in our lives, we both ended up seeking the options a metropolis had to offer."

"You never ran across Nate in those new haunts, I'm sure, so we can skip over those days. You report your first contact as a fancy meetin' of the minds. What about plain old lusty thoughts?"

Hot whispers.

Insistent kisses.

Probing hands.

Crushing embraces.

"Nate set a striking figure with his black hair and ivory skin. In spite of outdoor life on the farm, he neither burned nor tanned. Although tall and wiry, he was strong, and his muscles were supple, so his movements were smooth and never startling."

"Such poetry! I heard the way he ran things out here saved his precious strength."

"Black as coal, his eyes were alert, constantly searching. A special look promised undivided attention, making his targets feel important."

"Always calculatin', it seems."

"His hands were communicative, but his fingers were hypnotic. When Nate was talking to you, you were never sure whether he was controlling you with his hands, eyes, or words."

"A great blend. Like the poet said, the ever-paired hand and brain."

Misinterpreted, out of context, and beyond Browning's intent to boot, this quasi-intellectual reference did show Beach had had some education, but he did not use it accurately. Nevertheless, he grasped truths intuitively, and, having witnessed Nate do the same thing, it was frightening. Beach could not have known of the disappointment in romance, indeed in love, within our marriage, but I suspected he sensed it. This hard-nosed brute threatened to uproot my secrets. The longer and deeper he rooted, the more careful I would have to be.

Hopeful for food again, Molly was prowling under the table, nose to the floor. When disappointed by Beach after time, she nestled down at my feet and fell back asleep in a second. Perseverance bought her space, but practicality brought her to me.

"So we've got this charmin' character, Nathaniel Brewster, on the prowl. How'd he happen to pop up in crappy old Concord?"

"Seeking change—if not opportunity. After being been pulled down to the city, he was drawn back to the country. That was another of the curious parallels in our lives."

"Like you were preordained lovers? You were a real stargazer then, but as I look at you now, I'd say you've crashed back down to earth."

I could not have looked as badly as I felt. I had made a mistake. Rambling in front of strangers had never been my inclination. Yet a growing sense of competition, a challenge beyond my control, was sweeping over me. I felt a compulsion to test this man—and myself—in direct dialogue. Like two kids dancing around a peculiar Maypole, unable to tell who was leading and who was chasing, we could skip from fact to fact without ever reaching the truth.

"I can't believe your husband settled in a place more rural than where he grew up."

"It's not that way at all. Concord is bigger than Brattleboro. It is almost a city, by our standards."

"But it's no Boston. I guess he was fatally seduced by your feminine wiles."

"After we met at church, Nate dropped by the farm almost every day. At first, Father was perturbed because, with a young man hanging around, I was not doing my chores, but Nate started pitching in, and that soothed Father."

"So the hero rode in on his white horse, and it wasn't long before you two got married, was it?"

Father losing.

Nate gaining.

Loyal daughter.

Future wife.

"You might say I got carried away, but I also reasoned marriage would be a good thing for all of us."

Serve them breakfast in bed.

Bring their pipes to the porch.

Freedom and independence submerged.

"I can honestly state I felt a great desire to make him happy."

"To make who happy? Your lover or your father? But, seriously, did you get swept off your feet? Carried into your boudoir?"

"There was a certain magic to Nate, that is true. In contrast, Father was eminently practical. He could spot a bargain when he saw one. He was delighted to make our marriage imminent." I dealt a pun in what had been a game of solitaire for Beach so far.

"Bravo! A clever twist of tongue. And so, you pleased your papa."

If I could manipulate this lewd man so easily away from an image of coupling for pleasure into a belief in a marriage of convenience, surely I could deflect him in other matters. "In morality and religion, Father was orthodox. He was as pleased with Nate's proposal as the two of us were."

Beach had a pragmatic side. He would not let a minor thing like manners stand in his way. "Which begs the question of whether a shotgun was involved."

"You are dead wrong thinking like that, and it is insulting to boot."

"So it was a marriage made in Heaven?"

Promising bachelor.

Triumphant husband.

Useful farm.

Handy wife.

In that order.

"Nate did all he could to make our wedding day memorable."

"And the weddin' night?"

Guests gone at last.

The husband came to his bride.

Climbed into bed.

Rolled on his side.

Snored in a second.

"We did not take a honeymoon. We did not need one."

"It's probably none of my business." It was not. "But correct me, if I'm wrong. Didn't I hear a speech about bein' a complete woman a little while ago?"

Bed and birth.

Baby or body.

Childless or child-free?

My fault?

His fault?

Whose fault?

Their fault.

"According to Doctor Otis, this was not to be. That was difficult for me to accept, naturally, as I yearned for a child to raise."

"The second reason God put women on earth."

"I see your mind likes its place in the gutter. Be that as it may, after I left the farm, I became prepared for the possibility of not ever being a mother."

"Aha! Are you sayin' the real reason you left the farm came back to haunt you?"

A woodpecker's rat-a-tat-tat deep in the forest hardened my determination. "You are being ludicrous. I am referring to what I learned in a biology course at Radcliffe. Lord knows, I brought my new knowledge back here and applied it to one of my favorite things. Tending baby chicks or a new calf was a treat for me."

"Sounds like a real shindig, but tell me how'd your husband take to your barren state? Not being able to have children would be a blow to any red-blooded man."

Making the bed was what housewives did.

Ticking, batting, and padding.

A growing reef between two lagoons.

"Nate accepted it the way most men would."

"Does that mean he accepted it—or not?"

Seeking rescue and relief.

Searching rhythm and release.

Would I swim someday in warmer waters?

"At least, I resigned myself."

"Good thing for him he wasn't to blame."

"Nate did not blame me—unlike you."

Further explanation was not something to hand over to Beach. Although all might come out in time, I saw no reason to make it now. I liked the feeling of having power over a man; I had not had the chance very often.

Then, as if scared to be in such racy territory, Beach made a surprising confession. "I don't know much about intimate matters, as you might already have figured out." But the quick rebound from this revelation was no surprise. "It seems your infertility could only have added fuel to your husband's fire."

We had only begun and were there already. Sledgehammer statements from a vulgar man. "I forbid you to trundle out any tales about Nate gadding about. I have heard them all."

"Oh, I suspect you have. Like everybody else. But, after all, you brought the subject up."

We could have argued that point all day. If I had stumbled by introducing unsolicited information, slowly stringing Molly's long setter tail through my fingers out to its tip stiffened my control. A sunshine shaft streaming onto her coat turned her markings into flames. In that instant one could understand why dog breeders called brown streaking in white hair orange.

"At least you're not denyin' what people say about the way your husband filled his barn with fillies. The same way he stocked his hive with worker bees."

More comfortable discussing worker bees than wayward mares, I addressed the business of getting work done on the farm. "Everyone pitched in on Granite Ledge. My husband worked side by side with my father."

"Which didn't last long, I gather."

Nate backed the horse into the stall.

Hollered for help.

Father slammed the door shut.

Winded by the effort.

Side by side.

Nate praised Father.

"At first, Nate let Father call the shots. As one got weaker, the other helped more, but Nate still made it seem as though the decisions were still Father's."

"Phooey, I'll bet your father figured out pretty quickly Nate wasn't the selfless helper he pretended to be."

"That happened only gradually, but the wondering did become visible in his face. Although Father didn't talk about it, I could tell he had trouble admitting to himself he was losing."

"His life—or his farm? Actually, was it true your husband was more suited to run a farm than your father was?"

"Nate was suited for whatever he chose to undertake."

"My guess would be your husband seized every chance to shape things to his own likes."

"That came later. Slick but sure."

"Did your father give up knowin'ly?"

"Knowingly but not willingly. Father was stubborn. Once he realized things were changing, he tried to fight back."

"Did they get into actual fights—like cats in a bag?"

"There were not any physical fights, if that is what you are asking. There were differences, and then disagreements. The domination on Granite Ledge did not come until much later, after Father was gone."

"I can hardly see your husband waitin' to be handed the reins."

The hay wagon was loaded.

Nate beat Father to the seat.

Grabbing the leathers.

A beggar on horseback.

"It is true, as Father deteriorated, Nate took over. Father lingered on for a long time, fighting death in a way my mother never did, but Nate was making all the daily decisions."

"So did you let him take over without a fight?"

"It seemed good for the family's interests."

"Especially good for your husband's interests."

"My husband only did what was in his interest."

"In town I heard people talk about Nate's kingdom, which says it all."

"I was thankful Father got the chance to pass on what he knew about the farm."

"At least he had a smart apprentice."

"Nate could always tell a hawk from a handsaw."

"Your country terms are quaint—even if they make no damn sense."

Revelation was my antidote to reproach. "In fact, the meaning is very clear. 'Handsaw' is a corruption of 'hernshaw', which comes from 'heronshaw'. Both mean 'heron'—so the proverb does make a lot of sense."

All of a sudden, Beach scuttled from chair to rail and scared away some chickadees brave enough to have come back. Not needing to stoop, the short man planted his hands on the rail and squared his back to me.

"This is no time for you to run off. For someone so late on the scene, you have gained remarkable insight into my husband's personality."

"It wasn't hard to do. A probe here and there made things very clear."

Our family existed in the dark on Granite Ledge Farm. For outsiders to shed any light was next to impossible, but a newcomer was now closing in on the facts the way a barred owl finds its prey at night. Beach was relying on what he heard and not what he saw. In the same way, the owl learns more from its facial discs and asymmetrical ears, which are both especially developed for hearing, than it learns with its big eyes, which are so highly touted for seeing. I was skeptical Beach could have learned so much from talking to townsfolk, reading the newspaper, and listening in court. I feared he had tapped other sources—like Harley, Myles, and Luke.

"Wherever and whatever I've learned about your husband, I can't make the life insurance thing fit."

"I have told you I knew nothing about it."

"That's a paranoid response to a question I didn't ask."

"What I meant is that should be a fish in your basket."

"A what in my what?"

"Forgive me. I forgot you are new to country life. It means a settled issue."

The policy had brought Beach back to the edge of the pond where he seemed poised to plunge for a trophy catch. "Knowin' what I do now about your husband and you, I can't figure why your father would have taken out life insurance on Nate. Why not himself—or you, for instance?"

"Do I have to remind the company agent that the beneficiary is a trust? It is not any one of us, not even the dead man's widow."

"True, but—"

"I project Father figured we would be lost without Nate, so he tricked him into providing us with resources. While Nate thought he was stealing the farm for himself, he became the means of keeping it in the family."

"But wasn't that like writin' a death warrant for the guy?"

Nate left Father.

Ankle-deep in pigpen slop.

A broken shovel.

A leaky bucket.

Father's eyes daggers into Nate's back.

Who first said it?

If looks could only kill.

"Father was not malicious or vengeful. Since he did not tell anybody except Nate about the insurance, no one had a financial incentive to wish my husband on his way."

"It's hard for me to believe he didn't tell the family. Not to tell his loved ones what the master plan was. That seems a strange way to provide for 'em—unless your father liked to play the devil."

"On the contrary! Father lived and breathed the Ten Commandments. He did his very best to get us to live up to them, too. If some of us erred down the road, it certainly was not for lack of effort on his part."

"Hallelujah, praise the Lord! Now that you've taken to sermons, I'm ready to hear about the errant Harley Poor."

Beach turned to be sure I saw the grin on his face. I flirted with marching into the living room, bringing back the family Bible, and smacking Beach over the head. Rather I snatched up a dried crust missed in my earlier cleanup and flung it as hard as I could right past his head.

Beach did not flinch. The change to a blank look meant he did not get my message or was too focused to notice.

A man may drink and no be drunk.

—Robert Burns
"Duncan Davison"

HARLEY POOR

The missile landed way out on the lawn. When I had heaved it over the rail, Molly looked puzzled because I had not asked her to speak for the treat. She knew barking on command was required on every other day. Unaware of his close shave, Beach started only when the dog bolted off the porch. Aware of my narrow escape, I counted the creaks of my rocker on the floor. We had covered ground much faster than I had intended. We were approaching territory I had not planned on visiting. Out there was a no-man's-land Beach must not reach.

Beach returned to the rail to watch Molly's dash, but because he was soon bored with her pleasure, he shuffled back to Father's chair. Reinstalled like a judge on his bench, he reopened the hearing. "Enough fun and games, Mrs. B! Let's get on to poor Harley."

Had my nephew, Myles, heard this reversal evoking Dickensian memories, he would have twittered with delight. Since the appellation did not seem accidental, I wondered if perhaps Beach did use his brain on more than insurance claims, girlie calendars, and racing forms.

"Harley comes from local stock."

"Meanin' behind the ball from the start?"

"His family's farm is down the valley that way." I pointed along the top of Black Mountain. Stretching from south to north, it was the valley's compass.

"You have to imagine it from here because it is the one after Cleve's spread." You could not see either of the other two farms from our place. They lay hidden in the cul-de-sac of stone where the valley ended.

"Harley was one of many sons. All the brothers went off and joined the Army, except for him. He thought the others were wrong not to stay home to help his parents."

"Obviously not a world-beater like your husband."

"Harley was born with simple tastes. All he wanted was a small plot of land, a good wife, and some ordinary kids."

"None of which he ever got, accordin' to what I've learned. He really tried, I suppose, but missed the mark, and I look to you to shed some light on that. For example, tell me how your sister happened to take over his life."

"The Wimples and Poors went to the same church. While the adults talked about serious matters at the socials, the girls and boys horsed around together."

Constance a beacon.

Male moths encircling.

Eyes blind to the warning.

Wings close to burning.

"She liked to be in the center of things. I enjoyed the attention the boys paid us, of course, but my sister lived for it. She had an animal quality that attracted boys and, later, men like filings to a magnet."

"Or flies to flypaper?"

"As we matured, Harley started keeping his distance from Constance. At first, I thought he was shy, but that did not fit since he had grown up with us. I finally figured he was in awe of her."

"I heard it was you who hooked 'em up again."

Mischievous matchmaker.

Come and see the Queen.

"He seemed like a good match for Constance. Even as he grew into a man, he remained straightforward and considerate."

"Would you say your sister liked your selection?"

Suitor introduced.

Slave inducted.

"Some might say Constance liked to take prisoners, but it was really just a need to care for someone. Although he was not the first to court her,

48

Harley offered a no-strings-attached devotion that made him appealing to her."

"You're always hintin' you don't like men very much, and I get the picture you didn't like this fellow at all. Your expression 'even as he grew into a man' was not complimentary."

"Oh, but I did like him—really. Harley was loving, attentive, and loyal. He kept that up after they were married, too, which isn't always the case."

Two grosbeaks alighted on the rail. After a little strutting, the one with the rosy red ascot, the male, took off on a mission to find someone new to impress.

"I picture one of those scruffy mutts that hang around circuses—underfoot, scroungin' all the time for scraps." The criticism was directed at Molly as well. "I imagine Harley made a nice pet for your sister, the way your damn dog does for you."

The analyst shooting for an accurate comparison missed the mark. My dog was not a pet. Companionship, affection, and amusement wrapped into one package, Molly kept me going. She had long since found the tossed scrap and returned to lie beside my chair. Chin on top of my foot to let me know she was there, she was ready for action if needed.

"How quick did your sister decide to make Harley her husband?"

"Once Constance saw how nice it could be to have a man around the house, it was natural for her to get one for herself."

"Meanin' she was jealous of the happy couple—Patience and Nate?"

I used to read out loud to Nate.

He swore I made books fun.

Constance hung around with us.

She never read any books.

She liked to listen to Nate.

"Constance did not pay much attention to us. In fact, even if Nate had not been around, I think she would have married Harley to quiet Father down."

"Quiet him down?"

"When young men started dropping by to take Constance to town for her so-called errands, Father worried openly. That activity came to a stop after she married Harley. It was hard enough being her sister. I was ready to let her husband be her chaperone."

This slip—intentional, if you believe Sigmund Freud—popped out before I could change my mind. Sensing my transgression, Molly rose to her feet, hopped onto my lap, and coiled up. While settling me down, she was ready to spring to my aid, which did not become necessary because Beach abruptly changed the subject.

"Four of you already trippin' over each other up in this little house, and you added one more. Didn't anybody foresee your husband and brother-in-law bangin' heads?"

Beach's switch away from examining my sister's inclinations was not in deference to her memory or out of concern for my sensibilities. The mention of female fertility had closed his mouth earlier; the hint of female sexuality throttled him now. Likely ignorance and inexperience explained his ambiguity in dealing with feminine issues. If the man felt threatened dealing with a woman, I was hardly sympathetic.

"We were running a nice family home, not a barroom or barracks, Mr. Beach."

"Men in conflict come to blows sooner or later, Mrs. B."

Potato-grubbing time.

Harley worked the hoe.

Nate held the bag.

Accurate counting was the argument.

The artifice provoked no counter.

"Nate and Harley put their brains and brawn together to get the work done."

"Your brother-in-law probably let your husband push him all over the lot—like he did the rest of you, I suppose."

"We used to laugh about Harley's extra rush to please because he was always forgetting the basics. Like brushing his wild brown curls—buttoning his fly—tying his shoes."

"Would 'sloppy' fit?" The shoe fit Beach.

"Harley kept clean, mind you, but he let his soles wear out. When we went to the Concord fair, he would go to buy things for us, but would have forgotten his billfold."

"Seems to me, given her popularity and choices, your sister would've been more selective."

"Having someone at her beck and call was something she liked. She did walk over him a bit, but there was no complaint."

"Hobnailed boots and all."

Censure was characteristic of the cur before me—a mix of basset, bulldog, and bloodhound. In contrast was the purebred on my lap—still, silent, yet ready. I bet my money on the bitch.

"What did your father think of the newlyweds?"

"Father was happy for Constance. He liked Harley, too, since he was a willing worker who jumped right in."

"Sort of the way you described Nate pitchin' in at first?"

"Harley was not as picky as Nate was. For example, he thought nothing of mucking out the stable."

"It's funny how you country folk measure people's worth."

"Harley was very cooperative. Father said he fit in well, while I saw a welcome change."

"Change from what—from Nate?"

Warmth reflecting off the hillside behind the house spread onto the porch. I could see and feel the sun bouncing off the bleached dirt and rocks, but what was uncomfortable was the heat from my visitor.

"That was merely an innocent mistake in word choice, Mr. Beach. I was not comparing my brother-in-law to my husband. I meant an addition. Father gained something he did not have before. That is, a reliable worker and faithful friend combined—like a good mule."

"Or a jackass?"

"It is true Harley and Father had different brains, but as farmers they spoke the same language. They spent hours together trying to forecast when the geese would honk high and the trout would rise. Each fall they would count the squirrels' acorn harvest and try to predict the length of winter. Each spring they would eye the height of the woodcock's climb and try to envisage its success rate in mating."

"Could they really talk on the same level? I get the sense they were worlds apart."

"Father and Harley lived off the land the same way. Each pulled nourishment for soul and body from it. They were very happy in that."

"Simple pleasures for simple folk."

Beach had no experience with what I was describing. The unaware often defend themselves by throwing up a façade of feigned acquaintance that prevents further enlightenment. Therefore, they remain unaware.

Molly rolled over onto her back, making Beach flinch. Forearms crooked, toes to chest; thighs askew, pads to the sky; white down falling away from pink belly—she was only asking for a tummy rub.

"Speakin' of pleasures, let's get back to the happy couple. What went wrong?"

"They seemed happy. We were so delighted."

"Were you delighted when Constance got pregnant comin' out of the gate?"

Their bedroom next to ours.

Rushed insistence.

Muffled persistence.

I went to my kitchen.

Warm stove for aching cold.

"We were as proud of their accomplishment as they were."

"In court you had to answer questions directly. I don't give a hoot about family pride. I want to know exactly how you felt about the prospect."

Gradually more intense, the sunlight spread farther onto the porch. The barn roof gleamed. The ridge beyond turned from green to gold, from gray to silver. The kiting hawks above got lost in the blaze.

"The birth of Myles brought happiness onto the farm—I was one of the recipients."

"But how happy was his mother? They said she never fully recovered from that delivery."

Myles cried and kicked.

Alive and well.

Constance complained.

No more hell again.

Not for any man.

Soon dead asleep.

There it was again. Beach must have had sources I was not aware of. I still did not know if he had gained access to the imprisoned men. If he had, I hoped they had not told him too much. However, since Beach had managed to trick me into revelations, there was no reason to expect my male relatives would have performed any better. To identify them as resources would be to acknowledge any information Beach had extracted. I would stick to blaming the reporters and gossipers.

"The paper wasted a lot of ink on that subject, Mr. Beach. That Constance broke down after the birth of Myles was pure conjecture."

"Come, come. Something determined her neglectful treatment of Myles—and, perhaps, what happened with Luke. Can't we agree to call it depression?"

"I will admit much of her spark went out, but that is a long way from clinically significant depression."

"If it wasn't a breakdown, what was it? How do you explain her behavior?"

"Good Lord, it was all physical. Things happen with childbirth. New mothers lose all sorts of tissue, blood, and fluids. They get worn down."

Not wanting to be soft on Beach, I poured the female juices on. Revisiting pregnancy and delivery was not comfortable for me, either, but letting Beach discover that would be detrimental. Better he think he was the weak one than know I had problems with the same issues.

"Motherhood automatically changes every woman. Why would it be any different for Constance?"

"Okay. So how'd your sister do as a mother?"

Thick black hair.

Adorable but helpless baby.

The mother would not act.

The sister took over.

"Constance did what she could. I was happy to help where needed. Sort of a second mother, you might say. It was not a big deal."

"Not a big deal to ignore her own child?"

"She was extremely weak and tired. Kids are hard work. You have no way of knowing what mothering involves."

Whenever I was concrete on feminine issues, Beach turned to chalk. "You're right. I do have some trouble with that, but I can guess how a man might feel. How did the father of the boy respond?"

Harley cringed at cradling.

Timid.

Tense.

Troubled.

"Harley said he was very happy, but, like a lot of men, he was uncomfortable holding a baby. He was afraid he would squeeze it too hard—or not hard enough and drop it. As the months went by, he got very quiet. He withdrew."

"Like your sister?"

"Similar. But his reaction was not as obvious as hers. He would still do his work, but you could see life was not as much fun anymore."

"Is that when he took up the drink?"

"No, I do not believe so. He slunk around, but he did not disappear until later on."

"The relationship between Mr. and Mrs. Poor had started to turn to dust, I imagine."

The bedroom noises stopped.

Harley kept busy at chores.

Nate seized the opportunity.

"I did not recognize any obvious problems between Harley and Constance—except that they were not talking as much and did not whisper secrets anymore."

"If the rumors about her next pregnancy were true, there must've been a big problem."

"The next pregnancy was difficult for Constance, if that is what you mean. She was forced to bed much of the time."

"That wasn't my point at all. I wasn't referrin' to the fact that pregnancy put her to bed. I meant that she went to bed to get pregnant. But we'll delve into that later on. For now, just tell me how your sister's confinement put the load on you."

Windows shut.

Heavy air.

Curtains pulled.

Sunless room.

Unmoving Constance.

Patience changing Myles.

"I was glad to assist my sister whenever she needed my help."

"You're a loyal one, that's for sure."

"A bonus was the fun Myles and I had together, especially when he learned to communicate with me. It was too bad his mother was so weak and tired."

"Not too weak and tired to have another child right off the bat."

"Constance was never too weak or tired to make babies."

"I've got a good picture of how those days went. She ditched her responsibilities, fooled around, got pregnant, and—whammo—it killed her." Beach folded his hands together, not in prayer but in conclusion. "Not very smart to try and have another brat so soon."

"She did not 'try' to have children. Pregnancy was a secondary risk Constance accepted to satisfy her primary need. She could not conceive that might bring her demise."

"But she could, most definitely, conceive."

I shared the blame for this play on words. I had abstracted the conceptive act for a long time. Denying its physicality combated its power. Aware of how harmful these impulses could be, I wanted to prevent further injury.

I had even called on Doctor Otis for help. A trustworthy, ethical physician who listened, he had done his best. It was I who had failed the examination—not the probing of my body, but the exploration of my mind.

The remedy would be a man with lips that only kissed and hands that only touched. A man who offered and did not demand. A man who could only love and never hate.

Cleve's dog, Monty, ran up the steps, crossed the porch, and nudged Molly off my lap. Rib to rib, the couple bounded off to hunt together.

"In any case, I'm really not interested in the life histories of either of those boys right now, Mrs. B. But I do want to hear how Harley reacted to the second birth."

With appetite for details about Harley and distaste for facts about Myles and Luke, did Beach have Harley on his carte du jour as his primary suspect as Nate's killer?

"Harley acted bewildered once again."

"It must've been the black hair—once again."

"Your finger-pointing is cruel. Even if unschooled in genetics, my brother-in-law had seen enough animal births to understand his brown might be hidden by her black."

"But bein' so very black suggests brown and black may not have been coupled at all. Maybe it was black and black. After all, there was some reason Harley dropped out of the picture the way he did. Tell me about that."

Constance dying.

Harley sinking.

"Many things started changing after Luke was born."

Father going.

Nate rising.

"And especially after Father died."

"That was a sad day, I guess, but your father did live to see two grandsons."

Father asked to hold my baby.

I let his error stand.

"Father was very proud of my sister's babies. But as they grew, he shriveled. They basically passed each other in the doorway. He exited as they entered."

A whinny rolled down the hill from the barn. Every day that was dry and not too cold, I let our old horse out for air and exercise. I loved watching this ancient soldier parade in the sun, but today Beach stood in the way.

"But to have two male heirs must've pleased him mightily."

"You must be good at your work, Mr. Beach. Father had little chance as a grandparent to cash in on the years he had invested in his children."

"Your father followed your sister rather quickly. What knocked him off?"

"Doctor Otis called it emphysema."

"Even I know that's a long, slow, chronic process. Why so quickly, I wonder?"

"I believe it was his heart. In spite of their disagreements, Father loved Constance very much—more than Mother—much more than me."

"I guess one only has so much love to spread around."

The old horse had quieted down, a hush joining the dead air on the porch. I hoped he forgave me his lost opportunity.

"But tell me, Mrs. B, with the loss of those two warm bodies, how'd you people get along, seein' as how you had a lot more chores to spread around?"

"Oh, yes, it did get harder to keep the farm going. We—"

"You'd expect the men to pick up the slack. Which reminds me, you kinda got me off track just now. Back to Harley, the husband and son-in-law of the two deceased. How did he react?"

Harley milked the cow.

Left the pails on the steps.

Patience carried them in.

"Harley took over most of what Father had done."

"And the double-in-law of the two deceased? Did he lend a hand?"

Nate picked the apples.

Left the baskets on the steps.

Patience carried them in.

"Nate put his hands to work to a degree, but he concentrated more on the brainier things that came up. Because the rest of us had our hands full, it was not easy to carry more—but we all tried in our different ways."

"I'm not interested in what you did or didn't do with your time. I want to hear how you folks got along. You know, communication and things like that."

"Well, Harley, for one, did not have a lot to say, if that is what you mean. He was like a house mouse. You knew he was around, but you rarely heard him. When you did run into him, he was pretty mum."

"So, did he just mope around?"

"Oh, no! Nate never would have stood for that. Harley did his chores and then some, but more and more he preferred to be by himself."

"Did the sloppiness you mentioned before show up in his work?" Worrying about another's sloppiness was hardly appropriate for Beach.

"All my brother-in-law's work was up to snuff, at first—but as he took longer and longer, Nate complained louder and louder. Whatever the case, Harley eventually got the job done. So did I. We could not just give up because we were short a few hands."

"The townsfolk said Harley began to come into town frequently—on his so-called errands."

"That was no secret. Although he could not go to town very often, he made excuses to go in, so he could hit the bar. He was probably just seeking some consolation with his friends, but my husband put a stop to it once he found out."

"But Harley was no fool, I understand. Since they figured out in town he had switched to drinkin' on the farm, didn't people out here see that, too?"

I tripped over Harley.
Sleeping in the shed.
My knee banged his head.
A knot blew up.
He never moved.

"Harley stopped eating—I should have spotted that and sent him to Doctor Otis. He would have figured it out."

Sunken eyes.
Hollow cheeks.
Rotting teeth.
A sorry jack-o'-lantern.

"I would have liked to help him, but without Constance the kids took a lot of care, and the housework piled up. I barely had time to throw things together for meals."

"It sounds, in fact, like you spent a heck of a lot of time in that damn kitchen of yours. I'm surprised you didn't wait at the table, so you could hear the men rave about your culinary achievements."

Ignoring the latest insult was smarter than talking back. "As I've already said, there were leftovers on Harley's plate. He obviously was no longer hungry, but I failed to pick up on the reason why."

"Once again I'm surprised you missed anything, but it does explain why he looked so bad at the trial."

"Yes, it does. Skin and bones—like a horse in a desert."

"So eatin' stops—wish I had that problem. The key is, did your brother-in-law ever let on exactly what was eatin' him?"

A muffled voice.
Harley in the shed.
Wrenched my ankle.
Stopped to rest.
Sobs and slurs.
Bastard Nate.
Goddamn bitch.

"No. I never heard him on the subject. I did not know a thing."

"I guess the same bug that bit your sister bit him, too. I mean the depression one, which we agreed on a few minutes ago. Since you're so fascinated by what makes people tick, I'd like to hear your diagnosis, Doctor."

"The only couch we have is in the living room. Father bought it as a memorial to Mother—the one who never liked to see anyone take a break. Even though he had a generous side, he maintained her prohibitions, so he did not allow feet on the couch, let alone lying down on it. Father also displayed his proudest possession, the Wimple family pipe stand, on a curly maple table in the living room. He went there twice a day and was reminded of Mother."

"I asked you about what was goin' on with Harley, not with the family ghosts."

Equivocation served me better here than agreement. "After Harley's chatty humor and boyish enthusiasm dried up, he still cracked the occasional joke."

"I'll bet he never joked about the shenanigans of Nate and Constance or the results. I get the strong sense their foolin' around caused a lot of the troubles out here."

All of a sudden, announced by rustling leaves, a breeze swept through the yard and blew away the heat—adequately explaining my goose bumps.

I took some carrot ends up to the horse.

Familiar bedroom sounds from the loft.

Harley dozing in my rocker on the porch.

"We do not really know if there was anything to that, do we, Mr. Beach?"

"No more than we know about what bears do in the woods, Mrs. B."

It was too late for Beach's condemnation to affect me much. I had heaped so much upon myself already. I did not hate them. I loathed myself. They were not at fault. They were only answering needs. I was at fault. I had given in to desire.

"My sister is dead and buried all these years, so I was hoping you might have skipped those questions."

Beach did not relinquish his advantage—or me. "Tell me, even if

Harley forgave his wife, which is extremely hard to believe, he must've been ticked off at Nate."

Crows rooted our dump daily.

The stuffed owl did not work.

Nate put a scarecrow up.

A likeness of its creator.

"Did Harley lift his hand?"

Harley passed by.

Ax in hand.

Into the shed.

"Not really."

"Didn't he even hint he was angry?"

Harley said vandals had struck.

Chopped up the scarecrow.

Nate never found the culprits.

"Harley kept on plugging away in silence. There was no way to know how he felt."

"You expect me to believe he wasn't pissed off? Aw, forget him. Since it was your husband with your sister, what in hell did you do?"

"Another time I would not have been so passive."

"You needn't apologize to me. Didn't you speak up, either?"

"What would you expect me to say?"

"I shouldn't have to tell that to someone who talks fancy the way you do. Didn't you do a thing? If nothin' else, tell me what you thought about it? With what was happenin' I'm surprised it didn't drive you to drink, too."

"We do not know what, if anything, happened, Mr. Beach."

"Jumpin' Jehoshaphat! In your own home—under your very nose. People say Nate and Constance messed around for years."

"Those rumors only came up later because some thought Luke began to look like Nate."

"And, if you look back, Myles had black hair like Nate, too. Surprise! Surprise! What did you make of that?"

"There's another of your asinine insinuations. Harley gave Myles wonderful curls and Constance gave him beautiful black."

"Pretty steamy stuff for staid old Concord, it seems to me."

"The Bible teaches forgiveness—not to mention being kind unto others.

You would benefit from some Bible lessons." Given my dissembling red hair, if I could not be convincing, I could at least be pious.

As life deteriorated on Granite Ledge Farm, I had given up on church but not on God. Consciously transfusing God into nature, I reasoned a homespun religion. Denied the chance for worldly activity, I combined the spiritual and natural into a personal enclave, my own version of a Fruitlands or a Brook Farm. The men were a burden, to be sure, but there were many women—Emily Dickinson came first to mind—to help me bear them all.

"Forgive and forget? Turn the other cheek? Thanks for the sermon, Mrs. B."

Skipping the chance to give a benediction, I took a utilitarian approach. "My brother-in-law stuck to his work. He did the heavy jobs with our horse. Short of that, he broke his own back—lifting, carrying, pushing, and pulling."

"That we learned from the trial. Your brother-in-law must've been real strong, if he did what Luke said he did."

"Luke was referring to Harley's help with the ladder in the shed—not anything that happened up at the barn."

"If that ape wasn't accusin' Harley, then I'm a monkey's uncle." The thick lip rolling out below his grinning teeth did look simian.

"That was completely uncalled-for." A burst of wind punished my flowers, slapping down the tall ones—irises, daffodils, and tulips—one right after the other. I was trying to stand tall in the face of Beach's assault.

"Back to Harley, Mrs. B. Passive or aggressive? The newspaper and court testimony led me different ways on that one."

"If you are asking lamb or wolf, he remained a gentle soul."

"I wouldn't call shootin' deer from here on the porch the act of a gentle soul."

The blast drew me to the window.
Harley sitting on the rail.
Eyes shining.
Face serene.
Twelve-gauge on his knees.
Red on the rump of a white-tailed deer.

Running for the woods.

Bloody trail in the snow.

"You are off base with that accusation. Because snow had buried her usual fare, a starving doe came into the yard to strip bark from the trees. The harsh winter threatened her with a slow and agonizing death."

"Come on now. What about the shotgun? I've heard their tiny pellets are meant for little birds—hardly right for big game."

"That is where hanging out in the city shows you up. You can take deer down with 'buckshot'—that is why they call it that. It is perfectly legal in New Hampshire. So that is quite enough from you."

"If you want to talk legal, I know you're not supposed to shoot a doe."

"My, my, first time out in the country and you are already a huntsman."

"And if you don't hit a lethal spot, you get a maimed critter. The poor thing runs off to suffer and bleed to death."

Jabbing with his pipe stem, the citified marksman took aim and put his final shot right on target. "Even if the victim happens to survive the wound, it's apt to end up a cripple, unable to search for food or escape enemies—that, I will admit, I learned in court."

"All of which has little to do with my brother-in-law. He is a hunter, and he happens to be a good shot, but he is not a killer."

"Humbug! It shows he's a murderous son of a bitch."

"If putting an animal that is better off dead out of its misery makes one a murderer, everybody on Granite Ledge Farm qualifies. Perhaps I should tell you about the bull moose that fell through the ice in the pond last year. He had to be put down. Why, once even I put down a mother rabbit with a broken leg. I made myself do it because I knew it was the right thing to do."

Out in the sugar bush, the maples were dancing in the wind with their dull green leaves turned over, coyly exposing their silvery white bottoms for all to see.

"You don't understand what I'm after, do you, Mrs. B?"

"Actually, I think I do, but why not spell it out for me just to be sure."

"Okay! The party line is that one thug did it, but I don't think they picked the right guy."

"Well, you have heard me on that subject already."

"For that matter, it could have been two of 'em. Not to mention—but I will—whatever role you may have played. Somethin' fishy went on out here. I've tried to figure out those charades, and they've kept me awake at night, which is too bad because I'm the sort of fellow who needs his sleep."

"My sleep patterns have changed, too. Once everybody is satisfied with the how and why, I expect I will get some relief. I am willing to cooperate with your little investigation because I welcome any chance to help those in the family who deserve it."

"I guess that means we can sample the other dishes on the table. Your nephew, Myles, is the logical next course—which reminds me, can you tide me over till lunch?" The toothpick shredding between Beach's teeth proved the hunger gnawing at his belly.

"By all means. I will go right in and see what delights I can rustle up for you."

The desire for food was not the problem; the appetite for information was what worried me.

On my way to the kitchen I schemed about what stuff to feed him. Poison came to mind.

MYLES POOR

No, filling the belly of Benjamin Beach was not the problem. Some cookies left over from a splurge for Molly and me did the trick, for when the plate hit the table, he started wolfing one right after another. It was a plateful, which gave me time to wonder how, if events on the farm seemed a game of charades to him, Beach would have described the trial proceedings. A mind reader, he opened up right there.

"It took the trial to get a good fix on Myles. I had a pretty good idea what your nephew was like, but I wasn't completely sure—not till I saw how he behaved in court."

"You did not see the true Myles. He was nervous and frightened."

"I'm real good at readin' people by their looks—though, at first, he was a bit hard to pigeonhole."

"Fancy my nephew as a flamingo, confident in his pink plumage, wading in muddy water, indifferent to dirtying his legs. That is Myles."

"You could knock me over with a feather after that portrait. But did you describe a bird—or a Martian?"

"Myles is from another world, Mr. Beach. Absolutely!"

"I saw him more like a jumpy circus poodle."

"I can agree with the circus part—that whole trial was a circus."

Attracted by a shower of falling crumbs, a tufted titmouse family landed on the porch rail, but the birds hesitated in front of Beach's frenzied feeding. His hulk was a threat to them. At the same moment, Molly returned from her romp with Monty. After a few of her circles around Beach's chair reassured the birds, bobbing and pecking heads speckled the floor.

"When did it become clear your nephew was—shall we say, different?"

"It was clear from the beginning my sister was not cut out to be a mother, but she—"

"You are always so complimentary of your sister."

"You can criticize me, but not her. She is not here to defend herself, but I certainly can. Constance did the best she could. After she died, naturally I tried to mother Myles, so it was easy to pick up on his romantic inclination."

"Pick up on it? I'll bet you promoted it. Your nephew preferred to be with you rather than anyone else, didn't he?"

Song sprang from pastries.
Fanciful flight following flavors.
Cookies a favorite.
Cake he could not resist.

"We had fun in the kitchen together. Myles flitted about, a parrot yakking about wonders in an imaginary world."

"How'd you get your work done?"

"Myles helped with everything I did and anything I asked."

"It's beyond me why he'd want to do all that she-stuff." A raised upper lip betrayed how uneasy he was in my comfort zone.

"We developed strong bonds. It was mostly because I answered basic needs in raising Myles—as newborn, infant, and child."

"Plus his psychological needs?"

"As Myles passed through childhood, struggled with adolescence, and became an adult, I was there to respond."

Beach jabbed. "Martyr?"

I parried. "Mentor. I cultivated his fertile mind."

"Nuts to that psych nonsense, but he must've grown like a weed to be so tall. Not at all like Harley, his—um—father."

"More flower than weed. His mind was way ahead of his body in growth, and I was there to nourish his intellect."

"To judge from the way he looked at the trial, he doesn't have the body of a real man yet—if he ever gets one."

Walked lightly.

Stood weakly.

A sorry pout.

Disgust with his lot.

"He is a man in his own way."

Did his own laundry.

Enjoyed that woman's burden.

To escape the barnyard.

The grime of the others.

"Myles is attentive to how he looks. He likes things neat and clean."

A blue jay fluttered down to the porch rail. Finding the floor bare of food, the scavenger scanned for trophies to line its nest. Dressed in crested cap, blue jacket piped with white, black choker around its neck, the bird could not be sexed from its appearance alone. However, the way it strutted its fashion up and down the boardwalk meant it had to be a male.

"So much for your nephew's namby-pamby looks. Let's get into that brain you admire so much. Let's get into his education."

"I devised a home program for him, one designed to replace Concord's antiquated method."

"That may have made you, the schoolmarm, feel good, but what did the men think of that?"

"We agreed schooling here on the farm was best for him."

"I should think most men would want to see a male child go to a regular school, just like they had."

"Each man had different reasons to accept my plan."

"All selfish reasons, I'm sure."

"Your insolent attitude annoys me. Please be so kind as to hear me out."

"A straight explanation for the warped way you think would suit me just fine."

"I argued Myles was too bright. His talents would be wasted in Concord's one-room-schoolhouse approach."

"So, naturally, you became Professor Brewster."

"You might say so. I did take on full responsibility. The result was that we connected on a mental level even more strongly."

"You went beyond the simple ABCs, accordin' to the talk." Beach must have dug to China in his quest. "What books did the little scholar like to read?"

Beach's interest in the boy's library suggested Myles, rather than Harley or Luke, might now be his primary suspect as Nate's killer. I decided not to play librarian.

"They were mostly books I already had, and the Concord library filled the gaps. It was a wonderful opportunity for us both. To pour out knowledge to someone with a thirst for it was a pleasure."

"Did you sign all your hopes and dreams over to your nephew?"

Jane Austen.

All three Brontës.

Harriet Beecher Stowe.

Louisa.

All the great mistresses.

Tea and conversation every day.

"We read, we sang, we dreamed."

"You read together. You sang together. You dreamed together. What else did you two do together?" I let this off target rocket fizzle.

"As I brought Myles to adulthood, he carried me back to childhood."

"What'd the men think of his pantywaist activity?"

Myles on the porch.

Spring bonnet.

Shoulder shawl.

Sunday pumps.

"It provided change. They found it amusing."

Mama's boy.

Disgusted men.

Better to paddle Patience.

"They tolerated his behavior, even if they did not understand— particularly in the later years, as Luke turned out to be an even bigger enigma."

"Sort of out-of-the-fryin'-pan-into-the-fire?" Accurately applying a saying was not Beach's forte.

"Surviving in this environment required pacifying the men, a nearly impossible task for Myles and a hopeless one for Luke. I had to play defense for both of them."

"Did you study how to play-act at Radcliffe, by any chance?"

"We looked to the animals around us for support—the mundane farm animals and more exotic wildlife."

"That sounds exactly like the stuff you'd feed them, especially the bright one."

"I helped Myles appreciate the ways of animals, hoping he could extrapolate from that to accept—if not comprehend—the human way."

"A cock-and-bull approach, for sure."

A splendid bird was now sitting on the porch rail. Sporting a tall crest, a long tail, and the red only a cardinal has, it was tracking the tidbits falling about Beach once again. Less flamboyant in color but with the same orange bill, its mate was hiding within the laurel beside the porch. Spying a snack, the male glided to the floor and hopped to the treasure. One peck and away he flew to his bride, lunch secure in his beak. As she craned her neck and opened her mouth, the groom stuffed his wedding gift deep within her gullet. Seeing a male defer to a female was exhilarating. It was the reason the cardinal was one of my favorite birds.

"That guy's just bribin' her so he can have his way with her." Anticipating a different spring ritual, Beach missed the point, but at least he could tell male from female. The real surprise was I thought he had been ignoring the birds.

I was grateful for all living organisms and nonliving objects in the natural world around me. Observation and interpretation of nature sustained me, especially when confrontation and interaction with humans frustrated me. A substitute for the matriarch I never had, Mother Nature supported me. Although the men all thought it was silly, I worked out answers to my questions by talking to her offspring—my friends.

"Like that cardinal, Myles was considerate. For example, as soon as he was tall enough to reach the suet feeder, I could count on him to keep it stocked with fat. And look at that squirrel over there at the back of the yard."

Myles had strung a wire between two trees. Dried corncobs hung down from its center on thin, waxed cords. The birds enjoyed the easy pickings, while the squirrels had yet to solve the conundrum. One bushy-tailed stuntman had mastered the tightrope dance, but shinnying down a string was not in his repertoire. As Beach and I watched the plucky critter climb and fall, I doubt we drew the same conclusions.

"Well, Harley had a different take on his personality. In court, he called Myles driven and ruthless—a demon possessed. I would agree with him that takin' an ax to a beaver dam is not standard behavior for the nature lover you talk about."

Myles frantic and feverish.

Ripping the beaver house apart.

Probing the ruins with his ax.

No resident to be found.

"That was a total overstatement, one designed to make Myles look mean and vicious. We all understood how, with the water rising so fast, that beaver dam threatened the planting in the field nearby."

"You forget I'm no farmer." Forgetting that could not have happened.

"A few days of flooding would have cost us a whole summer's crop. In fact, Nate scared Myles to death and forced him to open the dam as fast as he could."

"Myles could've done the job and not destroyed the home—even I can figure that out."

"Your concern for the beavers is admirable, but you do not understand. Once the dam was open, the pond was finished, rendering the house nonfunctional. Fortunately, they would set right out to create another dam somewhere else. In fact, I believe beavers enjoy house-building."

"House-wreckin' is what I'd call it. But I guess that's not as bad as cuttin' the legs off frogs. Was that just child's play—or a misguided science project you introduced to your nephew?"

Squirming frogs in a pail.

Flashing kitchen shears.

Twitching legless bodies.

Creepy lily pads on the pond.

"That was not mean or vicious, either. We had read a book about life in France and discovered a popular delicacy there was frog legs. Earlier we had learned that injured frogs could grow new legs. Myles was exploring both concepts. Surely, with your scientific bent, you can appreciate that."

"Hell, no, I can't! That's the twisted thinkin' of an evil mind. If it had been a valid experiment that would've been a different matter. As a matter of fact, did you know Volta invented the battery almost a hundred and fifty years ago based on experiments with frog legs?" Our science-versus-arts dichotomy would continue to widen. "What other nutty stuff did you tempt him with?"

"All subjects interested the boy. I was unwilling to be a censor."

"That's not what I asked. If you didn't dictate the choice of subjects, you did have control over his use of time, didn't you?"

"Not really. He would disappear, and a hunt would find him curled up with a book."

"Did he have favored hangouts?"

"Often he'd go somewhere new and be unaware when we called for him."

"Was that a way to ignore you?"

Low lair.

Nate's fist or foot pried Myles out.

High nest.

Flying sticks or whizzing rocks.

"Actually he did not seem to hear us calling him. When you found him, you had to bring him back to reality."

"What'd he do, when it got too dark to read?"

"Hunker down on the hearth. I used to joke about having our own built-in Abe Lincoln."

"The arrival of electricity must've been a joy to you all."

A cricket sat under the doorsill. A true house cricket descended from the family that serenaded us before electricity, she was waiting to jump indoors to the hearth.

"Father condemned electricity as unnecessary, expensive, and suspicious. He thought having it in the house would be dangerous. We respected his opinions for years."

"What rubbish! Electricity is a prime example of the wonders of science."

"When Nate finally had it brought in, it was handy, but it took time to pick up enough fixtures to make this a well-lighted modern home."

"Those aren't the words I'd pick to describe this gloomy old farmhouse."

Beach flicked our home over his shoulder with the back of his wrist. A daddy longlegs traversing the chair's top behind his head wobbled on his spindly legs in the draft.

"Never mind the pains of life in the backwoods. Let's hear more about how the family didn't get along. For instance, how'd your husband treat the pansy?"

Nate stole his shoes.

Thrust him into muck.

Took away his hat.

Put him out in the sun.

Hid his gloves.

Drove him into the cold.

"Nate tried to ease Myles back down to earth."

"You gotta stop flyin' all over the place and cut to the chase."

"Nate found it challenging—like trying to press a butterfly into a gang of workers."

"What a bunch of misfits—a slapstick comedy."

Concord had been debating for years whether to let a movie theater open up. The proponents were eager to have romance; the opponents were scared of facing reality. Neither group foresaw their potential manipulation by films. Beach demonstrated this danger in his cinematic lingo.

"Keystone Kops or Our Gang? Did Nate beat up on the boy?"

Nate ran faster than Myles.

Walloping was standard.

Sometimes hands around his throat.

Other times pillow over his face.

"Nate never brought out the paddle, although a few times he resorted to an old-fashioned spanking."

"Did Harley defend Myles?"

Once Harley put out gloves for Myles.

Nate found them right away.

Harley had no other ideas.

"Harley tried, but was not up to the task. With his mind outstripping his physique, Myles was too much for Harley to contend with. He was not equipped to deal with a son brighter than he was. Since Harley was not used to applying brains over brawn, Myles became a burden for him."

"A burden? I thought you did all the work to raise the boy."

"I'm not talking about work but the classic male predicament—that is, having a son who did not match the expectations of the father." Luckily, Beach did not inquire about the expectations of fathers for daughters.

"You mean somethin' Harley couldn't bear?"

"It jostled his paternal role."

"I find 'jostled' a curious choice. Is that because Luke grew up to look more like Nate than Harley?"

"We are talking about Myles, not Luke, Mr. Beach."

That both boys lacked hereditary credentials in support of Harley as their father meant ruthless attacks by Beach, but I could raise a shield against his slings and arrows. "I can tell you Myles looked like his mother."

"But your sister wasn't tall, nor is Harley."

"Myles had her black hair."

"Or was it Nate's?"

"What made me sad is Constance never got to enjoy Myles as a child, son, or companion—the way I did."

"So I see. What the boy needed was a real mother."

Scolding Myles.

Gripped my gut.

Squeezed my heart.

Warden not woman.

More matron than mother.

"My success made me stronger—even as a surrogate. The times I did fail him, I tried all the harder." I did not cave in here.

Beach tunneled in another direction. "I'm sure you did a great job on matters for a woman. But what about real work? Could Myles pull his weight?"

"Myles was not happy with a hoe or ax."

"Was that unhappiness out in the open?"

If displeasure draped his face,

Hope scrubbed away the look.

"Myles was upbeat about the future."

Exhortations of what he could do.

Projections of what he would do.

"He delighted in telling me his dreams, and I did not tire of listening to him. It became a way for both of us to escape."

"Did he discuss that freaky wanderlust with you a lot?"

Dallying in London.

Strolling in Rome.

Paris our Mecca.

Myles would make the Grand Tour.

The one I never would.

"Enough for me to tell it was going to determine what Myles would do with his life."

When the men were out of the house, Myles flew around after me, a canary out of its cage, singing songs of freedom. I wanted for him what I had never had. My deprivation was not his fault, and his deprivation was not my fault. Blind to the improbability, we saw only the possibility.

When the men returned from their chores, we shut our books, closed the maps, and put away the travelogues. Once age stole Myles from my side to labor alongside the men, we traded knowing looks whenever we passed on separate missions or joined for common meals.

Since talking to Beach about Myles also exposed me, I worried he might penetrate my perimeter. But, instead of counterattacking, I created a diversion. "A walk would do us both some good. We could go into the woods, where it is shady."

"As a matter of fact, I can't resist a stroll down that path any longer." Euphoric in the mushroom of his own acumen, Beach was easy to deflect.

From the back of the house, we headed off to the right, on the flat, into the stand of maple trees. Leaves switching and branches swaying overhead, the sun painted bright spots and dark shadows on the canvas of the path. Ahead of us, Molly's nose parted a nameless group of squirrels in a rush of flicking tails and trailing titters.

"Squirrels down home are nothin' but a pain. We hate 'em—call 'em vermin." At least Beach was beginning to pay more attention to nature around him.

"Squirrels up here don't have to share with humans. They don't complain about men—they laugh at them." Maybe he was ready to learn how insignificant he was.

We could see the shed well before we got there, but the ladder was nowhere in sight. I was glad it had spent the winter lying out of sight up on the ledge. Normally it would have been sticking out of the shed because Father chose to store it in a shelter too short by several feet. Suggesting he might keep it in the barn had brought only dismissive shrugs. So, like the glacier erratics that confront New Hampshire farmers when clearing their land, the ladder in the shed became just another tripping hazard on the farm.

Silence was often Father's way of handling inquiries. It was a tactic Mother had taught him—if one ignored difficult questions, they usually went away. One could say I learned the silent treatment from both of them. But the technique was more widespread than that. My experience in Concord and Cambridge taught me it pervaded New England.

Sometimes, when Father ran up against one of my special sulks, he sensed he would be happier if he explained things to me. That had never occurred with my husband. Nate always protected his control with silence, never justifying his commands or listening to any resistance. Repairing the barn was a typical example. After the storm last September had tossed a limb through the roof of the barn, Nate waited and waited until suddenly he summoned the other three men to fix the hole. Climbing up and working on top of the barn looked safe enough—but only to the team captain.

As Beach and I moved along into the sugar bush, everything was still winter-wet, and mud pocked the path. Finding a site for my cane was tricky. Where it was hard, it slipped. Where it was soft, it plunged. Beach had no trouble at all. It must have been his big flat feet. Halfway into the woods, he detoured to study the interior of the shed. Not only did he spend too long inside it, he was making notes when he came out.

It was a short walk from the shed to where the outhouse sat secluded in a thicket under the maples. Its cloak of shingles was resistant to wind, rain, and snow, but porous to sound, odor, and temperature. At the corner of the outhouse, Beach pivoted and peered back along the path.

"The outhouse and the barn aren't that far apart, Mrs. B. The transit time for Myles was important to his alibi, but I can see now it would've been an easy run for a youngster."

"I cannot see the outhouse from my rocker on the porch."

Although I had made my point, Beach cold-shouldered my remark. "Well, I've seen all I need to see of this stinky place. So we can head back to the porch and talk turkey."

For the second time, Beach nearly ran me over to get where he wanted. Not only that, ignoring the flagstones I had laid to protect the lawn—none of the men paid them any attention, either—Beach tramped right across the grass on an angle toward the house. I hoped the bees would defend their clover and sting his ankles.

He stamped to the top of the stairs where, sides heaving and mouth gasping, he sucked enough air for a bluster. "The dumbbell's the next one on my list."

Expecting the boor to hear me, I set to snapping off dead heads in my garden.

LUKE POOR

By the time I pulled myself up the steps onto the porch, Beach had seated himself at the table. In a swipe with one finger, the last smidge of butter went from pot to mouth, advertising the guest was getting ready for lunch.

Molly had reached the porch ahead of me, too. Poking open the screen door with one paw, she had disappeared into the house. Her destination was a given—on our bed, curled cheek to croup, she would be filling the hollow where I slept.

Whenever Molly joined me in bed, which happened every night, she left me room, but always stayed in contact. If she did not lay her muzzle or paw on top of me, she would lie against my trunk. When I could not sleep, which used to happen every night, she was all ears. As she soaked up my sounds, whether words, whispers, sniffles, or sobs, her tail patted the covers. Someone loved me; I had someone to love.

Whenever Nate came to bed, which happened late each night, he left me room also, always staying way over to his side. During the quilt-yanking, pillow-thumping, and body-crashing, his fist, foot, and mouth drove Molly off the bed. She did not come back up but waited at the bedside on a throw rug. I got up early, so we could go together to the kitchen.

With Molly sleeping and Beach eating, I took my rocker seat. Eyes closed, I shut the glutton out and, mind open, sketched out the next biography. I was ready when the interrogation started up again.

"The next suspect, Mrs. B, was the last to join your happy family, but he didn't trail the other boy by much, did he?"

"It was in the second year."

"Hot stuff. They wasted no time in takin' the dog for a walk." Sexual innuendo was another of Beach's weaknesses, but I could tell he was not really comfortable with it. It was much like a moth and a candle.

"There was no joke about it whatsoever. That pregnancy was not an easy one."

"For who? I'd guess both of you."

Constance flat in bed for weeks.

I brought food and water.

There was no conversation.

The men paid no attention.

"It was not so tough on me. But try to be charitable, if you can, because Constance went through hell—only to die as her baby was born."

"How?" The short inquiry was long on insensitivity.

Sea of blood and pus.

Waves against her body.

Damp black hair.

Dying, bloodless face.

"For no apparent reason, Constance had developed an infection in her womb."

"And the baby, too?"

Silent.

Stained.

Swimming in the ocean.

Where his mother drowned.

"That is hard to answer. At first, Luke seemed to be healthy. It took some time to tell he was not progressing the way his brother had."

"Well, somebody saved him nevertheless." If that opinion was accurate at birth, later it was questionable, but I did not want to admit it to Beach.

"You might say instinct ruled. I took care of the baby, while the midwife tidied up."

"What about the father? I mean Harley, of course—without makin' any assumptions."

"Harley did show concern for him."

"Maybe concerned about another head of jet-black hair."

The taunting had to stop. "Mother washed our mouths out with soap.

I give you a choice, Beach. Lye or Fels-Naptha." Too thick to pucker, his lips were speechless.

Constance a stone on the bed.

Harley lifeless on the floor.

The baby alone between them.

"Picture a newborn and dead mother, side by side. It was awful."

"You must be proud of what you did for those boys—not to mention the men." Compliments, even if counterfeit, were better than censure. "It must've been tough on you." Maybe I was getting somewhere with Beach. "Very tough indeed to raise a couple of monsters." No, clearly I was not getting anywhere.

Luke wept and wailed.

Myles whined and whimpered.

My silent screams for their mother.

The men heard it all, but did not listen.

"Raising such cute little tykes was not as difficult as you might think. Both were cooperative and easy to please."

"How did Mother B determine her little Luke wasn't—well, shall we say, ever gonna set the river on fire?"

"Looking back, it is possible to appreciate that Luke was slow from the start. But I was slow, too—in accepting he was delayed in getting to his milestones."

"What did you finally notice?"

"The most obvious thing was language. It took forever for Luke to utter a word."

"When did he stand? When did he walk? I've heard mothers brag about that stuff."

"Let me finish with his language before we go on. Even today, Luke's speech is essentially monosyllabic."

"Yup—nope—hunh. I heard 'em all in court, Mrs. B." Calling me B demonstrated the force of single syllables.

"I know Luke comprehends way more than he articulates. Once I learned to interpret his oral expressions and body language, I appreciated that. It is heavily nonverbal communication, to be sure, but it informs me about his thoughts and emotions."

"It seems you're the only one who truly gets him. What about the other functions? You know the usual baby stuff—sit, crawl, stand, and walk?"

"All came along late, especially compared to Myles. But I could remember from my college courses that even when children lag a bit, most eventually catch up."

"How long did you hold out hope?"

"I am still praying for that day—although I know now I will not get the chance to help Luke catch up."

Some assertive quacking announced the time had come to learn how to swim and dabble. A family of mallards—born early in the spring because the parents were hardy, year-round residents—had been nesting in the field east of the house. Now, the mother and her ducklings, followed by the father, were taking a shortcut across the lawn on a trip to the beaver pond. Moving to the edge of the porch, I leaned on the rail to watch the show and block Beach's view. He had already disrupted enough of our life on the farm.

"What was the attitude of the other grown-ups?"

"Father did not live long enough to form an accurate opinion. The other two were distressed to see yet another boy who did not live up to their concept of what a man should be. Still, they tried to understand. Of course, I was looking through the eyes of a woman."

"They didn't have your she-cat vision, so when did they first see the light?"

"It was the first time one or the other, I do not remember which, realized Luke did not respond to his special demands."

"I don't get it."

"The little things added up. For example, when Luke was tickled, he did not laugh or smile. Both Harley and Nate expected Luke to gratify them."

"To be an errand boy?"

"Not that self-centered. At last, the two agreed with me there was something wrong. When I suggested calling Doctor Otis in, they did not argue—they were frightened by the prospect of having to cope with Luke by themselves."

"I'd like to have seen more of that doctor than I did in court. You make him sound like—like Hippocrates."

"Doctor Otis determined that the same infection that took Constance had damaged Luke's brain. The good doctor was quick to admit he might be wrong and humble enough not to predict the future."

"Even if we men aren't that hip about babies, whichever one was the father should have—"

"You're too persistent about this father business, Mr. Beach. It doesn't matter a hill of beans who the father was. My brother-in-law and husband had the same attitude. 'A man's got to be a man' sums it up best. But can you blame them, since they were in territory they knew nothing about— just the way you are now?"

"Their personalities differed, so their behavior should have differed, too."

"Now I am the one who does not get it. Are you referring to the adults or the children?"

"I suspect you're tryin' to deflect me." He had made it clear everyone would be dissected right down to the bone, sooner or later. "I'm interested in your husband right now."

"Nate was just as impatient with Luke as he was with Myles, so he applied the same techniques."

"You mean he beat 'em both into submission?"

Red welts on his back.

Myles fell from a tree.

According to Nate.

Bruised buttocks.

Luke slipped on some rocks.

According to Nate.

"My husband was not a physical person and was reluctant to punish them for their sins. He tried hard to ignore them. I told you before there was some spanking, and he got out the belt a few times. Mother used it on us, and we turned out all right."

"That depends on who you listen to. Am I to understand your husband really didn't pay much attention to 'em?"

"Nate was always aware of what was going on. He did not speak to them very much, but, even without saying a word, he was like a bogeyman to them."

"Because he punished 'em?"

"No—because he insisted there was only one way to do things—his way."

"So the boys learned to stay out of your husband's way?"

"They learned by trial and error. As in touching a hot stove. Or putting a finger in a light socket."

"Isn't that the way we all learn?"

"Learning should not require burning or shocking." Teaching the boys had been one of my greatest pleasures on Granite Ledge. Had I been able to stay off the farm and complete my education, I would have settled into a teaching role somewhere or other as my vocation.

"To each his own, Mrs. B. Luke must've had a lot more burns and shocks than Myles."

"As each got big enough to work, Nate tried in turn to teach them. However, he did not recruit them, he drafted them, and they ended up pawns in his hands. You must understand that discipline is considered integral to education in these parts. So you can imagine what the teaching atmosphere was like."

"What kind of a teacher was Harley?"

"He was not much for book learning, as you might have figured out from what you heard in court. But he knew a lot of practical things, much of which Father had spoon-fed him. However, Harley ran into an electric vacuum in Myles and, unable to fill him up, he stopped trying. He tried to pass things on to Luke, too, but once he concluded Luke would never grow up, he adopted an approach more like Nate's."

"You mean he threw in the sponge?"

I had kept on watching the convoy of ducklings waddling behind their mother. The clutch was still fuzzy with no feathers. The yellows were gone by now, and they were all brown—still too young to display a hen's mottling or brandish a drake's green.

"Their mother was dead, so did Harley help with Luke in the day-to-day sense?"

"He was willing to change diapers."

"I would've guessed that's one thing all fathers try to escape."

Back from the swimming hole.

Dripping wet.

Blue with cold.

Shorts bulging in front.

Happens often with growing boys.

Harley hurried Luke away.

"Harley guided Luke in the manly things, Mr. Beach."

"Are you speakin' pruriently or prudishly, Mrs. B?"

His word choice left me almost wordless. "Some things are better left unsaid."

The duck children were wandering off. While the mother raked them in, the father ambled away, looking for an unencumbered female. Mallards led their lives this way. Maybe, in the long run, it was better the fathers did not stick around.

"How did Myles relate to his younger brother?"

The helpless one pulled me in.

The able one got pushed away.

The morning eggs arrived all cracked.

The kitchen floor was tracked with mud.

The cookie dough would taste of salt.

"Myles was friendly and attentive to his little brother, at first. Once he discovered Luke could not participate in his special world, he drifted away."

"That smacks of boyish disappointment. Was there any jealousy or anger?"

Myles failed to do his chores.

Dirty water in the barn.

Ashes filled the stove.

Snowy steps unshoveled.

"Myles did not openly complain about Luke, if that is what you are driving at. What would make you think otherwise?"

"Just that they remind me of Fat and Skinny."

"Their difference was an intellectual gap. Still, in his own way, Luke was a good candidate for homeschooling."

"Are you suggestin' he was not a good candidate for the Concord system?"

"Are you suggesting that the school in there is a good one?"

"No. I'm suggestin' the school out here was not."

"Whatever would you know about how things were out here? If you think the adults on Granite Ledge responsible for these youngsters had selfish motives, you are dead wrong. We spent our lives trying to bring them up properly."

"I would say 'weirdly' better describes those efforts. But let's not debate the method. The question is whether the retard could be schooled at all."

A burst of quacking drew Beach over to the rail. Together we watched the mother thrusting one straggler with her bill. If Beach saw reprimand, I saw encouragement. "Of course, Luke could be schooled. All he needed was some attention—and a lot of patience."

"The patience of Job. Your father named you appropriately." Although submitted swimmingly, he failed to bow.

I curtsied in response anyway. "I did what I had to do."

"So you were basically all alone in how the kid was brought up?"

"It was easy because Luke was a lovable little boy."

"He didn't stay little for very long. Gadzooks, he was bigger than any man in the courtroom."

"Even when Luke was a full head taller than I was, he was still a boy to me."

"Does that translate into 'large body, small brain'?"

Empty eyes.

Expressionless face.

Scant activity behind.

Slight grin.

Nodding head.

Sudden output.

"Luke offers a lot—it is just a matter of learning to read him."

"Just how defective is he?"

A message.

Not the message.

But some message.

Response delayed.

Often inaccurate.

Sometimes inane.

But a response.

"That is a brutal way to describe someone a little slow in development."

"I got it from where he is now—the State School for the Mentally Defective."

"That term is a brutal way to describe the condition. It is unfair for anybody to focus on disabilities that way. The approach should be to enhance the positives, as I tried to."

"You really are a dreamer, aren't you?"

"I simply strive to make things better in the future—to act to control one's destiny."

"No, madam, you took control of someone else's destiny. I don't think you or anybody else, for that matter, has that right. But I'm not interested in a wrangle about the future. I want facts from the past. For example, when I listened to Luke talk, it was hard to believe he was anythin' but retarded."

"My nephew's testimony did show he has the vocabulary of a child, but—"

"But one perfectly adequate for a farm worker, it seems to me." Ignoring this childish slur was the adult decision.

"Given some time, Luke was able to learn to do the physical tasks of any adult."

"But could he actually reason for himself?"

A puzzle with a hole remaining.

Fingers turning the jigsaw piece.

The brain could find no place.

"Luke does have insight. He is simply not good at building conclusions upon it, which makes him slow in deciding how to act."

"He may have performed those functions very well last fall."

"There is another thing that might surprise you. While Luke cannot count high, spell well, or put together complex sentences, he can read what you want him to do quite well, even when you do not say very much. You can see the recognition come into his eyes."

"I could see from my close-up seat in the courtroom his eyes were deadpan. If you told me he was blind, I'd believe you."

"It is more than a look. His eyes seem to open a bottomless hole. You can see into his brain."

"That can't be real."

"Well, no matter what you think, Luke eventually responds to you or ignores you. He does what you want or he walks away. Even if poorly articulated, his answer is clear—a raw yes or no."

"I suspect you're the only one who can read method into his madness. Still, no matter how far-fetched it might be, I suppose any way to explore his role in the ladder goin' down with your husband on it is better than none. Let's take up something a little more concrete—like his strength."

Sturdy frame.

Bulging muscles.

"Luke is very strong—"

Slow reflexes.

Jerky motion.

"But not coordinated. Sophisticated acts like throwing, kicking, running, and dancing are real tests for him."

"In that case he wouldn't make a very good circus bear. But at the trial he did seem kind of—well, cuddly—till you heard the testimony."

Crying, fussing, crying.

No end in sight.

Calming fruitless.

Cheering futile.

Good mothers never quit.

I had to rest.

"My nephew was neither unhappy nor demanding. I came to love him as if he was my own."

"That last part I have real trouble with, even if it comes from the mouth of his biggest supporter."

"Luke would watch a mosquito sucking his blood, and it could count on flying away with a full belly, unharmed. One summer Luke blundered into a hornet's nest up in the barn. Eyes swollen shut from stings, he wrapped himself around the ladder to the loft, so no one could climb up and destroy the nest. Harley had to sneak up there after bedtime to do the job."

"A different barn story counters the one you just told—remember the very first portrait of Luke in the *Granite State Times*?"

That newspaper kept on cropping up, as if Beach was beating me over the head with a rolled-up copy. This time his reference set me to reflecting about the power of words in print. At first, the reports had made the case appear open-and-shut, a mere formality to prove the Poors guilty of murder. They had teamed up to send Nate down to his death and then arranged the ladder to look as if it had slipped out under him, by accident, when he was climbing down. However, in the wake of the three defendants changing their stories on the stand, an editorial by Charles Troubadour, Editor in Chief, had floated new questions: had Nathaniel Brewster earned his fate? Had Patience Brewster defended the culpable by insisting on an accident? Had Cleveland Parsons responded to the minor barking of that dog for a major reason? Had Constance Poor poisoned the three Poor men? Had Morton Wimple spawned a school of piranhas? Were they not all, in some way, guilty creatures?

"It's time to come back down from the clouds, Mrs. B. How do you explain the time Luke snagged those bats in the rafters and drowned 'em in a bucket of water?"

Luke in the loft.

Glowing face.

Curious smile.

Furry body submerged.

Frantic flapping wings.

"It was the innocent experimentation of an impressionable child. Luke had learned to make funny sounds underwater in the bathtub, and he knew bats did not talk. He thought he could teach them by holding their heads underwater."

"Good thing he didn't try that technique on one of those toddlers on the farm up the road."

Beach was showing again how far and wide his explorations had been. There were no children on the farms at our end of the valley, but kids did crop up on the farms closer to Concord. Those families gravitated toward town naturally, so we did not run into them often. Beach could not have learned very much about us from them—at least anything accurate.

"Like any other child, Luke could learn from his mistakes. He never tried that again."

"So what about the other time his viciousness came up in court? When Myles described how Luke pulverized that squirrel with a sledgehammer?

You know how much I dislike those rodents, but that's pretty bad." The elephant did not forget.

Crushing hammer.

Compacted corpse.

Chortling Luke.

"That was humanitarian. The facts explain his actions. That poor squirrel had lost its tail in an accident or a fight. Essentially helpless, it was doomed. Luke came up with a quick way to put it out of its misery."

"A very stylish solution for a stupe."

"Luke has empathy for anybody in a predicament. It is as easy as that."

"Isn't 'anything' the correct term, Mrs. B? Violent acts like that concern me, especially when committed by someone who isn't completely with it. Did he react that way when the men treated him so badly?"

Luke left an ax out in the rain.

Nate locked him in the shed.

Luke kicked the walls.

Luke pounded on the door.

Good thing Nate put the ax in the barn.

"No, Luke brushed things like that aside, even though his elders were rough at times. He understood it was for his own good—all part of growing up, as Father used to say."

"Did Luke even understand what a father was?" Beach's sudden shifts were less surprising now. Controlling my impulse to strike back was easier, too, although unsatisfying.

"Actually, Mr. Beach, I submit Luke—in an ironically intelligent way—did understand there were two father figures in his life, but they were of no use to him."

"You're liftin' off the planet again."

"It was tough. When he looked to one father, he got rejected."

"You're on a balloon to the moon."

"When he turned to the other, he got the cold shoulder there, too."

"Come on now! I doubt the average person would have been able to figure things like that out."

"I do not mean to imply Luke is average. He has no awareness of conception, birth, or parenting. In his world, people are like pigeons."

"Pigeons? Whatever are you talkin' about? To associate us with animals all the time the way you do makes us look bad."

"Why, you misunderstand me. I love humankind and nature."

"But, somehow, it's men who always come out on the losin' end in your scheme of things."

"And appropriately so—men behave like untamed beasts most of the time."

Abrading Beach's ego was soothing to mine. Because he was unfamiliar with my style, he was easier to chafe than my other male challengers had been. Nate looked through me, and Harley turned his gaze away. Myles daydreamed, and Luke played.

"But getting back to people and pigeons, Mr. Beach, do we ever see baby pigeons? No, we do not. All we see are pigeons—young and old, male and female, they all look alike."

"Now I get what you're drivin' at. Since your nephew never saw a human born, he wouldn't have known about the mother thing and couldn't have connected the father part. But isn't that sort of a complicated way to say he's naïve and inexperienced?"

"Although Luke had seen plenty of animals mate and have babies, he could not transfer that act to the humans around him. Still, what he did see in the animal world made him trust we would care for each other."

Soaked diapers.

Reddened skin.

Luke just had to wait.

"And that is what we did."

"The whole kit and caboodle? But what about the wild beasts you just mentioned?" Beach was still smarting from my comparison of men and beasts.

"All the beings of God's realm. Luke had a good home here at Granite Ledge."

Sometimes.

I did not wash or dry.

I had to sleep.

"The way I cared for him conveyed all that."

The backyard was quiet without the duck family. A breeze rippled through the trees, but their leaves trembled in silence. Blossoms stretched towards the sun. A sparrow couple poked the thatch without discussion. The female was seeking food for her young, the male for himself.

"So, let's return to practical issues, Mrs. B. You contend your nephew couldn't have known Nate was his actual father—in spite of what his lawyer argued in court."

"Any discussion about who might or might not be his father was and is utter speculation."

"Ignorant or not, Luke might have attacked his own father and sent him to his death."

"Two points. First of all, we do not know that Nate was Luke's father."

"And a ball doesn't roll downhill."

"Second, and more important, I know Luke did not attack Nate. He had outgrown experimenting—the same way Myles did. Luke would never hurt a flea or step on an ant. How could he kill another man?"

"Now here's my point. Nate treated Luke like a dumb animal. The boy-man's reaction was predictable. A crescendo of hateful vengeance would've been a normal response."

"No, I say that would be an abnormal response."

It was time for Beach's first Bible lesson of the day. "Do you recall ever hearing this? 'If thine enemy be hungry, give him bread to eat; if he be thirsty, give him water to drink.' The Book of Proverbs, chapter 25, verse 21." I was confident Beach would not know how the passage ended and did not instruct him in it: 'for thou shalt heap coals of fire upon his head, and the LORD shall reward thee'.

Earlier, while discussing Harley and Myles, Beach had not probed into the projected murderer's mind so deeply. Exploring behavioral theory this way now suggested Luke might be his primary suspect as Nate's killer.

"You, Mr. Beach, and all those buzzards in the court are good examples of how society takes a notion about someone and never changes its view regardless of the facts."

"And your wisdom is?"

"Being retarded does not abolish effective cognition or prevent moral awareness."

"What gibberish! In fact, if I were to believe the way you sugarcoat it, I'd have to wonder if he just faked it and played slow for years."

"What an absurd notion."

"Maybe he learned to play dumb to get special attention where he could and, where needed, to shield himself from the ruthless Brewsters and Poors."

"Our doctor and the psychiatrist did not come near to suggesting that in court."

"Hey, maybe the patient tricked his primary therapist—you, Mrs. B."

"That is quite a stretch. The psychiatrist used up-to-date techniques of psychological and intelligence testing. His conclusion was Luke lacked the ability to deceive and manipulate the way you are suggesting."

"You don't have to be a pro to read people. I pride myself on careful, unemotional evaluation, just the way you do."

"Besides, the psychiatrist testified that my nephew's retardation is not the cause of his behavior—rather, it is merely a brush that colors his conduct."

"But that same doctor stated that same nephew should do his color paintin' within the confines of a state institution—rather poetic for a man of science don't you think?"

"What in Hades do you know about poetry? Or painting? You're like Seurat—reluctant to concede that a scientific approach does not always work. I am only repeating the psychiatrist's opinions about Luke. His diagnosis was that Luke simply had a limitation in mental capacity—without potential for dangerous behavior, I hasten to add. That condition made Luke better suited for the controlled life of a state institution, which is why the psychiatrist made the recommendation he did. It was simply a question of safety."

"Whoa, Mrs. B! The question is, whose safety?"

"You hold it, Mr. Beach! 'Whoa' is for horses; 'wait' is for people. I will reiterate—it was a question of safety—his own."

"You're right, this is a good place for us to stop because we can't seem to agree. As a matter of fact, we've run through the whole menu now, and it's about time for me to pick the main course. By the way, I could sure use a bite to eat."

"I will see what I can do to help, for I realize you must satisfy your belly god." Always being a good hostess was one of Father's lessons. "I will go into the kitchen and put something together." What I really intended to do was unwind.

Leaving Beach in his corner, I withdrew to mine, hopefully still ahead on points in the fight.

However, in another sense, things were heading backward.

It was the same old story.

I was waiting on another needy man.

'Tis well to be off with the old love,
Before you are on with the new.

—Charles Robert Maturin
Motto to *Bertram*

IN THE KITCHEN

While I puttered about in the kitchen, Beach hunkered down on the porch. Window spying, I found my guest had helped himself to my rocker. Facing off the porch, he was hungering for details up on the ledge. Even though I was going to stuff the pig with food, I would be sparing with information.

Molly had not defended my chair and was nowhere in sight. In the past, a move into my rocker by Luke, Harley, or Myles would have earned them explicit stares and Nate a special growl. That is why my rocker rarely warmed the seat of a man's pants. Beach must have learned from my example and tricked my guard with some cookie bits thrown over the rail. What decoys would he be setting out for me?

While my brain stockpiled responses, my hands gathered things for lunch. There was thick-sliced bacon, smoked salmon, and a small wheel of cheddar cheese. These I added to the day's fresh bread, yesterday's homemade butter, and a several-days-old piece of rhubarb pie. Only when finished did I recognize the coincidence—this lunch was identical to the one Nate did not live to enjoy. Handing Beach this meal was to repeat the menu of that fateful day. The thought of it was delicious, even if I might regret the provocation.

"Is everything okay?"

The voice coming from the pantry did not startle me. The other outside door to the kitchen opened there, and it was on the end of the house nearest to the farm next door. Besides, if Cleveland Parsons, a man of few words, asked a question, he did not insist on an answer. The reticence of his speech offset the demands of his size. Tall and rangy—"rawboned" was the local term—he telegraphed strength without threat, stability without domination.

Both hands came to mine. The handshake was firm, not wanting to let go, but soft at the same time, shunning insistence. We had adopted the habit of shaking hands, even if we met more than once in the course of a day, and that had been happening more lately. It was not hello or good-bye; it was "glad to see you" and "thank you."

"When I went by on the road just now, I couldn't help noticing a strange vehicle in the drive. Thought I'd stop and check on you." His eyes read my face, while his ears waited. If I never said a thing, he would not complain.

"How nice of you. I do have a little visitor. Not so little, as you'll soon see, but he's no surprise and assuredly no risk to me."

"You should know how I worry about you, all alone over here." Chin pulled against his neck, eyes peering through his eyebrows, Cleve was embarrassed, not by his concern but by the mention of it.

"Why, Mr. Parsons, you know very well I'm not alone. I have Molly. Could I ever have a more loyal friend?"

Idiot! The hero rides in to protect the damsel from an aggressor only to hear her tout her dog. I could do better. The heat of the oven might explain the warmth spreading over my cheeks. I hoped they were not too red.

"I sure do appreciate your stopping in. I trust you can tell."

Cleve brought out the coquette in me. To flirt was fun. What is more, I could explore, theorize, and ventilate without fear. Self-expression was not a crime. There was no punishment for feeling. For the first time in years, no hurt followed. Myles had been a good listener, but he was only a boy.

"Cleveland, it's comforting to have you nearby to pull me out of hot water. Still, you and I must bear in mind how Father preached the importance of standing on my own two feet. That's a big part of being a Wimple."

"I not only remember, I understand. But, shucks, I'd like to hold you up when I can." Imagining strong arms around my waist did not hold me up; it made my knees wobble. "At times like this, when the going gets tough for you, I'd be right proud to be of help. No one has to see a thing or even know about it."

Cleve had always been discreet—when his wife ran off, when his daughter moved away, and when my husband fell to his death. Why should I be worried about appearances or rumors if a sensitive, caring man was willing to help?

A change of subject followed on the heels of a look out the window. "Who's your caller anyway? Doesn't look like he's Salvation Army. Is he a tax collector?"

"No. He's here about the policy."

"Not that foolish thing again. Keeps popping up like a goldarned weed."

"I can tell you that policy doesn't mean any more to this fellow than it meant to us when we chatted about it the other day. He's supposed to be an investigator for the insurance company, but he's here on a different mission—as if he's going to unlock some giant mystery on Granite Ledge Farm. And do it all by himself."

"That's not a great way to start a nice spring day like this, Patience, when you could be picking flowers or walking the dog. Want me to edge him along?" That was about as assertive as Cleve would get.

While Cleve's presence bolstered me, I hoped I would not need any more direct aid. He had been doing so much since Nate had died. He shoveled the drive and paths after it snowed. He got the vet when the horse went down. On his way back from town, he always checked my mailbox, and if there was mail, he brought it in. I was writing more letters, hoping for more in return.

Years ago, Cleve had made similar kindly gestures, but Nate had rudely put a stop to them. After that, we had not seen much of our neighbor from the farm next door, except for the occasional days it was clear my husband was off running errands in town.

"I'm positive I can handle this fellow by myself. You're forgetting I've already had experience with some difficult ones."

"Not on your life, Patience. That's something I will never forget. I could tell bad things were going on, even when I didn't see them directly. Just because I never did anything doesn't mean it didn't bother me."

"I'm fixing lunch for my visitor right now. Care to join us?" I still had trouble adapting to a man saying nice things—that had not happened for a long time—but I was working on it.

"No. Thank you anyway. I wouldn't be comfortable sitting in on all the money talk and fancy words."

"Oh, we won't get near the insurance again. He's already buried that. He's bent on resurrecting another little issue, which you needn't be concerned about."

"I wouldn't be comfortable with it, whatever it is. But if you think he's going to be a problem, I'll stick around." Cleve was not forceful, but he could commit—the way Father would stand up for me when Mother went too far.

"Don't worry, Cleveland! I'm betting we'll have a jolly time. Why, we'll be strolling hand in hand up to the ledge in no time at all."

"How can you joke about that? Thinking about what went on up there still gives me the creeps."

"I don't try to deny what happened. I'm at ease with everything I've said and done, so I'm not scared of more investigating. You could call it the courage of conviction."

Cleve had conviction of another sort. A humble rustic, he was a man of the earth who drew sustenance from his land and, when that was not enough, from his God. He went to church because he believed, although he could not elaborate on what he believed or why he believed it. Steeped in the Bible, staunch in the Sabbath, Cleve had been urging me to come back to church for some time now. I was not ready for that kind of formal deity. I had not sinned. I did not feel guilty. After all, I was a victim.

"Perhaps you'd like to meet the man with the slings and arrows."

"You're right. That snoop needs to know you're not all by yourself. I'll do just that."

Hefting the tray before I could blink, Cleve headed off. He balanced the tray on one hand, hauled the door with the other, and jockeyed the screen open with one hip. He hit the porch full stride, uncharacteristically jawing.

"How do you do, Mr. Insurance Man?" That salutation was a shock—Cleve never attacked. "The delivery boy is here with your lunch."

On his feet in a snap, Beach stepped back without verbally giving ground. "Am I supposed to know you, sir? Or do strangers around here just drop in for lunch?" Beach was lying. A figure and a force in court, Cleve had been unforgettable.

"The natives in these parts use drums to spread the word about intruders, mister. Didn't you hear the rumbling as you were driving out from town? I thought I better have a look-see."

Since I had not told Cleve about today's appointment, he must have been keeping an eye on things. In spite of what he had said, seeing a vehicle in the drive when passing by on the road was near to impossible. He was not spying on me; he was watching out for me. I liked the feeling.

"Are you tryin' to make me feel like I should eat and run?"

The tray clanged on the table, and the men locked eyes. As if each was trying to beat the other through a narrow doorway, the two needed a gatekeeper. "Mr. Beach let me introduce Cleveland Parsons, one of my neighbors. He often stops by on his way back and forth to town. You should remember him from the trial. He was the voice of reason in it all."

It was nice to have the chance to thank Cleve in public for what he had done. Because he underplayed his useful role, acknowledging his deeds in front of others would show him how much I valued him. Otherwise, we would never talk about it. New Hampshire was not a place for extra words. Actions measured folks better than words.

"Ah, yes. I do recall the deliberation of his testimony. He was quite the Johnny-on-the-spot. The minute your damn dog put up the ruckus he came over in a rush. It was very, very convenient. I was dyin' to trip him up on that, but didn't have the chance, of course."

The lunch break was over before taking a bite. "Why in hell—Parsons—would a few yips from a dog bring you runnin' over? Made me wonder about a prearranged signal between you two."

"That's an easy one—Beach. Molly's not the kind of dog to bark without a damn good reason."

"How could the stupid mutt have known there was a problem? It was way down at the house at the time."

"Coming from a city slicker, that's a question to be expected. Why, it's the sixth sense of animals. We see examples of it out here all the time. My dog woke me when my daughter got the croup. Saved her life, for sure. Monty's got that special ability, and so does Molly."

Whenever Cleve used Molly's name, he always gave her a pat, but he skipped it today, which was definitely not a good sign.

"Dog smells something fishy. It barks. Parsons dashes over. Pretty weird."

"You're a skeptical son of a gun, Beach."

"Weird, because I recognized you in your courtroom performance as a cool and collected sort of chap—one who didn't get ruffled—not that you didn't do a pretty good job yourself, Mrs. B."

The noisome nickname for me perked Cleve's ears. I felt him reconsider staying for lunch. "Your prying into things irks me, but if need be, I'll tell the whole story again. Just so the truth gets out. By the way, Beach, what's your first name? Sandy?"

Beach likely missed the color rising in Cleve's cheeks, not easy to see beneath his beard. That Cleveland Parsons would defend me to the hilt should have been clear to Benjamin Beach by now. It was time to step between them, before it became too late. "Why, Mr. Parsons, that will be enough of your little jokes!"

No matter how helpful Cleve might have been, I preferred to be on my own. Doing it alone was a challenge. He could share in the victory celebration later on. "Mr. Beach is here on serious business—something he and I mean to settle alone."

Cleve's hat, always doffed at my door, crumpled under white knuckles, betraying a temper better not seen by Beach.

"Too many have knocked heads on this porch before. You best run along."

"Whatever you say, Mrs. Brewster." And Mr. Parsons meant it.

"I will see you to the door."

Grasping my ally's elbow, I steered him into the house.

"You'll give me a call if he's trouble? Just ask Molly to bark!"

"Should there be any problem, it's nice to have someone to call."

During the jaunt to the front door, his broad hand covered mine, sealing the bargain.

The sun heading for the mountain threw a shadow of the house onto the walk. When Cleve burst bright and strong out of the dark onto the drive, he stopped and turned. Twinkling eye and smiling lips, he raised his thumb up to the sky. That was another goodwill sign we shared.

Out back again, in the shadows, Beach was packing his briefcase. "That friend of yours ruined my appetite."

"What a shame! Under other circumstances you two would have found something in common." My lie cancelled lunch for me, too.

"I'll be back tomorrow—hungry again."

"That will not work for me, Mr. Beach. I have some important errands to do. I'm sorry, but they will take up most of the day." In fact, I was delighted to fend him off.

"What could be more important than gettin' to the bottom of the mess right here on Granite Ledge Farm?"

"I'm going into town to see the men."

"Well, I guess that is important. 'Cause you owe them. You could've been a lot more specific when you testified in court. You didn't help those guys one bit."

"I let the facts stand for themselves and simply told the truth."

"Who gets credit for teachin' you your holy integrity? Morton or Molly?"

"If you do not trust my answers, you should stop asking questions. Why did you ever bother coming back out here?"

"Hell, I can tell the difference between a silk purse and a sow's ear." Chalk up another misconstrued proverb for Beach. "Expect me for lunch the day after, then. You owe me, too." All I owed him was a kick in the pants.

"Make it about noon, if you will. That will give me time to get ready." As if I would ever truly be ready.

Benjamin B. Beach barged out as fast as he had barged in.

Reject your sense of injury and the injury itself disappears.

—Marcus Aurelius
The Meditations, Book Four

TRIP TO TOWN

The coating of snow that had fallen from the gray overcast was not a good omen. Because we were in the New Hampshire mountains, it was not too late for snow. Despite the downturn in the weather, I looked to the day as an upturn. These would be my first visits to the incarcerated men since the trial had begun. Of course, I had seen them every day during the process, but had no chance to talk to them. I wanted to bring a little light into their gloom.

In my hurry to get going, I had rewarmed coffee and leftovers for breakfast. While doing the dishes at the sink below the back window, I spotted Cleve coming down the shortcut, a path through the woods he never used when the men were around—except the day Nate went down.

Cleve came in through the back door in the pantry again, but only after knocking the snow off his boots and letting Molly out to play with Monty. A new approach on Granite Ledge Farm, consideration like that was something to treasure.

"We certainly have smart dogs, Mrs. Brewster. They must've known it would snow. They slept with their coats on." Early birds who never stayed up late, we had a running joke about failing to be wise.

The stove had heated the kitchen nicely, but I brewed a fresh pot of coffee to warm and welcome Cleve anyway. While he sipped, I packed. From within the punched tin panels of our pie safe, each of three different pies went into the open-weave baskets Father had saved from his storekeeper days. Finally, there was an occasion to use them, although I wondered if it would be the last. It does not make much sense to make a pie for just one mouth unless it was a very special event.

Once bundled up, we loaded up and headed off for Concord.

Cleve drove the farm truck, which had replaced the buggy when the horse got too old, not because that is what men did when it snowed, but because I was too keyed up. While he studied the road ahead, I mused about the reunions to come.

"I made each man his favorite pie—like the old days."

"I hate to sound presumptuous, but I'd be mighty pleased to try them all."

"I had forgotten the pleasure I got from cooking for others. It all came back to me last night. Maybe I should start baking again."

"I hope you haven't hidden any files inside." His chuckle covered up my giggle. If he thought it was feminine modesty, I knew it was girlish anticipation.

"You know, Cleveland, I do wish I could help them escape—each and every one of them. What happened wasn't their fault. They were victims of a force they weren't prepared to contend with, a power they could not have hoped to overcome."

"Well, it happened, no matter who's to blame. I don't mind saying the situation with Nate was pretty tough on all of you. Now you're free, and they are, too—maybe not in a perfect sense, but better than it was."

Cleve rarely spoke about matters on Granite Ledge, but I knew he had always been paying attention. He had worked on understanding the problem and, now, on accepting the solution.

"No, Cleveland, that's not completely true. Although it may look liberating, it's a tight state of affairs for each of them. All they have to look forward to is loneliness, and I haven't figured out what, if anything, to do about it."

"I'm guessing, because you're compassionate and considerate, you have tender feelings for them that are nearly impossible to resist."

"Whether they're thoughts or feelings, they've been nagging me a lot. I guess I'm particularly sad because I can't see how what happened could have been avoided. I wish there had been a better way around the mess and things had not been decided by fate. I'd liked to have played a different role. That's the disappointment for me."

"There should be no disappointment the way I see it. When I think about what was going on, every one of those guys deserves whatever he gets. They were nasty to each other. Most important, not one of them was nice to you. Why—"

"Please don't talk like that! I don't want to look back at all. It only makes things worse. I want to feel good about what's going to happen, about what I'm doing today."

"You must be wondering how the men will receive your visits."

"I sure am. I doubt any of the men will be the same as they were before."

"Especially the one condemned. But I'll bet it'll be okay. Don't worry." The giant apologized by patting my knee. "I didn't mean to upset you."

Already weakened by remorse, I sagged under his strong hand, and we rode the rest of the way into town in silence.

The State School for the Mentally Defective was the first stop. Its location on the outskirts of town proved Concord's rejection of its residents. The crumbling bricks, peeling paint, and overgrown grounds showed how much New Hampshire cared, too.

We pulled off the highway into the visitor parking lot, which was empty as usual, where I got out. Knowing he should wait outside, Cleve signaled the dogs and took them off on a walk. I felt tense entering the building, like the first time I went into school by myself. I knew what Father would have said: I was about to reap what I had sowed, lie in the bed I had made, and so on. He liked to emphasize his points.

It took some red tape, a short staircase, and a few corridors until I was outside Luke's door. After glancing inside the pie carrier, the attendant hesitated before he unlocked the door.

"You won't have much time with 32. The board is meeting this morning to review the case." A number and a case, Luke Poor, my nephew, was no longer a human being.

"Which reminds me to take that fork. Residents aren't allowed to have any sharps in their rooms." His check on my gift had not been as casual as it had looked, and he was careful to leave the spoon in the basket.

"Any problem, you hit the buzzer on the wall. I'll be just down the hall." If I were heading into the cage of a wild animal, this warning would have made sense.

Luke stood before me. He looked the same: large frame, big muscles, deadpan face, dull eyes. He moved the same way: slow motion, head bobbing, shoulders hitching. He was still a boy in a man's body. When I moved to him this time, however, instead of grinning, he frowned.

"Here. It's blueberry pie." Luke pulled back from the basket.

"Remember the fun we used to have picking the berries?" I shook the gift a bit to coax him to take it.

"Rubbing the ripe ones off the bush into our buckets?" Luke did not answer.

"You don't have to eat it now. It'll keep a few days."

Luke jerked the basket off my hand. "No like pie no more."

Luke did not open it. "No want it."

"I can pick the basket up later."

"You no come back."

Luke used to call me Auntie. Now I had no name. His eyes were different, too. They were shiny black, glistening with anger.

Dumping the pie plate on a table, grabbing the spoon falling with it, Luke scooped a hunk of crust and dripping berries into his mouth. Then, switching from tool to handfuls, he packed away chunk after chunk. Eyes closed, still frowning, he chewed long and hard without swallowing—until, all of a sudden, he spewed everything back onto the plate. Blue teeth and cheeks, his anger came back as he thrust the mishmash at me.

"You coulda said Luke not touch the ladda."

Speechless, I reeled to the wall—and the buzzer.

Soon I was free outside the door.

Luke was stomping on the basket.

Part of me stayed behind in room 32.

The sky seemed grayer and the air colder when I reached the truck. The ground must have been warmer, for the snow was shrinking away. Overjoyed to see me, Molly and Monty quieted down after a few pats. Cleve was slow to speak up, ever sensitive to my sadness.

Back on the road, it was not far to the State Prison Hospital, but slogging along in the melt, there was too much time to think. Before, I had feared what Beach might have learned from the men. Now, I was afraid of what they might have learned from him. I prayed for a better reception at the next stop.

102

The hospital was the same vintage as the school, both built to house the overflow from overcrowded jails. Identical cubes of rigid red brickwork, the bricks came from the same kiln, and the bricklayers had been brothers. Judging from the identical rundown look of things, the State custodial crew spent more time traveling between the two facilities than they did maintaining them.

The remedial approach in play at the time meant housing Harley with a bunch of other patients on what they called an open ward—except for its locked doors and barred windows. The nurses were also guards. The patients were inmates, cooped up for their crimes, captives for medical treatments, too.

"What's that you're bringing in, miss?"

"A little something I made for my brother-in-law, Harley Poor."

"Well, you're in the right place but maybe with the wrong thing. What exactly is it?"

"A pie—rum raisin—his all-time favorite."

"Give it here! That's booze. You can't feed rum to a liver patient."

Her rough hands snatching away the basket, which cracked down the middle to boot, reminded me of another nurse I had run across years before. This one vaunted the same white uniform, angry face, and grouchy voice. Because I was much older, it did not surprise me this time, but I was not less sensitive.

Most of the patients were lying under covers, some were sitting on their beds, but no one was walking around.

Harley's hair was longer and wilder. Bulging out of his skull, his pupils floated on yellow. His jaundiced skin had scabs and bruising. He was never still, hands fluttering and feet flipping.

"I brought you the pie you've always loved, but the nurse said you couldn't have it, so she took it at the door."

Turning a blank face up to me, Harley propped himself up on one elbow. "Wouldn't eat it no way—not from yer damn kitchen."

"I just wasn't thinking about your liver, Harley. I was worrying about you."

"Not as much as yer mutt."

Savoring the sting, Harley smiled, soundless. Some bedsprings behind me spoke. Their prisoner rolled over to see as well as hear.

"If you saw the way Molly mopes around the house, you'd know she misses you, too."

"I don't have the brains ye have, but I've figured it out. She cares, and ye don't. Ye're a liar."

Moving down the row towards us, the nurse passing medications brought the eyes and ears of all the patients along with her. I was more on stage here than in the Concord courtroom.

"But I do care a lot, Harley. I can bring in good home cooking to build you up. Just tell me what appeals to you."

"Being alone—as far from stuck-ups as I can get. Ye're so selfish." His bright yellow eyes paled beside the bile erupting. "Like the way ye left me on the ledge—just like ye ditched me in court. Ye could've said I didn't touch the ladder."

Collapsing back on the bed, Harley did not look at me or speak to me again.

I fled without sounding a buzzer this time, but no one missed my exit.

Back at the truck, the dogs barked and wagged just as much as before, but Cleve did not say a word. The drive from the hospital into town proper was dismal. The deeper we plunged the dirtier the snow. The street poked through in broadening black ruts. Some had shoveled the sidewalks, and others were awaiting the thaw—a simple matter of how much a merchant needed the business.

In the center of town, white clapboarding soft-pedaled the jail as an ordinary link in a chain of look-alike buildings ringing the public green. From one side, the County Jail scowled across the communal grass. From the other side, the Congregational Church smiled back. Sinners had an obvious choice. I was torn between the two.

A simple door into the jailhouse brought me face to face with a complex web of iron rods. A lone policeman barred me from approaching the metal that stretched floor to ceiling, splitting the room in half.

"And what do we have here today, ma'am?"

"Something I made for my nephew."

Educated on the routine by now, I handed the basket to the jail keeper, who opened it, poked around, and took out the fork.

"These sorry tokens always take two forms. They're either apologies or prayers. They'd work a helluva lot better if they were bribes for the sheriff." This was the only enforcer who smiled. Wisecracking must have lightened his chores. "Understand, my dear, all visits have strict limits. The clock starts ticking as soon as the jailbird alights in the cage."

Waving one key on a ring of many, he beckoned me forward to where a horizontal slot in the vertical barricade leered at a chair on either side. The gap would let sitters shake or hold a hand, but that was it. Unlocking, stepping through, and relocking a hatch, the jailer disappeared through a doorway into the dungeon beyond.

"Up and at 'em, sonny boy. There's a nice lady here to see you."

"No way!" The scream of cell door hinges was not as shrill. "I'm not coming out. I'm way better off in here."

"Come on. Come on. She brought you this tasty little pie."

A thud and a splat told me what had happened. The pie basket hit a wall and crashed to the floor. There would be lemon and meringue oozing out of the broken basket. I kept seeing broken baskets.

"Tell that old bag to hit the trail!" I envisioned Myles dancing about.

"She came all the way to town for you, son. Give her a chance."

"I'm not coming out—not for that crotchety old witch—ever. I'm done with her silly dreaming." Myles would be trembling, out of control. I wanted to call to him, to soothe him, but I could not speak.

"Making things up all the time—she built me up, then chopped me down." The excited voice was familiar. The angry words were brand-new.

"If I ever get out, I'm long gone." Myles would be clenching his fists, flailing his arms. I felt like I deserved it.

"Jail or not, I won't ever look at her again. All she had to say was I never touched the ladder." His eyes would be squeezed shut now, his lips pursed to spit.

I did not wait for the guard to let me out. As he was locking Myles back up, he would have known I had fled.

I had walked from the State School. I had stumbled from the State Hospital. Now, I ran from the County Jail. Right outside the main door, to my surprise, Cleve stood ready to greet me. His handkerchief was ready, so I did not try to hide my tears. Although his arms were ready, my distrust of men had come back.

Riding back to Granite Ledge was gloomier than coming in. It was colder, wetter, and darker. To cheer me up, Cleve talked about the future: clearing out brush in the cut between our farms, getting a new cow we could share, and—yes—fixing the barn roof. Once he realized I would not join in, we finished the trip without another word. Although we were three pie baskets lighter, it seemed to take twice as long.

By the time we reached the farm, I was not feeling much better. I had tried to apologize, but they had rejected me. If they were finished with me, I still had to go on. Regrets growing, resolution dwindling, I was trying to look ahead again.

When Cleve walked me to the door and lingered on the stoop, I wavered and almost asked him in.

One of Mother's old excuses surfaced and came in handy. "Beach will be here tomorrow. I've got lots to do to get things ready."

Cleve nodded. Even if he did not believe me, he respected me. "I'm sure you do—and you will be ready. You're on your own, but I hope at least you'll let me drop by tomorrow night. I'd like to hear how you fared."

"That's a deal. In fact, I'll make you dinner. I'll even make a pie."

"That'd be mighty kind, Mrs. Brewster. I'll take you up on that."

"Who could have ever predicted this, Mr. Parsons? A man will get to eat his favorite meal on Granite Ledge again. That's not something that's happened around here lately."

Flushing, he left me, blushing.

Tails down, the dogs accepted the disappointment.

You are not like Cerberus, three gentlemen at once, are you?

—Richard Brinsley Sheridan
The Rivals, Act IV, Scene 2

ON THE PORCH

Little was needed to get ready for Beach. A night's sleep with Molly alongside was all. Still, I was not as prepared as I thought when suddenly, before I heard him, Beach was standing in my kitchen. That he had the gall to enter by the back door was troubling. Such violation of my personal space tested me. He was becoming too familiar.

"How'd it go yesterday, Mrs. B?"

"Three very pleasant visits, Mr. Beach."

"I kinda thought it would be rough on you."

"Rough?"

"They said such rotten things about you when they testified. Now that it's all over, I'd have loved to have heard what they said to your face."

I wondered again when and how often Beach had meddled with the men. Before the trial? During? After?

"By the way, what did that ungrateful trio call you? I don't mean names like they used in court, but how did they address you out here on the farm?"

"Myles picked 'Aunt Patience.' Luke found 'Auntie' easier."

"And the grown-ups?"

"Harley called me 'Patience' until Constance died. Then he switched to 'Mom' in the hope it would help the boys."

"Wasn't that like rubbin' salt in a wound?"

"One thing I treasure—as a woman—is my thick skin."

"And Lord Nate? What endearments came from him?"

Sarcasm.
Criticism.
"Mother" had many tones.
I heard them all.
I preferred being nameless.
"Nate did not use names. He gave orders. But you know that by now."
"Well, you won't hear names or orders anymore, but I'll bet you already miss not bein' important."
No ringing alarm.
No stamping feet.
No pounding tables.
No banging plates.
No disrupting men.
"To tell the truth, I do feel sort of adrift without the men out here on the farm. I am so sorry things turned out the way they did."
"And they've got to be sorry, too, since they've missed out on what's on the stove. It sure smells good." One man's likings took precedence over three men's lives.
I stirred the soup lest I hit him with the ladle. "The cold snap's over, so I've set up on the porch. You can head on out and get started."
When I came out onto the porch, steadying the tureen with two hands, Beach was slapping cold cuts onto bread with both of his. If he had a wife, which I doubted very much, I would have felt sorry for her.
Set between us on her haunches, cheeks aflutter, Molly weighed her options. There was lots of flaring, a little slobber, and a string of drool dangling from her flews, but she did her mistress a favor by not barking.
As Beach gobbled and gorged, we looked and listened. Most men ate like pigs, and Beach was no exception. At least Cleve had manners.
Luke smeared and splattered the table.
Myles drew on his plate, but only he could read it.
Harley left most of his food untouched.
Nate consumed his meal and the rest of us.
"You know, eating lunch out here on the porch was a great thing. It was very good for family togetherness."
"Since we lined up the characters the other day, we can get right on to

the big show. Still, if you want to postpone things and harp on your family feeds for a while, go right ahead. I've got plenty of time."

Memories of eating meals on the porch flooded my mind. While Father was alive, lunches had been family reunions, an escape from work. After his death, however, a more and more overbearing Nate ruined our meetings. Returning to work became the escape.

Nate preached sermons, fire and brimstone but not religion. Lunch started with bits of invective sprayed at random over us. He hurled acrimony after the first ones to depart and spattered those who remained with diatribe. Early exit bought early relief, but meant sacrificing a full stomach to save face. Once the others ran off, the table was mine to clear. Plates, platters, bowls, and flatware for five meant many trips to the kitchen and, worse, many returns to the porch—to listen to Nate.

Like thunderstorms pounding my ears, Nate's harangues became my lot to endure. One bluster in particular, which he often repeated, confirmed the height of his aversion toward the others, which was something I had watched develop for a long while. Nate's paranoia of losing control fueled his feelings, while their acquiescence to him fanned them. That an alcoholic, dreamer, and man-child could threaten a bright and able person like my husband was mind-boggling. Yet the three did worry the monarch, inciting him to crush rebellion before it occurred. Ever fearful his subjects would challenge his rule, the demanding king expected a docile queen. Needless to say, she was not a court favorite.

Our other meals were hardly more comfortable. Breakfast and dinner were overture and encore to lunch. Although excuses for missing Nate's soliloquies proliferated, there was only occasional success. Mealtime is a delight for happy families, but toward the end of our living together a meal with Nate was like attending a dinner party with bad food. You had to be there. You had to chew the serving. The task was to swallow it. Fortunately I did not lose weight the way Harley did.

"Hey, Mrs. B! I shouldn't have to be wakin' you up."

"I was just reminiscing. Lord knows, I have fed many hungry men. Farm work builds strong character and great stomachs. Please understand I was not trying to evade you."

"Well, I'm not sure I believe that, but I don't really mind. Just so long as I learn in the end about who chomped on who." He never seemed to stop. He was either chewing or jawing.

"Are you familiar, Mr. Beach, with 'the wolf and the lamb shall feed together'? You will find it in Isaiah, chapter 65, verse 25."

With his fingers flying from plate to palate and back with a speed never seen on Granite Ledge before, Beach polished off his lunch, while I sat in silence.

"You've run short on talk, Mrs. B, and I've got nothin' left to eat. Java with plenty of sugar will do the trick for both of us." Beach presumed I got up to do his bidding. I knew I had to get away.

"Hot stove but cold water. It is a guess how long it will take." There was no guessing about it. It would take as long as I needed.

While bubbles popped inside the percolator knob, I gathered my wits. Through the lens of the kitchen window, I could see Beach clunking about on the porch. One after the other, he dragged Father's chair and my rocker to the rail. It looked as if joining the coffee club he was setting up would lead to closer contemplation of the fatal ledge.

Back outside with a single mug of coffee, disconnecting the chairs a bit, I sat down near him, not beside him. As we stared straight ahead, he searched for lingering clues from last fall, whereas I contemplated the forward progression of spring. The snowdrops, skunk cabbage, and forsythia all sought admiration. They had no secrets to hide.

"That's a mighty steep climb to the barn, Mrs. B, and it looks pretty slippery."

Mornings I had to wait.

Fingers not opening.

Knees not straightening.

Ginger tea my brew.

Did wonders for arthritis.

Gentler than bee stings.

"It's not hard if you are familiar with the path. I get up it pretty well with my cane."

"Ledge has gotta be a tough place to set a barn up."

"But it is flat. On stone the barn will not settle, and there is never any mud, although it does get a little tricky when the ledge is wet or iced up."

"Now tell me why your husband was in such a hurry to fix that hole in the barn roof."

"We had been having a lot of rain during the fall, and suddenly there was a break in the weather, so the shingles were able to dry out. Nate figured this would be our last chance to fix the roof before winter because the almanac was predicting another long rainy spell."

"You farm people rely on such foolish notions."

"The signs also supported the idea that rain was coming in again. We had seen a halo around the moon the night before. When birds were not flying the next morning, that clinched it."

"Well, you can't plug a hole with myths."

"There was more to it than just fixing the hole. The entire roof was deteriorating. It was becoming porous as a crayfish trap."

"Whatever the hell that is. Why didn't Nate wait for summer, when it was drier and safer?"

"Because Thor had thrown his hammer early in the fall. It was September."

"You can leave out the stupid Greek gods."

"For your information, Thor is the Norse god of thunder."

"What twaddle! Mad gods and a hole to hell!"

Gale across the hole.

Shingles sailing.

Wind whipping.

Whirring in our ears.

"The storm was the first in a series of nightmares for us. Fixing the roof was the next one. The men dreaded the thought."

"Scared of a little hard work?"

"It was not just because it was a very tall barn with a very steep roof sitting on a big rock. It was way more than that. The barn symbolized the trials we had to face on the farm. Father accepted it, but it always bothered the others."

"Did it bother you?"

"I felt its power, too, but I interpreted it as positive. I liked the challenge it represented."

"Yet your roosters were afraid of the damn thing. In Boston, we'd call 'em chickens." Beach was learning about life on a farm, after all.

When the barn door swung in the wind.

When livestock escaped from a stall.

When the cock did not crow.

They all agreed.

Two investigators were better than one.

"It may sound ridiculous, but they started scrambling at mealtimes to sit with their backs to the barn. Looking at it reminded them of trouble ahead."

"The boys maybe, but not the men, I would hope."

Four of them. Boys or men? Childish or grown-up? I had wrestled with such questions for years. There were answers for some. Many I had to leave buried.

"Go on, Mrs. B. It's time to get to what really happened that day. Lean back in your rocker and spin your yarn."

Slats against my back.

Eyes squeezed shut.

It started with a bang.

It ended with a bark.

"I'll sit at your feet and gather your wool as you spin."

Beach's invitation was enticing. Daring me to tell all, he could serve as final arbitrator. Disturbed by the verdict, I could see the value of closure. Could there ever be a valid finale without the full story?

Despite the loose ends, the jurors had tied the evidence and testimony up into one knot. Even though the judgment was wrong, it was an ending for them. They went home to their families. I went home to none.

Now, competing with Beach was providing a double challenge. Contention was as important as conclusion. The fight was as important as the finish. The words rushed out on the heels of my thoughts. "I told the jury everything I saw and heard, but if you want, I am perfectly ready to go over it again."

"Your old testimony has nothin' to do with the price of eggs now. I'm after a new version—the real McCoy."

"I could not see the ladder! Those trees to the right block the view from here."

"We'll get to the big fall in time. I mean to start with breakfast that day and work up from there."

"Very well—I set out breakfast, the others took seats, and Nate hit them in the face with his plan. Although the day had started cold, the sun was bright and the air dry, so it would end up nice and warm. The time had come to fix the roof."

"And the response?"

Not a peep.

Cagey looks.

Did they know something?

Were they ahead of me?

"There were no outspoken complaints right away, but their lined brows said they were not very keen."

"Well, in the city you'd hire a roofer—and get him cheap."

"Well, in the country we do our own work—and call ourselves thrifty."

"On with the story!"

"Nate handed out his marching orders. The others would haul whatever was needed from the shed up onto the ledge." A junco on the rail had chirped in sympathy. "They would lug everything up the ladder onto the roof." A blue jay had shrieked in understanding. "They would fix the hole and replace missing and rotted shingles, working straight through the day into the night, if need be, to beat the rain."

"Sounds like your husband was out to see if he could break 'em."

Leftover shingles would go on the outhouse.

The laziest roofer would get that job.

On the hottest and smelliest day.

"I was worried for the others. I suggested to Nate he might build in some breaks. Since it was going to be like Hades up on that roof, I offered lemonade—"

"The whole disaster could've been avoided, it seems to me. Too bad your father wasn't smart enough to use steel." Beach's enthusiasm for modern science was on show again. "It's been available for years, and they still argue whether it was an American or English invention."

"Father built the barn with the wood off his lands and the sweat off his palms."

"Big deal. Did Nate pay any attention to your bright ideas?"

Stern eyes.

Taut lips.

Fingers a vise on my arm.

A slap was in the mail.

"Well, he acknowledged my interest."

Limp submission.

Temporary salvation.

I was a quick learner.

"But he dismissed my concerns. Petty fears from the 'chief cook and bottle washer' he said. He described his mother that way, too."

"That must've hurt!"

"I was surprised he said anything to me at all, but things like that did not bother me. Remember what Jesus taught: 'And unto him that smiteth thee on the one cheek offer also the other.' Saint Luke, chapter 6, verse 29."

Earlier in the same lesson, when Jesus had come down from the mountain, stood in the plain, and lifted up his eyes, he had said, "Blessed are ye that weep now: for ye shall laugh." Better for me to leave that part unsaid. I did not want my interrogator to learn too much about me.

"Well, well. We've heard from Luke, so who's next? Matthew or John?"

"That was when Nate slapped me with my personal set of orders. That is, I would serve lunch up at the barn."

"Wow! A country picnic!"

"I could tell they would be lucky if they even got to eat it."

"I'm surprised your husband was ready to omit his luncheon lectures."

I had never revealed Nate's practice to Beach. He must have learned about it from one of the men. Which one? Or ones? And how? To confront Beach now about these sources guaranteed approval of their accuracy. Ignoring his question would parry his thrust.

"Nate did not care what they got to eat so long as I brought it up to the barn. He was not going to stand for any dillydallying."

A horde of common grackles swooped down to scout the lawn for something, anything, to eat. Boisterous birds, they bobbed about, beaks combing grass, flipping leaves, and probing turf. Frustrated soon, the iridescent invaders exploded away. After the blast scattered the hairs off some balding dandelions, a chipmunk chewing on a pinecone restored tranquility to Granite Ledge.

"This place seems so relaxed it's hard to picture people hustlin' around like you say, Mrs. B." Was this man appreciating the positives in farm life at last? Or was he setting me up for the future? "On the other hand, it does reek of dawdlin' and delay." The nasty was up and running again. "Did your husband's picnic plan upset you?"

Pestle end crushing rhubarb.

A mess of mashed pulp.

Rolling pin squashing dough.

Oozing butter between bloodless fingers.

Hard to grease the plate.

"On the contrary, I was pleased. Any change from the day-to-day routine was refreshing."

"But him bossin' you around like—"

"Nate's style was a bit trying, to be truthful. But with a hurry-up lunch there would not be time for lectures—like the ones you guessed about a few minutes ago."

Searching for a flicker of acknowledgement, I drew a blank from Beach. Nate had used the same look. This man's methods mimicked those of my husband. I had run into a wall again, softer and flabbier, but still a wall.

Methodical in my own way, picking up Beach's half-empty mug, I started off for the kitchen. "Soaking ceramic cuts down on coffee staining." There was no resistance from Beach because he was not looking or listening. Head down, chin on chest, he was concentrating, not napping.

"I'll only need a minute." Putting a mug to soak does not take long, but all I needed was a short break. For months, I had not needed my kitchen coziness to recover from conflict outside on the porch, but I was back at it again.

Molly had used the break to sample scents down on the lawn, but the creak of the door as I came out, brought her dashing back to hit my lap on the first forward rock.

Beach had not budged his bottom from his seat in front of the porch rail, but as soon as I sat down, his words flew up the hill. "So, after breakfast was over, what steps did they take to get up there?"

Myles skipped down the path.
Luke stumped off to the shed.
Harley snuck into the house.
Nate stayed supreme on the porch.

"It's hard to remember exactly. Things happened fast. I do recall no one finished their breakfast—no, that's not quite right, my husband did."

"Come on. Don't wander the way you did in court. Actually, that's not fair, I guess." Could Beach be fair? "You heaped up piles of precision, only they were unimportant details under which you hid essential facts. You didn't fool me then and won't now. Can't you see I've done my homework?"

"Myles and Luke headed for the shed."

"And Harley?"

"Evaporated from the porch."

"Did he hide in the house?"

"I did not pay much attention. There is a fleeting image in my mind of the screen door swinging shut."

"I thought everythin' stayed fixed in that brain of yours." Censure not compliment.

"I was busy planning a fortifying meal."

"Meanwhile, Harley went after his."

"You're just fishing. Hope you make a good catch."

Under clothes in his bedroom bureau.
Harley put away his own wash.
Beside the cider in the root cellar.
Rum and cider look the same.

"I did not realize Harley had stashes in lots of places."

"People who didn't even live here suspected that. It's hard to believe your eyes, ears, and nose failed in such a conspicuous situation." At least, in criticizing my senses, Beach left common sense alone.

"That hogwash coming from complete strangers amazed me. The people interviewed in the paper barely knew us, but they had lots to say. Then came the next group of outsiders—the prosecutor and lawyers—spouting all sorts of insights out of the blue. Now, I have you to contend with, but you know what? It is too late for anything new." I prayed that this be true.

"The talk shouldn't have surprised you. There's nothin' like a murder trial in a small town to open a few closets." I pictured Beach running about Concord, all eyes and ears on a rubber neck. "What I've learned so far is you were stuck on this dismal farm with no alternatives. You still are. I imagine you regret that you ever came back here."

Books beside my bed.

Next to the kitchen chair.

Alongside the porch rocker.

No Nate kicking them away.

No Harley stumbling over them.

No Myles grabbing the pages.

No Luke whining for attention.

"There was never a dull moment with the men around. That kept me busy, and now I fill my time reading."

"Farm manuals and feed catalogs?"

"The expansion project at the library has brought in books I never dreamed I could get way up here in the country."

"You could satisfy your desire to thumb pages without livin' out here in the sticks—alone."

Beach could not appreciate the power of reading for me, nor could he understand how it strengthened me. Years ago, Jefferson wrote he could not live without books. Years ago, I found I could live only with books. Productive ideas in my reading displaced the dysfunctional creatures in my life. Intellectual application dislodged those physical dead weights from my mind.

"The reasons I live here—alone, as you say, when the correct term is independently—are hard to express."

"I haven't seen you have any difficulty expressin' yourself. Give it a try."

Explaining my choice—if he believed it was my choice—was worth a try. To challenge Beach with abstract and spiritual considerations was appealing. If nothing else, it would whip up some consternation.

"Since you insist, I'll start with how the rebirth of souls sustains me. Nature and Father join under God here on Granite Ledge."

His eyes and lips screwed up together, crinkling his nose. "What speech am I in for now?"

"Reading the Bible nights and attending church Sundays got me believing."

"Hallelujah!"

"Studying religion in college set me to doubting, but living out here as an adult reinforced my faith."

"This sermon is headed exactly where?"

"Don't you get it? Every day I delight in nature around me. It energizes me. It inspires me."

"Quack! Quack! Quack! You're daft as a duck." What would Beach know about ducks? Why, he probably thought wood ducks were decoys and carpenter ants built houses.

"When a hawk lingers over the house. When a squirrel watches me from the steps. When a dove does not flinch on the rail. They are all benevolent spirits looking after me."

Would Beach's bulging eyes burst the glass in his spectacles? "Preach on, Mrs. B."

"The grief of Father's death got in my way for a while, but he was reincarnated quickly, crowning everything—like a miracle, the cherry on my sundae. Today he sits with the last snow snug in the shade up on the mountain. Tomorrow he may be flowing in the brook. His soul has joined all of nature's spirits, all subjects of the Lord."

The inner strength flowing to me from this alliance kept the external intrusions in my life at bay. Granite Ledge Farm teemed with helpers, from mountain to river, from clouds to grass, from birds to beasts. This mechanism was at work in my clashes with Beach. The hand on my shoulder, the eyes watching, and the ears listening made his assaults tolerable. On top of that, there was a living human being who supported me the way Father, Molly, and my friends in nature did. Although Cleve had the option to talk to me, more often than not his reassurance was as nonverbal as the others. His stability had smoothed the upheaval on Granite Ledge Farm.

"That's quite a tribute, Mrs. B. Even if things like that can't be true, I suppose they will have some effect since you believe they are." Faced with the heat of my creed, Beach swiped his brow with his fingers. "Your nephew's speech in court was just the same—wild and crazy. I can sure remember how Myles wailed on about his need to escape this dreary place. I know what that really means now, thanks to you."

"There is a difference between Myles and myself. He was never happy here."

"He saw demons in this hole. I'm sure the good jurors of Concord never expected to hear a blacklist quite like his. No reincarnated farmer-father for that unhappy boy, no siree." A practical man unable to handle my intangibles, Beach was searching for an ending without a benediction. "So the lesson ends with you, wacky thoughts and all, worshipin' here evermore amidst the untamed spirits."

"Amen, Mr. Beach. Amen."

Beach rolled his eyes to the heavens above the barn. "Let's get back on solid ground. We left off with Nate and you on the porch."

With Beach plodding ahead in his hunt, strewing bait to set the trail was irresistible. "My husband was procrastinating. He not only had more coffee, he got it for himself. Nate never, ever waited on himself. I could not help feeling that something big was brewing."

"Too bad details like that didn't come out at the trial from you. The more known about Nate's habits, the more it might have helped the jury. Were you tryin' to cover up? To prevent 'em from knowin' what a bastard he really was? So they'd buy your accident theory?"

"When it's a question of a man dying or being murdered, how much coffee he drinks does not seem important."

"If it isn't important, why did you bring it up? More important to me, though, is to find out if the four of you were ever together that day without Nate?"

"We all testified that did not happen."

"Which doesn't mean it didn't happen. The whopper would be if you all teamed up to bump Nate off, which would perfectly explain the 'mysterious' fall."

"But you know perfectly well I was not a suspect. All three men said they saw me down on the porch when my husband fell."

"One of the very few things they did agree on. At first, I thought they wanted to protect you—until they started to blame each other. Then I realized any one of 'em would've fingered you in a jiffy if he figured it would've saved his rear."

"I would have needed a long rope to reach up from here and pull that ladder down. Besides, in the pretrial inquiry all three volunteered that

Molly's barking came from down here on the porch. Everybody knows she sticks to me like glue, so I had to have been on the porch, too. Even when they switched their stories later, that did not change those basic facts."

"A bag of fleas provides your alibi. You'd only get that in a fairy tale written by some damn dog lover."

Still not ready to abandon his theory of group complicity, Beach offered another postulate. "Okay. Suppose those three rascals teamed up without your help. They were in the shed together at one point. Maybe they dreamed it up then."

"That does not add up, either. Each man protects both of the others at first, but later singles out just one as the murderer. Yet no two agree on who that third guilty person is. That is unbelievable. It is hardly the behavior of a murderous trio working in cahoots."

"Since you've apparently been absolved of direct involvement, I expect to iron out wrinkles like that with your help."

"The men were going off on separate paths long before this mess happened. I suggest you work from that premise."

"Okay, you were all chargin' around this damn farm in different directions. Did Nate ever talk of any concern about collisions?"

"We did not talk about anything special or private, if that is what you are wondering. Exchanging ideas had fallen low on my husband's list. In any case, the work started in the shed. First, Myles and Luke carried the ladder up to the barn, which was easy. Next, they dragged the sledge loaded with shingles up the hill. Luke was heaving at its traces like a struggling ox."

"Did you mean to say 'dumb ox'?"

"Myles lent a hand from the back. Supervising Luke appealed to him. Being in control made him feel grown-up."

"The peckin' order was well established by this point, I assume."

"Nate was tweaking them with shouts over the rail."

Beach strolled to the rail and thumped his pipe on it. Never before had live embers threatened the tinder of dead leaves lying below. Fire on a farm belongs in a stove, forge, or fireplace. If Father could have witnessed this act, he might have strangled the man. My scowl burning into the offender's back, I had murder on the brain, too.

"Luggin' that thing uphill must've been hard for two boys. A modern device like an internal combustion engine would sure upgrade this antique shop."

Luke strained at the lead.

Myles pushed from the back.

Nate never lifted a hand.

Never offered the horse.

"You persist in calling them boys, but they did the work of adults. You should be able to appreciate that. Sweating is something most men can relate to."

Although Beach was only sitting, he was sweating. Salt running into his eyes explained their scrunched-up look. Propping his glasses high on his brow, he wiped his lids with the table napkin that had not neared his lips while he ate.

"Sure enough. The sweat and tears of our foundin' fathers built this country." As his glasses fell back down onto his nose, his lofty platitude plunged to a low dig. "But parenthood is certainly not on the plate for Myles or Luke, is it?"

"Once the sledge was up at the barn, my husband left the porch."

"Napoleon advances."

"A froth of curses churned in his wake."

"Aimed at the brother-in-law drainin' his reservoir? By the way, where did he get his booze?"

"It was a clever ruse. Harley met the fish peddler out at the end of the drive every other week."

"Girl's work!" Pigs snort like that, too.

"Harley claimed a passion for fish and a need for the freshest."

"Why would anybody trek all the way out here to sell a stinkin' piece of fish?"

"Why, don't you know if fish stinks, it's not fresh? The money the dealer made off selling rum to Harley made it worthwhile. When his buyer went to jail, he dropped me from his route, which is how I found out about the rum traffic."

"Aye, the demon rum. Cod and rum have been interdependent in New England for hundreds of years. I had no idea the connection reached all the way to this godforsaken place." What drivel! Beach could know nothing about godly choices.

"Molly and I do not have much call for fresh fish. She prefers salt cod and mackerel, which I can get at the general store."

"What a great life! A dog determines your diet."

"Our tastes in food and men are the same."

"Well, that's enough on that. Tell me, did your husband help with the ladder?"

"That question need not be asked. Nate surveyed the work. He was not about to help with it."

"Ah, the ruler of the roost."

"Even in his sovereign position, Nate was an inferior commander."

"It surprises me to hear you say that because the trial propped him up as such a superior individual. Where'd he fall down?" Whether Beach's cruel remark recalling Nate's fall was meant to hurt, bomb, or joke, at least he spared me the pain of his laughter.

Beach pounded and whacked his pipe on his palm.

I hugged and cuddled Molly to my breast.

Coarse versus smooth.

Varmint against vixen.

'The question is,'
said Humpty Dumpty,
'which is to be master—that's all.'

—Lewis Carroll
Through the Looking Glass

UP THE HILL

Whenever I needed to tune out from things that were happening on the porch, I had a little trick. I kept a rubber ball jammed in the crotch of the legs crisscrossing under the table. It was always ready for a game between Molly and me. Now, as I bent down to reach for it, she read my mind, slid off my lap onto the floor, and assumed the classic setter's crouch, nose on forepaws.

Bouncing the ball in rhythm with each step, I walked from the table to the top of the stairs leading down to the lawn. A polished red turning dull brown, the ball crumbled slightly in my hand, and bits of it flew off when it hit the floor. A lot of things had deteriorated over time on the farm. Molly pretended not to follow the tease, but her eyes betrayed her—the way everyone's do—round and brown rising and falling with the round brown ball.

When I lofted the ball from the top of the stairs into the garden at the back of the lawn, one tall iris dipped its head to the passing projectile. Molly scampered down the stairs, sped across the lawn, skipped over waves of daffodils and crocuses, and dove into a sea of violets. Her signal flag tail was all you could see above the ocean of flowers until her head surfaced victorious, and she raced back to drop the wet prize at my feet.

Our game of fetch was even more fun during the depths of summer. By then, the heat had coaxed the garden into a jungle of different blossoms with longer stems. The predominant inhabitants were black-eyed Susans—

123

whose yellow faces with brown noses had no eyes at all—that collapsed in bunches, ensnaring the dog. The more I picked the more they bloomed, and Molly enjoyed the greater challenge that presented.

A typical English setter, Molly only chased the ball a few times in a row because running after an object that would not fill her tummy did not make much sense to her. This day she persisted longer than usual, and while we played, Beach struggled to light his pipe, which he could do about as well as I could throw a ball. It took a bunch of matches burned down to his fingers before he was able to break off our fun and games.

"What a waste of time, Mrs. B! I suppose you two could do that all day long. Well, I've got better things to do than have some goddamn mutt hose me down."

Molly had gone to stand beside Beach and was shaking herself dry—an act so natural I had not even noticed. Sprinkled with droplets, boiling with rage, he was laughable, but I spared him by switching the focus back up the hill.

"Once Myles and Luke were up on the ledge with the ladder, Nate caught up with them and took charge of standing the ladder up against the barn."

"I imagine he didn't want to slow his project down."

"You are right about that. I could hear him bossing them around from way down here on the porch."

"Simon Legree is the image I got from the trial. Your husband alone picked the spot for the ladder—another of the rare points the defendants concurred upon."

"Bear in mind, I could not see the whole stage from here."

"Now that I'm here on your porch, I can actually appreciate that. There are so many trees." I was hoping he would not see the forest.

It was my personal arboretum. Hardwoods predominated: maples, beeches, birches, oaks, and hickories. In the understory beneath the canopy, berry bushes came up to the knees of flowering short trees, while ferns and wildflowers ran over their feet on the forest floor. As the forest climbed the mountainside, needles and cones infiltrated the leafy crowd. Pines and hemlocks made up the first surge, whereas spruces and balsams took over at the summit.

A favorite pastime of mine was hiking through the woods and visiting with the wildlife. My companions, winged and four-footed, came in numbers too many to count. Hours spent connecting my friends to their nests and dens provided me with long getaways from the men back on the farm.

"Not much to see out there but a bunch of trees, Mrs. B. What counts is they half hide the barn."

"So now you can accept that I could not have seen what happened."

"Your testimony was vague and ambiguous. It seemed odd to me you could describe the ledge, apple tree, barn, and roof, but not the ladder itself."

"As an honest woman, I could not describe what I could not see."

"In fact, since we've had a chance to talk, I'm more convinced than ever that you left some big-time details out—the same way the ladder did. It was central to the crime, yet unable to testify."

"And so, you are now determined to learn how Nate and the ladder plunged to the ledge."

"More than that! I don't intend to leave here without the fine points about how your husband rode that wooden horse down to his death."

The ladder and my husband hit together.

Trees blocked the scene.

Yet the image was vivid.

The sound was clear.

"Well, sir, I can only imagine what might have happened."

"Well, my dear, I have to believe you know exactly what did happen, but won't tell."

"I was under oath at the trial and told the court what I saw."

"Well, I was unconvinced of that at the time, so now let me tell you what I saw. The three defendants hated your husband and had no love for one another. On the other hand, you had positive rapport with each of 'em, and that included your husband, even if things might have slipped there a little bit. You had always worked for the men, so you dreamed up the accident gambit and, snivelin' in your handkerchief, took center stage in court. That worked to everybody's advantage because it deflected attention away from the crime, a trivial thing like murder."

"You have got to get it straight and stop trying to assign an active role to me. Remember I was asleep on the porch at the time."

"Which made it look impossible for you to have been involved at all.

How convenient! But we still need to run through whatever you did learn from down here. For instance, who you saw on the roof will tell us who went up the ladder." We were looking again where I wanted.

"Luke was first with a bundle of shingles. Next came Myles with a hammer and bucket of nails."

"Where was the big boss all this time?"

"On the ledge, but who knows what he was doing there? Nate did not do much physical labor. He farmed it out. The men had a term for his kind of help—hen's teeth. Nate's late appearance was no surprise to anyone."

"Your husband didn't come across as a man who would permit surprises."

"You have him pegged correctly."

"I would wager he was waitin' to see, by the success or failure of the other climbs, if the ladder was secure. Even if that point was not addressed in court, it speaks against your favored accidental death, which is exactly the sort of stuff I intend to examine as Johnny-on-the-spot out here."

"You are probably right about that. I did not mention the possibility because it was not my job. Besides, I was beginning to enjoy myself. I wanted to see if any of the lawyers knew how to examine a witness."

"Since you weren't at risk yourself, you felt free to play games, I suppose."

Father had taught me how to play many games, and in this one I could tell checkmate was a long way off. "I do not view this as a game at all. In fact, ever since I heard the verdict and started waiting for the sentence, I have been feeling guilty. I never imagined anyone would be convicted of murder."

"Well, I expected it, but not the murderer they picked. For now, we'll skip your little fun with the attorneys because I want to hear what happened next on the roof."

"They went at it like a state highway crew. Luke brought lumber to Myles, who started nailing it home. The foreman, who finally climbed up on the roof, was ever present but never involved. He just stood and watched."

"Both your nephews claimed your husband criticized their every move. It must've been pretty loud. Could you hear 'em down here?"

"Yes, but I couldn't hear everything they said. It was like being at an outdoor band concert. You can hear the music, but not every instrument and hardly ever the announcer."

"My impression was it must've sounded like a bunch of alley cats."

"More like a flock of unruly sheep."

"What do you mean by that?"

"Well, even though they were not bleating in complaint, I could see they were not all that meek."

"So Nate rode herd on 'em? Like the cowboys say?"

Nate brandished his fist.

Myles shook his head.

Luke looked away.

One picture told the whole story.

I did not have to hear.

"Nate was pretty scary, so each held his tongue as best he could."

"Did Nate single out one or the other?"

"Everybody was on the receiving end that day."

"Be specific for the record."

"Before they went up the hill, Nate threatened Luke with no lunch."

"And Myles?"

"That, too, plus he got a warning on how not to shingle. You know, poor placement and improper nailing."

"Did Nate forget Harley?"

"By no means. When my husband was not beating on Luke or Myles, he was cursing Harley, who had not showed up."

"Where was he? Wasn't it kind of late?"

The screen door slammed.

Harley lurched onto the porch.

Feet scrabbling.

Catching up with his trunk.

"I did not know where he had gone, but did know it was time to work and too early to drink. At last, there he was, heading up the hill."

"What'd he say?"

"Nothing to me. He was swearing at Nate. I wish I had never heard him."

"The other two men said they could hear him as he came up the hill, but I wonder if those were just stories they made up to protect their skins."

"Why do you insist on doubting everything? Even after feasting fully at the trial, you are still looking for dessert."

"All in a day's work, my dear."

"None of this should make any difference to an insurance man. There is no clause in that policy relieving payment of benefits in case of homicide. So what are you actually interested in?"

"For a new widow who only just learned about the insurance, you're quite familiar with the fine print."

"We must stop dancing around. We should home in on your coming out here and prying into things. You treat us like lesser beings undeserving of courtesy, manners, or decency."

Beach rose to his feet in defense. "Excuse me! I apologize for anything you have misinterpreted as rough or rude behavior. This case challenges me to the utmost, so I cannot help myself at times."

Beach was on target on only one of his four points. Apologizing was dishonest. Blaming misinterpretation by me was ignorant. Excusing his misbehavior because of the case was inappropriate. That he could not control his behavior was, however, accurate.

Beach's flop as a thespian brought me onto my feet. "The newspaper published all the pertinent facts about the insurance." The histrionics followed. "In your excitement, you forgot the fine print yourself. The sole beneficiary is an irrevocable trust, the Granite Ledge Farm Trust. Nothing goes to any of us." And concluded with a dash. "And do not forget all the lawyers agreed on the stipulation that there was no financial motive for murder."

"Do you mean to suggest a Veritable policy is like fool's gold?"

"Good Lord! That policy is not worth a tinker's damn."

"In my experience, which I assure you has been extensive, I've flushed out a lot of people who did a lot more than topple a ladder for a lot less." After pausing for applause that was never going to come, Beach appended a rider. "It may look like my interest in certain details exceeds that of your friendly insurance man, but you're mistaken if you're suspicious of that."

Look like? Mistaken? Suspicious? That more than a job assignment lay behind Beach's behavior had become indisputable. We both knew it, but pretended unawareness—who would crack first?

I was banging heads with a detective, interrogator, and voyeur, wrapped in one. Whatever the blend, the man was using his authorized position as a claims investigator to gather unauthorized details.

Perhaps I had failed to defend the family in front of the court. Yet, now in the one-on-one, I was confident of handling Beach. Although I could not predetermine the questions, I could lead him to the conclusions I wanted. Like a cat with a captured mouse, I would take command. I would push him around with a paw and bat him away as I pleased. If he started to get out of control, I would seize him in my mouth and squish him between my teeth. It was not time to stop the playing yet, but when the time came, I would break his neck and fling him away.

"My brother-in-law knew that he better get to work."

"You mean save his ass?"

"Maybe protect his sons."

"Do you really think he'd bother to protect those boys? I can't go so far as to call 'em his sons."

Staggering steps.

Steady oaths.

The goal the ledge.

The target Nate.

"Harley did not seem too troubled. I figured he would pitch right in."

"When Harley reached the ledge, could you hear what they said to each other?"

Nate commanding.

Harley cursing.

Myles and Luke complaining.

"Like screeching crows. You do not catch every word, but you still get the message."

"Did you get the idea of what Nate had to say?"

"Nate accused him of being late, lazy, and loaded."

"How'd Harley take that?"

"He stopped dead in his tracks and turned his back. I did not know what he was up to and did not expect what he did. One fist raised in a fig toward Nate, he stared down toward me, as if he wanted my approval."

"I'd be surprised if he cared a fig about your opinion, given his comments about you in court."

"Yes, that was a big surprise. It took some guts."

The tree beckoned.

Trunk a support.

"Harley headed for the apple tree and, trunk against trunk, slid down to the ground."

Ruby red hat against the tree.
Too large, too low for an apple.
"And went to sleep."

"Passed out is what you said in court."

"You could be right. There was no peace or quiet for ordinary napping up there. The awful clamor on the roof kept on."

"I say your brother-in-law was fakin' the whole thing."

"Well, things were a little different. Usually, even if Harley drank a lot, he stayed in control."

"That's exactly my point. To lose control was not typical for him, which makes me suspect it was all an act. What were the boys up to durin' all the theatrics?"

"Just wanting to get away."

"But instead they watched the show."

"They did not have a choice. They were trapped on the roof with Nate."

"And the Poor boys didn't object?" The secondhand pun crashed at his feet.

"Myles kicked a bundle of shingles off the roof. I saw pieces flying before I heard them hit the ledge. I had no idea he was so upset."

"Did the bomb wake Sleepin' Beauty?"

"Harley never moved."

"How about you?"

"Right then and there, I figured it was a good time for lunch. I dreaded climbing the hill with the basket, but I wanted to stop the racket, if not end the war. I was hoping I could interrupt them."

Beach interrupted. "What a great time for us to go up on the ledge. You can tell me the rest on the way up. I'm hungry to inspect the scene the way the jury did."

Intent on a feast thanks to Beach, a parade of ants heading up one table leg caught my eye. "We're getting into ant season. I need to tidy up first."

Bald spot looking back at me, he paid no heed to my housekeeping.

The enemy sat down to muster his forces.

I fled the battle zone for my kitchen.

Little strokes fell great oaks.

—Benjamin Franklin
Poor Richard's Almanack

ON THE LEDGE

Beach ignored my return onto the porch the way he had my exit from it. Scanning the sky over the barn, he had his eye on a hawk, searching the earth below. The man was contemplating his climb; the bird was planning its plunge. Out of the blue, the raptor peeled off like a dive-bomber and, stooping for speed, vanished when it ran out of sky. You knew it had not crashed. Quickly, wings thrashing the air, target locked in its talons, the bird rose in slow motion back up into the blue.

"While I was in the house just now, Mr. Beach, a peculiar thought popped into my head." I wanted to bring the dreamer back down to the porch, to get him back under my control. "You might be interested to hear that the lunch you rejected the other day was what I took up for the men's picnic—save the wicker basket and butter pot that are no more. And I left fruit off their menu since some apples fell off the tree when Harley flopped down against it."

"Things were fallin' all over Granite Ledge that day." The taunt stung, but I held my tongue. "Incidentally, I've noticed the way you limp, so I wonder why didn't you have one of the men carry the basket up?"

"Why, bless my soul and body, that was work for a woman alone. Remember who was handing out the orders."

Straining to his feet and stomping down the steps, Beach trailed his set of orders behind. "Shake a leg, Mrs. B. Off to the barn!"

Apprehensive but curious, I tailed along. During the winter after Nate

131

fell, I had avoided all the trips up to the barn I could. A lasting snow cover had made that decision easy, but it was not the main reason. "Sometimes this climb's a bit too much for my knees."

"But you ought to know exercise is good for arthritis." Spinning around to launch his latest jeer, Beach threw off a shower of sweat, which broadcast his need to rest. Although I wanted him to think my joints made me reluctant, I could not resist passing the man, a grape on course to becoming a raisin.

The competition ended with us cresting the hill together and turning to survey the valley below. The path we had climbed was as ordinary as it looked from the porch, but the view beyond transformed dullness into discovery.

The sun was nibbling away at a doughy strip of fog concealing the lowlands. Light bouncing off the opalescent barrier dazzled the eye. Clumps of trees on higher ground punched like fists through the mist. A few pillars of chimney smoke perforated, too, but as they wafted up into the sky, the wind skimmed them away. A flight of green-winged teal darted by on a journey north, tracking the invisible river below by instinct. Far overhead, tracing the same line in the same way with same goal, a string of Canada geese inched along under a dome of blue.

The scene swayed utilitarian Beach—a bit. "It's too beautiful for a murder site."

"Well, that is one thing we can agree on. Being so high up, it is usually like this, but when I was standing here last fall after my husband fell, I did not check the view."

"I'm surprised you didn't look because you must've had well-rested eyes. I remember how in court you claimed you took a nap right in the middle of the hubbub. You certainly picked a perfect day to snooze!" Even if Beach agreed on the view, he continued to doubt me. "And you know what else? The way you and Myles traipsed up and down this hill still bugs me. Try as I might, I haven't got a hold of what was goin' on with that—at least not yet."

One finger tracked a swallow slanting down from the barn into the sugar bush. "Maybe this new vantage point will help me see things clearly. Let's go over that testimony again right now."

"What are you unhappy about? What do you want me to clarify?"

"While the men were up here, you stayed down at the house. Right?"

"That's correct. Preparing lunch."

"When you brought lunch up, you met Myles on his way down. Why so?"

"Pure chance. Myles was going to the outhouse."

"A courageous act in light of how the boss enforced his rules."

"Evidently my nephew could not bear any more berating, so he left."

"On his way to see a man about a horse. You bought his outhouse story?"

"What does it matter? Call of nature or not, Myles dropped his hammer, climbed down the ladder, and headed down the hill. What took him so long in the outhouse is nobody's business but his own."

"I don't care about his business. I want to know what was goin' on in his head. I can't remember what he said when you two met up."

Pretending forgetfulness was a ruse to draw me out, a way to find a hole in my story. His cunningness had threatened me at first, but now it motivated me to block his metamorphosis from creep to champ. I was confident because, after all, I had outwitted most men so far.

"I'd like to hear again just what your nephew said."

Jaw jutting.

Teeth gnashing.

Fist hammering.

"He stepped politely aside to let me up the path."

"And said?"

Myles bit his tongue.

Red spray gushed out.

Poison intended for Nate.

"He seemed upset. Whenever we crossed paths during a day's work, he would usually toss a quip that lifted me up into his world."

"Back to terra firma, Mrs. B! What the hell did he say?"

"Why, Myles mentioned my husband, the farm, and the whole State of New Hampshire."

"That I remember now. And the main point of what he bitched about?"

"He was going far, far away."

"Any place in particular?"

"No. It was not a great oration. He just wanted out."

"You always talk like you're givin' a public address yourself—better yet, a lecture—like the first woman to teach at Harvard College."

"So, then, you are aware that bastion of male domination is crumbling, as we speak?"

"That's either tittle-tattle or prittle-prattle. You see! I can turn a phrase myself." He could not. Spew insults was more like it.

"Well, you better be careful not to choke on it first." I moved along to evade his smart mouth. "I was struggling up the hill with the basket, and he was hurrying down to the privy. Conversation was not in either of our minds."

"I guess I have to accept what you say, but I don't have to believe you."

In another move to change direction, I stepped to the edge of the ledge and pointed the way to Beach. "Myles had to loop into the sugar bush and pass by the shed to get to the outhouse. As with most things personal, Father positioned the privy to limit intrusions."

Beach did change direction by turning on his heels. "No more sightseein' for me. The ledge is ripe and ready for Benjamin Beach to explore. Makes me wish I had my little Leica." Hearing about more inventions from the technologist was getting boring. "But usin' a spy camera is not my style." If Beach was not spying, I wondered what he would have called it, but I restrained myself from asking.

"When you first came up here with your picnic basket, how were things laid out? Exactly how was the arena set up?"

"It was not the Colosseum, if that is what you mean. Neither beasts nor gladiators were involved." I could not read from his look whether Rome was within his purview or not. "The first thing I did was go and set the basket down at the foot of the ladder, so I know that spot well. Then I took a few seconds to look around."

"Where were the other men?"

"Harley was in plain sight, over there against the tree. Close as I was to the barn, I could not see up on the roof, but I could hear Nate and Luke."

"Did you talk to any of 'em?"

"That is easy to answer. I did not feel like yelling up to the men on the roof or rousing Harley dead asleep on the ground."

"Dead drunk is what you mean. So, what were your thoughts as you stood there?"

The ladder shot to the eaves.

Tall pylon of hollow rectangles.

The basket squatted on the ledge.

Short fence of solid wattles.

Contrasting symbols.

Task and reward.

Tension and relief.

"I did not think—I acted automatically. There was no one to talk to and nothing more to do. It was only a minute or so before I headed back down to the house."

Concentration captured Beach's face in a flash. As though my description of leaving the ledge removed me from his mind, he began to pat down his pockets. A pair of field glasses that neither supported an interest in bird-watching nor suggested a passion for opera appeared. Was a magnifying glass next? Bowing to the competition, Beach's bottle-bottom glasses disappeared, demonstrating how much better he looked without them. A bonus was the easing I felt in front of eyes that could not see.

Beach walked to edge of the ledge and, pressing oculars against sockets, began to scan the layout down the hill. Searching the woods to the left, he should have seen the fully fuzzed out pussy willows. Even the family members I could not agree with admired that splendor, but Beach's silence proved he was not the type to notice. Because the spring-turning-to-summer foliage was thickening up, the outhouse was not detectable. The flash of forsythia way off to the left would have deceived Beach unless he remembered the outhouse was red. Father thought all farm buildings should be the same color, just as he thought all Wimples should be the same cut.

The surveyor swept from the trees to the house, where what he saw was mostly roof. The table and chairs on the porch were not in plain sight, demonstrating in a backward fashion how hard it was to see the whole barn from there. As Beach then moved along the ledge toward the apple tree, dragging me as if magnetized along with him, the furniture came into full view.

After staring below too long for my comfort, Beach inched his inspection up the hill to its crest where, in a sudden refocus, he turned his attention to the barn behind us. Here and there, sunlight reflected off the lenses onto the roof, and I sensed his paired eyes sliding over the shingles, plunging into the hole, erupting back out, and flowing down the roof. After a few minutes of tracking, a burst of light jumped off the eaves and died in the barn's shadow.

With binoculars down to his hip and goggles back on his nose, Beach switched to searching the surface at his feet. I guessed he was looking for where the ladder had planted its feet. He at last discovered a discoloration marking the rock several yards from the side of the barn. Closer inspection—Beach dropped to his hands and knees—revealed traces of a smudge adhered to the granite. Whether this was a human bloodstain or a police marker was not important to me. Where the ladder had let go, where it had landed, and where my husband had crashed were important questions for Beach. I did not need to know.

Nose and paunch down to the ground, Beach palpated the patch with the fingers of one hand, while the other probed a pocket. The magnifying glass I had worried about did not appear, but a piece of white cloth did. It could have been a handkerchief, except Beach was not a gentleman. He swabbed the spot and examined the rag. Held up to the light, it was tinged red—dirty, rusty, or bloody? The result of his sniff test I never learned.

Rag-testing complete, Beach stood on the ugly spot. "I'm convinced this is where your husband hit. Now show me where the ladder started out."

"I never thought I would forget any of the dreadful details, but now that I am back up here, it is really hard to be sure where the ladder stood." In truth, I did not know, so I picked a place to point to where the generally flat ledge sloped down slightly from the barn. "I would guess it was somewhere over there." I felt it would not hurt to try and build my case a bit.

As Beach studied the surface, a look of frustration spread across his face. Although there were small zones of textured stone and shallow hollows that might have stabilized a ladder, the rock looked smooth overall and downright slippery in several spots.

"You would think the cops would've marked the damn place, but have no fear, there are other ways to skin a cat." His doubt strengthened my conviction.

"Had I known the location of the ladder's feet was going to be crucial to my theory, I would have come back up here and painted a circle around it."

"Well, I can work from where he crashed."

While one hand drew an imaginary circle in the air with a flourish, the other palmed, then brandished a tape measure. Pulling a tongue of steel out of a head of brass, Beach handed me its tip. The showman stepped aside and motioned me, his apprentice, onto the spot where he was standing. Backing away from me, the magician-turned-carpenter uncoiled the tape, walked over to the side of the barn, and measured distances along several angles.

Once satisfied with those computations, Beach fixed his gaze on the apple tree and walked on a beeline to its foot, pulling more tape out as he went. When he got there, he sat down, leaned against the trunk, looked up at the roof, looked down at the house, and got up. He recoiled the tape by walking back to me, removed it from my hand, and buried the device in his pocket. Then, stepping from point to point on the stone surface, he performed a series of finger-pointing calculations, aiming from roof to ledge to house in a variety of pairings. In another sleight of hand, a stopwatch materialized from the treasure chest of his coat, and he hustled, clock to eye, from place to place, as fast as he could. Somehow, the staccato of the second hand sounded in my ears. The next thing I knew Beach was backing down the hill, only to halt as soon as his line of view was level with the ledge. The finger dance began again, this time tracing lines from outhouse to lawn to house to where he stood, as if connecting the dots. Once again, watch in hand, eyes on the dial, Beach raced to various spots on the ledge and back.

Would the time-and-distance expert climb next to the roof and run around up there? No. Instead, Beach sped across the ledge to the rear of the barn and stopped short where the ladder was lying alongside some bushes. Intact but illegible, it had not told the investigators much, so someone, flatfoot not farmhand, had hauled it to the far end of the ledge. The ladder was too heavy for me to move, and since it was the instrument of death, I did not want to touch it. The thought of it made even Cleve antsy, so the ladder had spent the winter there.

While I reminisced over its artistry and recalled Father, Beach plunged into its construction and envisioned a killer. First, he paced the length of the uprights and counted the rungs. Next, he retrieved his tape and measured the width from upright to upright and the space between the rungs. Then, he stroked both ladder ends with his fingertips, searching their texture to define their roles in standing, slipping, and falling. Finally, he marched from one end back to the other, stamping on each rung, where he stood still and summarized his findings. While searching like this could have weakened my accident claim, searching at all proved it was gaining strength in Beach's mind.

Whether satisfied or frustrated by what he found, Beach whirled with a whistle and, leaving me in his dust, he raced to the front of the barn and disappeared around its corner. Since he could not get into much mischief inside the barn, I let him be. In no time at all, barn swallows fleeing through the hole in the roof showed Beach was checking the loft. If he had climbed out onto the roof—a hazard I should not have wished for—I would have let him be.

Beach returned earlier than wanted, but he was empty-handed as expected. His face stated his disappointment, so we stood together, separated by silence. Too soon, mumbles and mutters started boiling forth. "Ladder. Angle. Flat. Friction. Push. Pull." Were they questions or answers?

Based on what I heard coming from his mouth, I speculated about what was going on in his head. All of Beach's investigative techniques so far had been disconcerting because he had not followed any formal rules of collecting and correlating evidence. Indeed, he had no rules at all, as with a grand jury of one or, worse, in a kangaroo court. So, how he might predict human actions from physical particulars like position, distance, speed, and timing concerned me now. Crackling, sparking, and flashing within his brain, bits of information coursing pathways and bridging connections might galvanize into an electrifying revelation at any second. Would I be able to short those circuits?

"Your head's in the clouds, Mr. Beach. It's your turn to come down to earth."

As if shot down, Beach descended as fast as he had catapulted off. "Just addin' things up in my bean. I have a better sense of what's likely to have gone on. It revolves around the ladder. Not that it fell—that's a given, but how and why. I don't for a minute believe its feet just slipped out under your husband's weight."

"But—"

"Yes, I know where you're comin' from. But that theory is off base, if you get the joke. Some additional factor, some force I've not yet figured out, was needed to make that ladder fall."

"If—"

"It's hard to conceive of any natural event as the cause—a tornado or earthquake, for instance. But a person could have put the ladder down in a second, and the bottom line is whether it was push or pull."

"You have my opinion. I am no ladder expert, but maybe—"

"Well, it's my opinion that the answer does not lie with the ladder over there." His roving finger was back. "It lies with whoever handled the ladder." At least, the finger was not pointing at me. "But, given the decision of the court, none of those canaries will sing again, at least not a true song. The convicted man is a goner. No one will believe any different tune that comes from him. The other two, who are off the hook, won't change their tunes at all."

The second wind firing up Beach was chilling me. "Which brings me right to you. I think you're the one who knows the most. I feel you hold the key, so we've got a lot more to talk about. A little while ago, we left off our discussion at the point where you dumped the picnic basket and headed home. Didn't your husband invite you to stay for the picnic?"

Two downies around our suet feeder.

The male would not let the female eat.

I kept it stocked throughout the day.

Intent on outlasting his arrogance.

"I did not wait for an invitation. I hardly expected one."

"Didn't you want to eat?"

"I was not really hungry. Besides, Molly knows a good thing when she smells it. I had to keep jerking her away from the basket, which was not fair to her."

"My God, Woman, you worried more about how you might hurt some dog's feelin's than how you could keep the food safe for your men?"

"Molly has rights, too. Plus I figured we both would be better off down on the porch."

"Where was your other pampered pet, Myles, at that point?"

"I have already told you. He had gone down the hill." Endless questions rolled over repeated answers.

"With Harley asleep and Luke too stupid to trust, I have to accept the story that you and Myles were not on the ledge together. But you could've plotted your next moves goin' down the path together."

"On Father's grave I swear to you I did not go down the path with Myles. I followed him down later. In fact, we were not even close together. By the time I reached the lawn, he had disappeared."

"Which puts you back on the porch all by yourself."

"Not by myself, Mr. Beach. Everyone—Myles, Luke, and Harley—said Molly was on the porch. too. That is where she was when she began to bark."

"Okay, okay. I've heard about her noise too many times already. You two were on the porch together, but that doesn't clear Myles."

"I am fed up with your implications and tired of defending every move this family made. So, I am heading back to the house right now, and Molly is coming with me. You are welcome to keep poking around up here. I will meet you down there, whenever you are done."

Going down off the ledge was a disturbing déjà vu, but viewing the path at the bottom, as it crossed the lawn out to the shed, provided some relief. Crocus heads crowded through the thatch along the edges. A garter snake basked dead center within a streak of sun where a circle of purple finches bathed under showers of dust. Curious about the status of my plantings, a woodchuck sauntered alongside the garden, while almost to the woods a partridge gobbled a dessert of grit.

These friends out on the path brought me much joy. From highflying fowl down through flora and fauna to lowly reptile, they were comfortable in their coexistence. There was little tension and no conflict—at least, for the majority. Even the wary ones, who were always respectful, if not bonded in trust, enjoyed a contented separation.

Crossing the lawn and climbing up onto the porch, I felt things closing in.

The porch would soon be cramped.

Once again today. Like two days ago.

Like so many days in the past.

And the four living creatures said, "Amen!"

—Revelation 5: 14

DOWN TO HELL

Wrapping myself in the shawl of stillness, I sank into my rocker. I was mulling over the uncertain road ahead when Beach thumped back up onto the porch. Molly raised her head off my lap and, ears peaked, eyebrows raised, nostrils flared, confronted the invader.

Like most English setters, Molly displayed human qualities. For example, she would often stand up like a person on her hind legs to watch the world go by. Supporting her trunk in an upright posture with her front paws on the porch rail, she would take up her favorite observation post. There, with simple head rotation, she could monitor the entire backyard. If some misfortune trapped her inside the house, while I was on the porch, her face would fill the kitchen window above her paws on its sill. Beseeching eyes begged for my return or her release. Barking came next. Out on the lawn, if a butterfly taunted Molly with overhead circles, she would stand and could even manage a few steps. Should a bat, devouring the mosquitoes intent on devouring the dog, arouse her by diving above her back, she would give the walking performance of her life.

Molly and I were ready for Beach's point-blank shot. "What'd you and that buddy of yours do when you got back on the porch?"

"You mean just now?"

"You know exactly what I mean, my dear." Sweet and sour were back on the menu.

"Tired by climbing up with the basket—not to mention the bickering, I dropped into my rocker."

"Safe and sound in your lousy rocker, but still with an eye on the barn. Or did you fall asleep right way?"

Body sweating.

Knees smarting.

"No, my knees were not doing well. I took a minute to rub them with Absorbine."

"Are you tellin' me that Absorbine Junior junk really works?"

"No, I certainly am not. Wimples only use the veterinary liniment. The junior product is inferior."

"I know now why Myles called you uppity. No wonder he griped about your greasy hands and their awful stink."

Fingers slipping.

Brain swirling.

"It is rather oily and costs a pretty penny, but it does help. I happen to like its fragrance, too."

"Well, Myles said in court the stench was terrible, and he wasn't singlin' out that one day in particular. It seems it was standard for you."

"Myles shocked me to the core with his comments. I never, ever realized he was so embittered toward me."

"Your belated discovery about how Myles really felt about you doesn't interest me. And I've heard enough about your snake oil. While you sat down here on your butt, what went on up at the barn?"

Pounding and yelling on the ledge.

Rocking and murmuring on the porch.

"I could not help falling asleep, so I cannot tell you any more. The last thing I remember is Molly's kiss on my cheek."

"How convenient! A perfect time for a siesta." Sarcasm trickled off Beach's lips. Not only had he not sat down, he was standing too close. "That you could sleep at all amazes me, Mrs. Brewster." A cruel inflection for my name so rarely used, the face behind the tone was even meaner.

Eyes shut.

Transparent lids.

Images beyond.

"I must have slept like a baby because I missed everything that went on. Even though Myles complained about me, he verified my napping. That I doubt you could forget."

"No, I can't, but perhaps you heard what happened?"

Thud and splat.

Rattlesnakes warn before striking.

Copperheads attack without giving notice.

"I did not hear a thing until Molly woke me up."

"Did Nate holler when he was goin' down?"

"How would I know? I was not listening, and you are not listening, either. I was asleep."

"Funny how nobody admits they heard a peep out of Nate. That's hard to believe. I can't imagine him speechless when he was crashin' down to his death."

"It could not have taken more than a split second."

"But there was enough time to name the guilty party. Nate must have known that day he was headed for trouble. That someone set the ladder into motion wouldn't have been a surprise to him."

"Well, I awoke in surprise. Here is something else for you to consider. Maybe when Nate fell, he did not call out anybody's name because no one was handling the ladder—except himself. There was nobody to name!"

"I can't buy that anymore. I picture a pack of wolves. I'm sick of all these lies."

"How can I lie about what I did not see?"

"So, all of a sudden, your damn dog barks. You'd heard her bark a lot before, but this time you were worried. What was the big deal? Why did a few barks upset you?"

Molly spoke a sinister prediction.

Then the shouting shut her out.

"Molly can smell trouble."

"Don't give that cussed hound so much credit. It's not a person."

"She is more human than a lot of the two-legged beasts walking around. Molly can tell me many things with her barking, and that day is a good example. I felt horrified even before I knew the truth. That sort of thing can happen."

"What claptrap. Imagination's not that good. Your brain couldn't have seen that comin' down the pike."

"Although you seem to have some, I take it you have never heard of extrasensory perception."

"The subject's not news to me, I can tell you, but it's nothin' but flapdoodle. To hope for things doesn't make 'em happen."

"I am not saying I was hoping for anything at all, but I do believe the mind can sense events in mysterious ways."

"Get practical! Talk concrete! What'd your peepers see first?"

Green cap.

Red shirt.

Blue overalls.

"Why, it was my nephew. Myles. Going up the path. Hitching up his overall straps."

"Both of the attorneys for Harley and Luke questioned that fact."

"However, the attorneys were not there at the time. I was."

"But Harley refuted Myles flat out. He claimed Myles had run from the ledge back down onto the path—after he pulled the ladder out from under your husband."

White face or neck?

Head or trunk turned?

Toes pointing uphill or downhill?

"I saw Myles looking up the hill. I did not bother to analyse it because I started heading up the path right away."

"Leave Myles on the hill for the moment. Who else caught your eye?"

Red hat.

Blue shirt.

Green trousers.

"Harley. I saw what looked like a moving apple bedside the tree become a red hat. Underneath it, Harley's face was looking toward the barn."

"Like a fiend enjoyin' himself? After, as Luke said, he had pulled the ladder out from under your husband."

Yellow face.

Big eyes.

Open mouth.

"That is absurd, Mr. Beach. I wonder what Harley could see, if anything at all. Do you still maintain he was faking a drunken state?"

"Depends on who you wish to believe."

"It is not a matter of belief. It is what I saw." I was testifying to what

I had observed at the top of the hill. Sticking strictly to visual reports would lead Beach where I wanted him to go. "To anticipate your line of questioning, I got a glimpse of Luke on the roof. Do not bother to ask me if it was as he pushed the ladder down, which is what Myles claimed Luke did. You already know my answer to that. And you already know I did not see Nate at all."

"We do know where your husband was—dead on the rock—and we'll go into Luke's whereabouts in due time. Your testimony as the innocent bystander, so to speak, is critical to each of those three villains, given their loopy claims. Since any one of 'em could have done your husband in, tell me what you saw once you made it up onto the ledge."

Center stage.

Alone.

Kneeling.

Facedown.

In a pool of blood.

"Harley and Myles were standing with their backs to me. It took awhile to locate my husband and then to figure out what I was seeing."

"Serve up some details." Hunger hung from Beach's tongue. Standing so close, he was almost drooling on my knees.

Haphazard heap.

Beside the ladder.

Flat and straight.

"The lump on the ground was Nate. I could not see his face, but I knew his clothes. He was not moving."

"No demands this time, I take it."

Arms splayed.

Legs folded.

Skull exploded.

"A circle of blood glistened around his head. His arms were extended forward. His knees were flexed under his trunk."

"Quite a strikin' figure, I'm sure."

"It was kind of a peaceful posture. The image of a praying Muslim flashed into my mind."

Beach's alternative was brutal. "Whatever that means. It sounds more like a failed Olympic dive to me."

"Red on black, blood coated his hair."

"My. My. That's colorful."

"Some cauliflower-like tissue protruded from his temple. My biology course taught me what that was."

"Did you just stand there and gape?"

White hands on gray rock.

Futile fending off.

Hopeless fatality.

"I was hoping my husband was only hurt."

Nate motionless and powerless.

At the same time.

For the first time.

"Maybe he was not really dead."

"He should be so lucky! What were the others up to?"

"Nothing. As I moved in, Harley and Myles stopped in their tracks. I did not see Luke. He must have been somewhere up on the roof. It became deadly quiet."

"So the mutt had stopped her racket?"

"Oh, yes. Molly stopped as soon as I headed up the path and, of course, she followed me. The quiet was broken by some clamor coming from the barn. Luke, it turns out, was stuck in the loft."

"How could you have known that?"

"I did not know it right then. The sounds were insistent, pleading. Myles ran off to explore."

"And Harley?"

"He took off the other way. Past the far end of the barn into the bushes. He was clutching his throat and stomach at the same time."

"That must've puzzled you."

"Not really. Raising two boys, I had witnessed such reactions before."

"Was it fear?"

"No. Nausea. As Harley disappeared into the bushes, I heard the retching."

"So there you were—all by yourself—with the body of your husband?"

"Not at all. Why, Molly was beside me. I was not scared."

Beach did not scare me, either, although he was still looming above me. Yet a wave of relief did sweep over me when he stepped back and sat on the rail. It was not a great distance, but I could breathe.

"After hearin' your description in court, I don't believe you, of all people, would ever be scared. So we've got Myles and Luke in the barn and Harley in the bushes. What'd you do, while they were gone?"

Brown ladder.

Green basket.

Red pool.

Gray rock.

Black body.

Inanimate.

Immobile.

"I was frozen where I was, trying to decide whether to call the doctor or the undertaker."

"You should've called the sheriff. But come on now, there's gotta be some details I can work with. Let's have 'em." Beyond insistent, he was insatiable.

"It was really messy."

"You mean your husband was a real mess?"

"The lunch basket had been crushed—the cover thrown open. There was debris everywhere."

"Those aren't useful details."

"The rhubarb pie had exploded into smithereens. The butter pot had cracked in half. There were yellows, pinks, and purples mixing with Nate's personal red."

"I don't intend to dig clues out of a pile of garbage. What happened next?"

Molly.

Driven hunter.

Soft pads on hard ledge.

Circling excitedly.

Wet nose to dry ground.

Sniffing eagerly.

"Well, Molly distracted me. She set to work, gobbling up what she could. I can still see her eager tongue inching toward all that blood—that shocked me back to reality. But, as I look back now, I realize she helped me get a hold of myself."

"Once again, a dumb dog determines your behavior. That's preposterous!" I did not wince beneath this whack.

"In any case, I collared Molly and was pulling her away when Myles came back with Luke. He said he found him up in the loft, shaking with fear."

"Or gloatin' without guilt."

"About the same time, Harley came stumbling back to join us."

"What a menagerie. I can just picture the four of you lined up, gawkin' at the stiff."

"We were not gawking. We were getting our heads together."

"Well, not grievin' in any case. Who felt triumphant and who felt relieved? There's one hell of a lot of possible combinations."

Weaving figures.

Bobbing heads.

Pointing fingers.

Still afraid of Nate.

"I cannot stand the way you make light of our tragedy. The men started talking all at once. They ended up arguing about how it had happened."

"But no one took credit, I gather. Hey, wait a minute. 'Arguin'. That's what you just said, but the records show that when they were first questioned, they agreed on most everything. Hell, even after they were arrested, they kept up the same line."

"Perhaps I should have said they were wondering out loud. The scene was so awful. I cannot be totally sure of what was said."

"Seems like somewhere along the way they cooked up a story, only to have it fall apart when the prosecutor started to sample the soup. That was when they started to blame each other. But come now, I know I can rely on you to be consistent in describing the events. What's next?"

"Well, that was when Cleveland Parsons arrived. We were all befuddled in the heat of the moment, but luckily he was the cool head. He sized things up in a jiffy and headed off to fetch the doctor."

"Four plus one makes five dancin' around a corpse. What still baffles me is the invitation to the party. Why would the simple bark of a dog have brought that guy all the way over from his place to investigate?"

"Well, there is—"

"Wait, Mrs. B! Let me guess. You're gonna credit ESP again. Well, I don't buy it. I'm suspicious Parsons knew a hell of a lot more about what went on out here than he or you let on. In fact, maybe he was lurkin' beside the ledge all the time. When he saw your husband head down the ladder and the others were occupied elsewhere, he ran over, pulled out the ladder, and took off before anybody saw him. That would've worked. Myles was down the hill. Luke was on the roof. Harley was asleep or passed out. No one saw Parsons up here but you, and you kept your mouth shut, of course. So he hid and waited a few minutes to show up and act all innocent and curious. 'Gee, folks, what's all the barkin' about?' Yes, that could explain the whole thing."

To spend so long talking at one time, and all in one breath at that, must have meant Beach really liked his latest theory. Why not ride this one together for a while to get farther away from the truth. "That is ridiculous. There is absolutely no evidence to suggest such a thing. Not one single solitary soul has even hinted Mr. Parsons might have had a role in what happened to my husband."

"Well, let me be the first. Maybe the guy couldn't stand the way Nate treated you people. Maybe he figured if he got rid of Nate, he'd get you as a reward for himself."

"That thinking is absurd. Cleveland Parsons was not familiar enough with our lives to get involved."

The big man did it all.

Opened doors.

Pulled out my chair.

Cleared the table.

Let the dogs out.

"In fact, he was the epitome of a good neighbor—which meant staying on his side of the fence and minding his own business."

"By the way, is he Mr. Parsons, Cleveland, or Cleve to you? You seem like real pals to me."

"Cleveland Parsons did not have much in common with my husband, or my father for that matter, and the boys paid no attention to him, so he did not come around very much. Plain and simple, he was not that aware about anything on Granite Ledge Farm. He was not that interested."

"So why'd he drop his newspapers off for you? You positively bragged about that the other day."

"That was a minor sociable gesture. Parsons has always done the right thing by us, If we were in a pickle, I am sure he would have helped out if need be."

"All he lacks is the shiny armor." Beach interrupted my song, and it was better the bird not sing anymore. "But, look, you lost your husband. I would think you'd have leaped to catch whoever did it. So, if you eliminated Mr. Nice Guy, who was the culprit? I'll bet you narrowed it down."

"I am not a fool. The men's speculation about what must have happened struck me as excessive, but they all seemed genuinely upset."

"And so, what did you conclude? Who did you suspect?"

Myles looked at Luke.

Who looked at Harley.

Who looked at Myles.

"In all the confusion, I do not recall thinking about that—and, of course, we did not know for sure that Nate was gone."

"In a-you-know-what's ass."

"What I do remember is being distressed by some finger-pointing, but it did not last long."

Beach's fingers were flying all over, too. "The guilt had to land on somebody's head. The innocent landed on his."

"Don't forget, since I had been down at the house, the men were talking about things I had no way of knowing about."

"Men or brutes? Each had reasons, big-time reasons, to want to get your husband off their singular or collective back. Even if you didn't work the fields, you must've seen that at the house every day."

A whirling mass on the ground.

An angry, dusty ball.

Four flailing arms.

Four kicking legs.

Six possible combinations.

Which two were at it today?

"My relatives got along pretty well, all things considered. What animosity I did observe I accepted as part of the destiny of Granite Ledge Farm. It had not been an easy life for any of them, and that had its effects.

Where we did not have rocks, we had stumps. It rained a lot, and snowed for a long time. The farm was too small, and the growing season too short, to get much more than what we needed to feed ourselves. And sometimes we did not even get that."

"That sums it up pretty well. I've got the picture now." Stretching his arms overhead, Beach yawned, moaned, and burped in succession. Out of the black hole beyond the yellowed teeth burst a closing bomb. "Lunch filled me up. And all that climbin' and rushin' around tired me out. It's been my habit to take an afternoon nap whenever my schedule allows. So I'm gonna leave you now and head back to my room in town. I've got a lot to mull over."

The weight was lifting off me, but it would fall again—likely harder. "Lately I have been snoozing in the afternoon myself, so I understand completely. You can appreciate I do not have a big clean-up after lunches anymore."

"Which means you'll have plenty of time for a little chore. Not the usual kitchen work, mind you. See here, I trust you noticed the papers I brought out before. Well, here they are again. They're copies of the trial testimony that yours truly edited to weed out the crap. I expect you to look 'em over before I get back tomorrow to talk about what they show."

After watching Beach lay out my homework, seeing him head for the door was a relief. While I wished he would never come back, I was committed to the end.

Dark shape framed in the door, a dreary daguerreotype, Beach trailed a promise.

"Benjamin B. Beach will be back—tomorrow—bright and early. Sleep tight till then, Mrs. B."

He was gone before I got up.

Had he known I would not show him out?

151

SPECIAL TESTIMONY

Fresh water would have rinsed out the bad taste of Beach. Upon demand, however, the cast-iron pitcher pump gasped for a prime, barely spitting in the kitchen sink. In the past, four males with a thirst and a well without a bottom kept the pump so busy it never lost its grip. Nowadays I had to keep several Mason jars filled with water, ready for the pump's frequent failures.

I solved every problem by myself these days. No Luke to fetch the eggs. No Myles to milk the cow. No Harley to buy the fish. No Nate to assign chores. While nobody helped, nobody hindered. Being without men was not all bad.

Fate took Nate and left the others helpless on the legal bar like ducks sitting in a row at a shooting gallery. All easy targets: dazzled Luke, distracted Myles, and dried-out Harley. The prosecution had three shots. Knock one down, any one of them, and the game was over. Left to myself, I concentrated on picking up the pieces and carrying on with my life. Now, however, the battle with Beach was forcing me to reassess the situation. Many considerations and concerns swirled around in my head, but floating on the top was one recurring question: what was the best way to rectify the error of judgment?

Given a jarful of water down the cylinder and a few seconds for the leather to swell, the pump was again squishing sweetly. The one time the well had failed him, Father was quick to point out how the spring beyond the shed was clean and pure. Its source was too deep for any animals to pollute it, and its flow too fast for bad things to grow in it. I noticed Molly preferred the spring to her bowl.

Pitcher and tumbler in hand, I went back out where the court recorder's mouthpiece lay ready to speak. Most everything about the man, be it dress, diction, or manners, shouted sloppiness. Yet, at my end of the table, Beach had laid out a line of four folders, each a different color, behind a single page, black type on pure white. The presentation proved precision.

Compared to my perky floral centerpiece, Beach's arrangement looked like fallen, flattened leaves. I built a stack of folders and started from the top. The single sheet was a simple preface:

1. The accompanying folders contain verbatim reproduction of selected portions of the testimony in the trial regarding the demise of Nathaniel Brewster.

2. Isolated question-and-answer exchanges between the prosecutor, the several defending attorneys, and the four major witnesses were extracted during the course of examination. These excerpts were combined and ordered in a sequence designed to create a generic legal representative who examines each witness in a logical progression. As a result, each person becomes a composite that delineates his or her testimony as a cohesive unit. In addition, the order of questioning was rearranged to facilitate comparing and contrasting the answers to similar questions by the four witnesses.

3. Superfluous and unnecessary details were deleted in order to preserve only pertinent facts and salient features critical to the case. Emotional or prejudicial commentary by the witness(es) and extraneous or noncontributory inquiry by the attorney(s) were omitted. Formal objections, whether overruled or sustained, in so much as they functioned as exercises in legalistic gyration by nitpicking manipulators,

were disregarded. Pertinent personal comments by the editor were handwritten within parentheses.

Forewarned by this smug introduction, I opened the first folder with humble expectations, wondering if I was equipped to deal with Beach's editing. If nothing else, it would be interesting to compare what I remembered with what he recorded.

Harley Poor's Testimony

ATTORNEY: You were asleep against the apple tree. Is that correct, Mr. Poor?

HARLEY: Yes, I was.

ATTORNEY: Yet something woke you up. Is that your testimony?

HARLEY: Right.

ATTORNEY: Did the barking dog wake you up?

HARLEY: Nah. I was awake before that.

ATTORNEY: Well, why did you wake up when you did?

HARLEY: Don't know. Just did. *(Was HP drunk or not?)*

ATTORNEY: Did you hear the deceased say anything?

HARLEY: Nah.

ATTORNEY: Not a yell or a scream?

HARLEY: Do you think the top dog would yap or whine going down?

ATTORNEY: A simple yes or no is in order, Mr. Poor.

HARLEY: Nah. Not a whimper. *(Everyone agreed on this.)*

ATTORNEY: Tell the court what you saw when you woke up.

HARLEY: Myles pulling the ladder down. *(This means the bottom went out.)*

ATTORNEY: We've heard testimony about the height of the barn and how precarious the ladder was. Are you sure it didn't simply fall by itself?

HARLEY: Darn tooting.

ATTORNEY: Does that mean you had no fear of using it?

HARLEY: I had no fear 'cause I had no intention of using it. Look, mister, I've been up and down ladders all my life. If ye put 'em up right, they're pretty damn safe. Nate knew how t' do it in spades. Myles pulled it down, I tell ye.

ATTORNEY: Where exactly did Myles grasp the ladder?

HARLEY: The bottom. With both hands.

ATTORNEY: His hands were at the very bottom?

HARLEY: Yep. Just said that.

ATTORNEY: Myles was beside the ladder with one hand on it. Is that correct?

HARLEY: Nah. He was standing in front of it.

ATTORNEY: Did he grab the uprights?

HARLEY: Nah, it was the very lowest rung. Pulled the bottom right out, quicker than ye can shake a stick. With both hands. *(No prints there! Were they wiped off?)*

ATTORNEY: Was Myles wearing gloves, Mr. Poor?

HARLEY: Don't remember.

ATTORNEY: Was he wearing gloves at any time that day?

HARLEY: I said I don't remember. What does it matter? His little lily-white hands did the trick. Gloves or not.

ATTORNEY: Did you see the deceased on the ladder?

HARLEY: Didn't see him till I saw the ladder falling. Just woke up, ye know. Just in time t' see it, but not in time t' save him. *(Did HP even get up off his butt?)*

ATTORNEY: Did he say anything?

HARLEY: Nah.

ATTORNEY: Did he holler or yell?

HARLEY: Already told ye. But I heard him hit. That was one big thud.

ATTORNEY: And you saw him land?

HARLEY: Sure did. I seen him splatter on the rock.

ATTORNEY: Where was Myles at this point?

HARLEY: Running back across the ledge. *(HP the sole witness to all of this.)*
ATTORNEY: Back or backward?
HARLEY: Jeez, mister.
ATTORNEY: Was he moving backward? Like this? *(Some comic relief.)*
HARLEY: Nah. He ran straight ahead like a house on fire, then turned around. T' look like he was just coming up the hill.
ATTORNEY: Are you sure of that, Mr. Poor? (*HP and PB don't agree on this.)*
HARLEY: 'Course, I am. He was pulling his straps down from his shoulders.
ATTORNEY: Or was he pulling them up?
HARLEY: Goldarn it! I said down. T' look like his breeches had been down.
ATTORNEY: Did he look at you?
HARLEY: Don't remember. Kept my eyes kinda squinted down under my hat. So he wouldn't know I seen him.
ATTORNEY: Did he say anything to you?
HARLEY: Don't remember.
ATTORNEY: Did you say anything to him?
HARLEY: Nah. Too scared, seeing what he did.
ATTORNEY: Where was Luke at this time?
HARLEY: Up t' the roof. I heard him up there.
ATTORNEY: Where on the roof was he?
HARLEY: He wasn't anywhere near where the ladder leaned. I figured he went down the hole or something like that. *(This helps LP.)*
ATTORNEY: Was Luke wearing gloves?
HARLEY: Don't have the foggiest idea.
ATTORNEY: Did he say anything to you?
HARLEY: Don't remember.
ATTORNEY: Did you say anything to him?
HARLEY: Nah.
ATTORNEY: Where was your sister-in-law at this time?

HARLEY: Down t' the porch.

ATTORNEY: Was she asleep?

HARLEY: Nah. She might have been asleep when I came out of the house 'cause she sits on her rear end all the time. But she was awake, standing up when I woke up. She was up straight. Like a ramrod. (*Confirms PB's porch position, but had she been sleeping or not?*)

ATTORNEY: Was the dog barking at this time?

HARLEY: Yep. I think Patience was trying t' quiet the mutt down. That dog's a real bitch t' get t' shut up. Wouldn't ye know Patience likes t' hear her talk.

ATTORNEY: Did you talk to her?

HARLEY: That stupid mutt?

ATTORNEY: No. Your sister-in-law.

HARLEY: Nah. Figured she'd come up the hill right away.

ATTORNEY: Did you go near the ladder?

HARLEY: Patience's the fussbudget for details around here. Ask her. She's always happy t' put her two cents in. (*Why did HP not answer this directly?*)

ATTORNEY: The question is for you, not her, Mr. Poor.

HARLEY: Nah. I never touched the dang thing. That's the truth, even though that sonovabitch says I did. (*He points at LP.*)

ATTORNEY: Luke said you pulled the ladder down.

HARLEY: Cripes! Don't believe that dummy.

ATTORNEY: We have examined that under oath, as we are doing with you now. Why don't you trust your own son? (*LP restrained by court officer. Must have understood.*)

HARLEY: I don't trust anyone anymore.

ATTORNEY: It is an easy enough question to answer.

HARLEY: Luke's too thick t' get it straight. Probably thought he was being asked if I helped with the ladder. Which I did. Down t' the shed.

ATTORNEY: Did you help Myles pull the ladder down?

HARLEY: No way. Never got up. At least not till Nate was flat on his puss. And Myles was back on the path.

ATTORNEY: I'll ask it again. Was Myles wearing gloves?

HARLEY: I'm pretty sure he was. *(He could not remember before.)*

ATTORNEY: But you are not completely sure now?

HARLEY: Yep. I guess I can't be sure.

ATTORNEY: Did you ever talk to Myles about killing your brother-in-law?

HARLEY: 'Course not.

ATTORNEY: Did you ever suggest to Myles he should kill Nate?

HARLEY: We didn't talk much. Never said a word about murder.

ATTORNEY: Did you help Luke push the ladder down?

HARLEY: 'Course not.

ATTORNEY: Did you ever talk with Luke about killing Nate?

HARLEY: Nah. But I always had t' be stopping him from some dumb stunt.

ATTORNEY: Did you and your sister-in-law ever talk about murdering Nate?

HARLEY: I never talked t' her about anything important.

ATTORNEY: What do you mean by that, Mr. Poor?

HARLEY: She's too stuck up. Always acting superior. *(This is new info!)*

ATTORNEY: Superior about what?

HARLEY: 'Bout everything. Always bragging about her brains. And her fancy education. It used t' make me sick. *(Noticed no reaction by PB.)*

ATTORNEY: Did you threaten to kill Nate in front of Patience that day?

HARLEY: Maybe drunk, mister, but not that drunk.

ATTORNEY: Did you mention the possibility on any other day?

HARLEY: Didn't never get that fuddled. Besides I wouldn't dare take Patience's precious time t' talk about my rotten luck. She didn't care. *(No PB reaction.)*

ATTORNEY: Once more, for the record, did you kill your brother-in-law, Nathaniel Brewster?

HARLEY: Not on yer life.

ATTORNEY: That is all. I have no further questions, Your Honor.

As I closed the folder, I was glad I was sitting down. Molly came to my aid, but I was eager to keep on going, so I threw a treat as far as I could off the porch, hoping it would her take a long time to find it.

<u>Myles Poor's Testimony</u>

ATTORNEY: You said that you raced up the path to the barn because you had been in the outhouse for such a long time. Is that right?

MYLES: Yes, sir. I was terribly afraid Nate would be hopping mad.

ATTORNEY: When you got to the top of the hill, what did you see?

MYLES: As I got to the top of the path, I saw Luke on the roof and Nate on the ladder.

ATTORNEY: What was Luke doing?

MYLES: He was holding on to the ladder top.

ATTORNEY: Was he using both hands?

MYLES: Yes, sir. On both uprights. He was so close to the edge, I thought at first he was holding on to keep from falling off the roof.

ATTORNEY: Are you sure he was not holding on to a rung?

MYLES: Silly man! The ladder just made it to the eaves. The top rung was real low. *(The fingerprint evidence is supportive if gloves not involved.)*

ATTORNEY: Was he wearing gloves?
MYLES: I don't remember.
ATTORNEY: What did he do next?
MYLES: He shook the ladder.
ATTORNEY: And?
MYLES: Luke pushed the ladder away from the roof. Bingo, down it went. Sort of like in slow motion. I keep seeing that in nightmares. *(Top pushed over, not bottom pulled out.)*
ATTORNEY: Was it possible the ladder went down by itself?
MYLES: Sure, it was possible. I've always been scared of ladders. Even if Harley says Nate was good at putting them up. Maybe that's why I had to go so badly. But I'm telling you it didn't just fall. I watched Luke give it the old heave-ho. Like they did defending castles in the old days.
ATTORNEY: You should stick to simple, straight answers, young man, and not offer opinions. That would avoid all the objections from the lawyers. What did Nate do?
MYLES: He turned over in the air. Fell headfirst onto the ledge.
ATTORNEY: Did he say anything?
MYLES: No, sir.
ATTORNEY: No holler? Nothing?
MYLES: Nothing. Yikes, sir, his head exploded.
ATTORNEY: What did Luke do next?
MYLES: It wasn't funny, but he smiled and laughed.
ATTORNEY: Did he say anything to you?
MYLES: I don't remember.
ATTORNEY: Did you say anything to him?
MYLES: Not a word.
ATTORNEY: Then, what did he do?
MYLES: Why he just flew up the roof. *(MP was the sole witness to all of this.)*
ATTORNEY: Did you see Harley at this time?
MYLES: Yes, sir. I did.

ATTORNEY: What was he doing?

MYLES: He was leaning against the apple tree.

ATTORNEY: Was he asleep?

MYLES: I couldn't see his eyes under his hat.

ATTORNEY: Did he say anything to you?

MYLES: No. I figured he was still asleep. I'm pretty used to seeing him drunk and passed out. He looked the same when I went down to the outhouse. *(HP getting edgy?)*

ATTORNEY: Did you say anything to him?

MYLES: I didn't say a thing. Luke had scared me, and I was thinking about what he was going to do next.

ATTORNEY: Was Harley wearing gloves?

MYLES: I don't know. I doubt it since he hadn't done any work. We were getting used to that, too.

ATTORNEY: Again, you must stick to the facts and don't give your opinions. Otherwise, you'll be up here all day. Where was your Aunt Patience all this time?

MYLES: Oh, she was sleeping in her rocker on the porch. *(Provides PB's alibi.)*

ATTORNEY: How did you know she was asleep?

MYLES: I could tell when I passed by the porch. On the way back from the privy.

ATTORNEY: Did she say anything to you?

MYLES: No, sir. I told you she was asleep.

ATTORNEY: Did you say anything to her?

MYLES: Of course not. I was jealous because she'd found a way to escape such a dreadful day. It was no picnic, if you know what I mean.

ATTORNEY: Was the dog barking?

MYLES: No, sir. Otherwise, she wouldn't have been able to sleep.

ATTORNEY: There has been testimony by many that the dog was barking, so you must have heard it, too. When did it start?

MYLES: Oh, you can be such a difficult man. You must be talking about later on.

ATTORNEY: All I want is for you to tell me when you heard the barking.

MYLES: Silly Molly started barking after I went past the porch, just about when I got to the top of the hill.

ATTORNEY: Where was your aunt at that point?

MYLES: When I looked back, she was waking up on the porch. Patting her doggie.

ATTORNEY: Did you go near the ladder?

MYLES: Not until it fell down. I think Aunt Patience said we shouldn't touch anything. You should ask her about that. *(PB played the cool customer.)*

ATTORNEY: You are the witness, Myles. It's not your role to direct the questions.

MYLES: Jeepers! I'm sorry, sir.

ATTORNEY: I do the asking here. Harley says you pulled the ladder down. Is that correct?

MYLES: It's correct that he said it, but he's a mean old liar. Luke pushed it down before I even got up there.

ATTORNEY: Did you help Luke do it?

MYLES: Don't be silly.

ATTORNEY: When you were up on the roof with Luke, did you suggest he push Nate down?

MYLES: Never! I'm not that evil.

ATTORNEY: Did you ever talk to him about murder?

MYLES: No way! I stopped talking to Luke because he was so dumb.

ATTORNEY: Did you ever hint to him about it?

MYLES: What? Luke being so dumb?

ATTORNEY: No. About murdering your uncle.

MYLES: No, sir. Never. Not even a little bitty word!

ATTORNEY: Did you help Harley pull the ladder down?

MYLES: That's utterly absurd. Of course not. I've already told you what happened.

ATTORNEY: Did you ever talk to Harley about murdering Nate?

MYLES: I didn't ever waste my time talking to him. He didn't care about me.

ATTORNEY: When you were going down to the outhouse and met your aunt, did you threaten to kill your uncle?

MYLES: I remember exactly what I said to Aunt Patience. I simply asked her what she had put up for lunch. *(MP and PB differ on their conversation.)*

ATTORNEY: Did you mention murder or killing?

MYLES: No, sir. Never. Besides, I really had to get to the privy.

ATTORNEY: We have heard testimony in this courtroom that you were threatening Nate. What is your comment about that?

MYLES: Don't believe that folderol. Everybody picked on me.

ATTORNEY: Does that include your aunt?

MYLES: Aunt Patience was getting old and crotchety. Just the way Nate said Grandpa did. And she always liked to invent things. She's so asinine. *(New slant on PB!)*

ATTORNEY: Were you not, then, very close to your aunt?

MYLES: She was always dreaming. She kept pushing me to get off the farm. I didn't like that. It got boring. *(PB shows no reaction.)*

ATTORNEY: Someone is not telling the truth.

MYLES: Well, it's certainly not me. That would be fibbing.

ATTORNEY: And you don't ever fib? Is that correct, Myles?

MYLES: I do have my pride and principles, you know.

ATTORNEY: Then, I'm sure you understand what it means to be under oath. Did you kill your uncle, Nathaniel Brewster?

MYLES: I swear to you I did not.

ATTORNEY: Your Honor, I have no further questions for this young man.

Molly was back, nosing me for another treat. I sent her off the porch again with a toss in a new direction. Luckily it made it all the way into the garden, which gave me confidence I had bought some more time.

Luke Poor's testimony

ATTORNEY: You do not need to be frightened, Luke. I have a few simple questions, and you will soon be done. You were positioned on the barn roof with your uncle, were you not?

LUKE: Hunh?

ATTORNEY: Were you on top of the barn?

LUKE: Yup.

ATTORNEY: Was Nate there, too?

LUKE: Yup.

ATTORNEY: Did Nate get on the ladder?

LUKE: Yup.

ATTORNEY: Did he express any thoughts to you?

LUKE: Hunh? *(Is the vocabulary too hard for him or is he faking?)*

ATTORNEY: Did Nate talk?

LUKE: Said no work, no lunch.

ATTORNEY: Where was Harley positioned at this moment?

LUKE: Hunh?

ATTORNEY: Did you see Harley?

LUKE: Yup.

ATTORNEY: Sleeping against the tree?

LUKE: Nope. Stand up.

ATTORNEY: Where?

LUKE: The ladda.

ATTORNEY: You mean adjacent to the ladder?

LUKE: Hunh?

ATTORNEY: Next to it?

Luke: Yup.

ATTORNEY: What occurred next?

LUKE: Hunh?

ATTORNEY: What did Nate do?

LUKE: He fall down.

ATTORNEY: How did that happen specifically?

LUKE: Hunh?

ATTORNEY: Did the ladder fall?

LUKE: Yup.

ATTORNEY: So it went down by itself. It was an accident?

LUKE: Hunh?

ATTORNEY: It slipped out? It gave way?

LUKE: Dunno.

ATTORNEY: I'm going to help you understand the question, young man. When the ladder fell, did some person, somebody, some man help it? Like this? *(Pulling and pushing demonstrations.)*

LUKE: Yup. He pull. *(LP picks the pulling example. The bottom went out.)*

ATTORNEY: Who? Nate?

LUKE: Nope.

ATTORNEY: Myles?

LUKE: Nope.

ATTORNEY: Harley?

LUKE: Yup. *(Leading, but no objections. LP is the sole witness to all of this.)*

ATTORNEY: Was he wearing gloves on his hands simultaneously?

LUKE: Hunh?

ATTORNEY: Gloves on hands? Like these? *(Puts one on.)*

LUKE: Dunno.

ATTORNEY: Did he pull the ladder? Like this? From the side?

LUKE: Yup. *(This puts prints on apple tree side.)*

ATTORNEY: Did the ladder fall?

LUKE: You ask that.

ATTORNEY: Did Nate fall?

LUKE: You ask that. Broke.

ATTORNEY: Did Nate say anything as he descended?

LUKE: Hunh?

ATTORNEY: I'll interrogate you another way.

LUKE: Hunh?

ATTORNEY: Nate talk you?

LUKE: Nope.

ATTORNEY: Harley made Nate fall?

LUKE: Yup.

ATTORNEY: What did Harley do following that?

LUKE: Hunh?

ATTORNEY: Did Harley go back to the tree?

LUKE: Yup.

ATTORNEY: Did Harley lie down?

LUKE: Back to sleep.   *(Note PB's version.)*

ATTORNEY: Did Harley look at you?

LUKE: Dunno.

ATTORNEY: Did Harley speak to you?

LUKE: Hunh?

ATTORNEY: Harley talk?

LUKE: Nope.

ATTORNEY: Luke talk Harley?

LUKE: Nope.

ATTORNEY: Did you see Myles?

LUKE: Yup.

ATTORNEY: Was he on the pathway?

LUKE: Hunh?

ATTORNEY: Was he on the hill?

LUKE: Yup.

ATTORNEY: When did he appear?

LUKE: Hunh?

ATTORNEY: When did you see him?

LUKE: Dunno.

ATTORNEY: Did he have gloves on? Like these?

LUKE: Dunno.

ATTORNEY: Had Nate already fallen?

LUKE: Hunh?

ATTORNEY: Nate on the ground?

LUKE: Yup.

ATTORNEY: Did Myles address you?

LUKE: Hunh?

ATTORNEY: Myles talk?

LUKE: Nope.

ATTORNEY: Did you speak to him?

LUKE: Hunh?

ATTORNEY: You talk Myles?

LUKE: Nope.

ATTORNEY: Sit down, Luke. Where was Mrs. Brewster?

LUKE: Hunh?

ATTORNEY: Where was Auntie?

LUKE: Molly talk. *(When?)*

ATTORNEY: Yes. We all know that Molly was barking. But Auntie?

MYLES: Hunh?

ATTORNEY: Auntie on the porch?

LUKE: Yup. *(All agree she was on the porch.)*

ATTORNEY: You could see her?

LUKE: Yup.

ATTORNEY: How did you get down off the roof?

LUKE: Hunh?

ATTORNEY: Did you go into the loft?

LUKE: Hunh?

ATTORNEY: Go in the hole?

LUKE: Yup. *(When?)*

ATTORNEY: Did you go near the ladder on the ground?

LUKE: Hunh?

ATTORNEY: Luke touch ladder?

LUKE: Nope. Auntie see. *(Each man looks to PB here. Why?)*

ATTORNEY: Did you help Harley pull the ladder down?

LUKE: Hunh?

ATTORNEY: Luke pull ladder? Like this? *(He gestures.)*

LUKE: No help.

ATTORNEY: Did you talk to Harley about Nate's murder?

LUKE: Hunh?

ATTORNEY: You know. Murder.

LUKE: Murda?

ATTORNEY: Kill. Kill Nate. Talk Harley?

LUKE: Nope.

ATTORNEY: Did you help Myles with the ladder?

LUKE: Hunh?

ATTORNEY: Luke push ladder? Like this. *(More gestures.)*

LUKE: Nope. Nope. *(LP agitated.)*

ATTORNEY: Kill Nate. Talk Myles?

LUKE: Nope.

ATTORNEY: Kill Nate. Talk Auntie?

LUKE: Auntie not nice. No talk. *(New info, no reaction by PB.)*

ATTORNEY: I think you know what to kill means by now. Did you kill Nate?

LUKE: Nope.

ATTORNEY: I want to be absolutely sure you understand the question.

LUKE: Hunh?

ATTORNEY: Did you kill Nate?

LUKE: Double nope.

ATTORNEY: That's the best I can do, Your Honor. Thank you, Luke. I have no more questions for you.

Molly was back and pawing for attention. Unable to wait to see what was in store for me next, I spoiled her with another treat right away. I threw it as far as I possibly could. Since it was the third time, she gave me a questioning look before bounding off the porch.

Patience Brewster's Testimony

ATTORNEY: You were asleep on the porch, Mrs. Brewster. Is that right?

PATIENCE: That is correct.

ATTORNEY: What woke you up?

PATIENCE: It was Molly barking. She has a sixth sense for trouble.

ATTORNEY: Describe for us, if you will, what you did when you woke up?

PATIENCE: I looked up the hill.

ATTORNEY: What did you see?

PATIENCE: I saw Myles at the top of the path and Luke on the roof.

ATTORNEY: Be very specific now, Mrs. Brewster. Was Myles going up or down the path?

PATIENCE: I think he was going up.

ATTORNEY: Could you be sure he was going up?

PATIENCE: I could not, but his back was toward me. He was pulling up his overall straps. It all fits. He must have been going up.

ATTORNEY: You tell us only what you saw, Mrs. Brewster. The jury decides what it means.

PATIENCE: If I see something, I am perfectly capable of drawing my own conclusions and deciding what it means.

ATTORNEY: Could Myles have been going down the hill backward?

PATIENCE: I suppose he could have. *(Unsure or cagey?)*

ATTORNEY: Could he have been pulling those straps down?

PATIENCE: I suppose he could have. *(PB and HP differ here.)*

ATTORNEY: Was Myles wearing gloves?

PATIENCE: I do not remember.

ATTORNEY: Did you see Harley?

PATIENCE: Not right away. But I did see him eventually. I remember the red hat.

ATTORNEY: Where was Harley?

PATIENCE: At the top of the hill.

ATTORNEY: You know what I am asking, Mrs. Brewster. Please, be more precise. Was he against the apple tree?

PATIENCE: I think so. At least near to it. *(Vague, uncharacteristic.)*

ATTORNEY: Was he near the ladder?

PATIENCE: As I told that other attorney, I could not see the ladder from the porch.

ATTORNEY: Was Harley standing up?

PATIENCE: I am not sure. I could see his hat, but I could not tell what he was doing.

ATTORNEY: Was he getting up?

PATIENCE: I cannot say.

ATTORNEY: Was he lying down?

PATIENCE: I just do not know. *(PB differs from LP.)*

ATTORNEY: Was he wearing gloves?

PATIENCE: I only saw the hat, I said.

ATTORNEY: Where was Luke?

PATIENCE: I have already told you that. On the roof.

ATTORNEY: If you cooperate, Mrs. Brewster, this would not take too long or be as unpleasant as it seems to be for you. Where on the roof was Luke?

PATIENCE: There was so much going on.

ATTORNEY: Was he at the edge?

PATIENCE: I do not know.

ATTORNEY: Was he near the ladder?

PATIENCE: I cannot remember. *(PB differs from MP.)*

ATTORNEY: Did you see your husband anywhere?

PATIENCE: My God, you know full well I never saw Nate. Alive. Why are you doing this?

ATTORNEY: Excuse me, Mrs. Brewster. I am only trying to get to the facts. Determining the guilt or innocence of each of these men depends to a significant degree on your testimony.

PATIENCE: They have always depended on me, and I am still trying to do the best I can for them. I have always done that. *(Sincerity? Truth?)*

ATTORNEY: Each man has claimed you could see he was not anywhere near the ladder. Is that correct?

PATIENCE: Yes, it is correct that they did say that, but I cannot be as sure about what I saw as they are hoping. In any case, it is an impossible question to answer because I could not see the ladder.

ATTORNEY: But you did see each of them, correct?

PATIENCE: Correct.

ATTORNEY: If you saw them but not the ladder, it seems likely that means they were not near it. Isn't that right?

PATIENCE: I thought I was only supposed to tell you what I saw and not try to decide what it meant.

ATTORNEY: That is correct. Perhaps, it would be better if I rephrased the question in a clearer fashion.

PATIENCE: That is also correct. *(Is she playing or obstructing?)*

ATTORNEY: Where was each man when the ladder fell?

PATIENCE: I did not see Nate fall.

ATTORNEY: That was not the question. I asked you about each of the other men, not your husband when he fell with the ladder.

PATIENCE: I did not see my husband fall, so I could not have seen the ladder fall. All the evidence supports that the two went down together. Would you not agree, Esquire? *(Judge admonishes PB.)*

ATTORNEY: Mrs. Brewster, I am not asking you if you saw the ladder fall. And I am certainly not asking you to interpret the evidence. That is for the good ladies and gentlemen of the jury.

PATIENCE: Meaning I am not a good lady? *(Judge calls lawyers to the bench.)*

ATTORNEY: In an attempt to spare you any more grief, Mrs. Brewster, I will not require you to describe the sight of your deceased husband. Nevertheless, I must ask you to define some essential details after the accident.

PATIENCE: That is the essential detail. It was an accident. *(Weeping? Hanky dry?)*

ATTORNEY: That was not a good choice of words on my part, and I do apologize. I should have said event. As you stood there after the event, did you form an opinion about the scene?

PATIENCE: I thought witnesses were not supposed to state their opinions.

ATTORNEY: In this case you may, so please tell the court.

PATIENCE: I am not much for mechanical things, but I do know if you put a skinny piece of wood up against a tall building, there is a chance it might fall. That is nothing but common sense. *(Quick recovery.)*

ATTORNEY: Since there were people all around, did you form an opinion about what roles they might have played?

PATIENCE: Not really. Why, I just figured the dice had rolled against my husband. Plus the others had been lucky the ladder did not go down under one of them.

ATTORNEY: This line of questioning is producing too much opinion and not enough fact.

PATIENCE: Well, you are the barrister, not me. You made up the questions. I am only responsible for the answers—and my opinions. *(Judge quiets laughter in gallery.)*

ATTORNEY: After the ladder fell, where were the men?

PATIENCE: It was pretty confusing up there. *(For PB? Really?)*

ATTORNEY: Please think very carefully now, Mrs.

Brewster. Tell the court who you saw and where they were.

PATIENCE: It is all such a horrible blur. I know I am under oath here. I would tell you if I could. I really would. *(Upset or evasive?)*

ATTORNEY: Please, Mrs. Brewster, I know this is distressing for you, but these questions are necessary. I understand that you did not see the ladder or your husband fall. But you did see all three of the defendants after the fall as well as before it. Is that correct?

PATIENCE: Of course, it is.

ATTORNEY: So, did any one of them touch the ladder?

PATIENCE: Of course. When they carried the ladder up the hill. How many times do I have to say it? *(PB smiles.)*

ATTORNEY: Remember, I ask the questions, and this question is directed specifically to the period after the fall, when you had arrived up on the ledge. Perhaps I erred in not making that clear to you.

PATIENCE: Now I understand and can answer that. No man touched it.

ATTORNEY: And that includes yourself?

PATIENCE: Aside from the fact that I am not a man, that is correct. You've have got me flustered. I should have said no human touched it! I was frozen to the ground. I could not move.

ATTORNEY: You will be able to leave the stand soon, Mrs. Brewster. I only have a few more questions left. Did you ever hear, at any time, any of the defendants talk about murdering your husband?

PATIENCE: Never.

ATTORNEY: What did you and Myles discuss when you passed on the path?

PATIENCE: He mentioned a bunch of little things, but I don't remember much of it. I just listened. *(Myles said it was just about the picnic lunch.)*

ATTORNEY: I have one final question about what you might have heard. Do you remember hearing anything from your husband before the dog woke you up?

PATIENCE: Naturally I remember hearing him before I fell asleep, but I did not hear him holler or anything like that when he was falling. If I had, do you think I would ever forget a thing like that? Apparently you have not been paying attention to what the others have said on the subject, either.

ATTORNEY: I'll remind you once again it is my job to ask the questions. And please remember to confine yourself to answering only the questions asked.

PATIENCE: But it is not fair for you to expect me to just sit here waiting for you to dream up better questions. *(Judge intervenes and explains.)*

ATTORNEY: Since you apparently have difficulty being certain about much of what went on, Mrs. Brewster, I can appreciate your desire not to want to hurt anyone with testimony about his actions. However, you should have no trouble describing your own actions. Remembering that you are still bound by your oath, did you, by any chance, act to kill your own husband?

PATIENCE: I cannot be held responsible for an act of fate.

ATTORNEY: A direct answer is required. Did you take Nathaniel Brewster's life?

PATIENCE: Not on your life.

ATTORNEY: I will accept that as a no. Did you, then, help any of the three defendants kill Nathaniel Brewster?

PATIENCE: Only if God blames me for keeping them alive on Granite Ledge Farm could I be considered guilty of helping them in the death of my husband.

ATTORNEY: May I assume, then, the answer to my last question is no?

PATIENCE: The answers to your last two questions are no and yes. In that order.

ATTORNEY: I will not provoke this witness with any further questions, Your Honor. Thank you for your testimony, Mrs. Brewster.

By the time I slammed Beach's last folder down, night was descending. The shadow of the mountain had already swallowed the barn on the ledge and was busy devouring the bats in the backyard. A cloud mass had eaten all the stars and was taking bites out of the moon. As the dark of night rolled down over my eyes, images from the trial rose up in my mind.

Spectators in the gallery—wall-to-wall vultures, every one of them.

Lawyers before the bar—all men with big mouths and no ears.

Jurors in the box—cattle with nose rings waiting to be led.

Judge on the bench—shaggy white hair: judicial wig, priestly tonsure, or royal crown?

What they had in common was they had forgotten Justice was a woman.

Though my husband's end was immediate and the court's conclusion was finite, definitive wrap-up for me now seemed so distant, so nebulous. Resolution is supposed to be refreshing, not exhausting. Benjamin B. Beach was the one to blame.

All of a sudden, boots clumped, hinges creaked, and light poured onto the porch. The shape in the doorway pulled my spirits up from the depths of my rocker.

"On my way back home from town just now, Mrs. Brewster, I got a hankering to drop in and check on you."

Even though I preferred Patience, especially the way Cleve wrapped his lips around my name, I was relieved to be Mrs. Brewster again and not Mrs. B.

"Why, Mr. Parsons, did you forget I was expecting you for dinner?"

"No, I wouldn't forget that. I just wasn't sure if this Beach thing might've made you forget. If you had, I was still kind of hoping you'd ask me to stay awhile." If need be, I would have begged him to. "I even brought along my pooch. Figured Molly could use a little company tonight, herself."

One eye open, muzzle to the floor, tail thumping, Molly was looking her visitor over. With his lustrous but water-repellent coat and merrily active, upward-curving tail, Monty was alert and athletic, the perfect golden retriever. Most times, Cleve playfully pulled Molly's ear upon coming into the house, and she would roll on her back, legs spread, inviting a tummy tickle. However, whenever Monty came along for the visit, Molly ignored both the pulling and the puller. After breezing through the required sniffing out, the two dogs blew off the porch to romp on the lawn. A jealous master and mistress watched their frolic for a few minutes in silence.

"You know, Cleveland, when you eat by yourself, meals get pretty boring. Besides, I like to cook for guests."

"Well, since I've got nothing much but leftovers at home, I'm mighty glad you asked me over for dinner."

Both of us had trouble expressing how we really felt. For years, all I got was back talk, and Cleve had had no one to talk to at all. Although our communication was getting better and better, now we became a gang of two and focused on plundering the kitchen instead.

"You're in luck. I baked extra bread this morning. I was afraid Beach might wipe me out."

"That fellow sure looks like he puts it away."

"Would you believe he butters both sides of his bread?"

Shaking his head and laughing as one with me, Cleve took the flatware and plates out to the table, while I sliced bread and poured cider. He was back to heft the hot and heavy crock before I had the oven door open.

"It sure smells good." Although Cleve was not filled out, he did not suffer from his cooking. Yet he always swore mine was better than his was. "Baked beans are my favorite dish, and yours are the best by far."

I had been using a lot of beans lately. The folks at the store wondered where all the molasses and salt pork went, too. I was uneasy at first about these trips to the market, but such a good reason for going there made it easy.

"You risk getting a swollen head, Mr. Parsons. I guessed my company might hang out here all day, so I put beans in the oven before he arrived, just in case. They benefit from a good long bake, and, lucky thing, now you end up getting the reward of that."

"No, Patience. The lucky thing is the pest is gone. I don't care for his manner a bit."

"Neither do I—not his manner or his manners."

"Well, at least you're done with him."

"I wish I could say that, but no such luck. He's coming back again tomorrow. He said 'bright and early', though you can be sure what's early for him won't be for me."

"What do you mean by that? Are you reminding me you get up early or are you hinting he's keeping you awake?"

An evening guest should not have to contend with the aftereffects of a daytime intruder. Taking the chair Cleve pulled out for me, I bought time to rephrase my thoughts by ladling beans onto his plate.

"Don't worry yourself, Cleveland. I'm not provoked. I figure I can handle anything Beach's got to throw at me. In fact, he left me some stuff to read that would make you laugh."

"Stuff to read? Tonight? What could he possibly have for you that was so important?"

"It's not. It's not important at all. Beach just thinks it is. It's a rehash of some testimony from the trial, sliced and diced by him in a way to make everyone look suspicious."

"That doesn't make sense at all. I can't see how chasing insurance crooks would prepare someone for examining murder suspects. Want me to take a look? Maybe a fresh approach'll help."

The folders would stay closed. Reading Beach's manipulations would only inflame things. Cleve would get angry with him and might be disappointed in me. An upset Cleve would not be an asset.

"There's nothing in those papers you don't already know about. In fact, you know a lot more than is written there. But you have to understand or, at least, accept that this is my fight. I want this Beach fellow to be the last man to try to put me down."

"This whole thing has been going on entirely too long. I knew the other day I should have moved him on out of here."

The hunk of bread chasing the last few beans around his plate telegraphed Cleve's actions-speak-louder-than-words style, the same way coming to the barking of the dog and going for the doctor had impressed the court.

"The shine on your plate says you're ready for more, I can see."

"I'd be right pleased."

"I wouldn't take no for an answer."

Thanks to the window light streaming from the kitchen we could see to eat. The cloud had gobbled up the moon, turning the whole sky pitch-black. The darkness showed me how I no longer needed to see Cleve's face to anticipate his thoughts. "I like it out here, even when it gets dark."

"I was just thinking you might let me fish a wire from the kitchen out through the roof. With a light over the table you could make out your dinner and your guests."

"That's a nice offer. I could read out here at night. Imagine how Father would have loved that, too. He'd probably have changed his mind about electricity and ended up buying stock in it."

"You know how I hate to stir things up, Patience, but I'm tired of all these people who think there's more to your husband's death than you say there is."

"It's not people, it's only Beach. Don't get alarmed. He's a nothing. Besides, since you're willing to stand behind me, that makes it easy."

"I'm not only willing, I'm determined. Thick or thin."

"You really must stay in the background. I don't want you sticking your neck out for me. I got into this predicament by myself, and I'll get out of it the same way."

"You're a strong, independent woman, Patience. That I liked about you from the moment we met, but it also explains my frustration now. You're all alone in the world, but you won't let me help. I hope you know I'll do whatever it takes."

"Again, I'm not alone, plus you've helped a lot already. I didn't say no to your friendship before, and I'm not saying no to it now, either. I just don't want to see you stuck in a mess you had very little to do with."

"I was hoping you'd say I brought something into your life. Anyway, since you've brought me more than I deserve, you can always count on me." The glass raised in my direction sealed his promise.

Molly and Monty rejoined us on the porch. Sitting face-to-face, tongues jumping with each breath, they licked each other's eyes clean. They were not in love; it was something they loved to do.

"I do like being with you, Cleveland. As a matter of fact, you're the first man I could say that to, but this is not the right time for rhapsodies."

"I know I can't replace your father. And, sure, we have our differences, but we're still pretty much two peas on the same plate. No wife. No husband."

"But, Mr. Parsons, for the time being we must be sure my apple trees stay separate from your pines."

"But, Mrs. Brewster, are you forgetting I have no cow and you have one in need of milking up in the barn?"

"What would they say in town? There's the obligatory mourning period, not to mention the penniless widow needing to settle with the Veritable first." To be funny was not my intention. To be prudent was. Cleve would have to wait. "If things go my way, I'll be done and finished with Beach tomorrow."

Without a word, Cleve came to me. One hand closed around my wrist, and the other took the knife from my grasp. Soon, with manly clanging in the kitchen, Cleve was cleaning up, leaving me in my seat to plan for the coming day.

Side by side under the table, Molly and Monty were sleeping now. In the tree beside the porch, a mourning dove cooed to her mate.

"Well, that was very, very nice, Patience. I best be on my way."

When Cleve poked his head through the doorway, I could not see his face, but I felt his smile and caught the kiss he blew to my cheek.

"Thank you for your company, Cleveland. When you hear Molly barking tomorrow—I'm sure it will all be settled by then—stroll on over. Success or not, you can rescue me either way."

Whistling Monty Parsons to his side, Cleveland Parsons headed home.

"Who saw him die?"
"I," said the Fly,
"With my little eye,
I saw him die."

—Tommy Thumb's Pretty Song Book (c. 1744)

EYEWITNESSES

Bright and early was right. We had just left the kitchen with a mug of coffee for me and a slice of bread for Molly, intending to enjoy breakfast outside in peace. Busting in through the front door without a knock and bursting onto the porch without a greeting, Beach was all business.

"You had plenty of time to peruse the testimony I selected. Had to have been pretty illuminatin' for you, if I do say so myself."

In a ploy to look bigger, Beach took a lesser Windsor and, drawing himself up, fisted the table in a magisterial manner. His heavy ham was a slapstick gavel, and his mussed-up suit a ludicrous robe. "I'm ready for your reaction, Mrs. B. Begin wherever you want."

"I read your collection with great dismay. You selected only the parts where the accused were running scared in front of the unjust system society has created."

"You call it unjust? It's not unjust to ferret a killer out of a pack of liars."

"Although we might agree only one person is guilty, in effect, they are all being punished. Life will never be the same for any of them."

"Wouldn't it be better to not criticize the system and try to collar the culprit instead."

"The system is the culprit."

"It's human nature to want to know exactly who to blame."

"That is not what the Bible and Father taught me."

"I hate to talk religion the way you do, but what about an eye for an eye and a tooth for a tooth? A man has been killed, and the court has convicted the wrong person as his killer. I intend to be the one to get to the bottom of this mess once and for all."

I sensed a confession was coming, so I held my tongue.

"At this point, I look to you to bring me what I'm after."

But I could not resist one simple question: "So, why not state directly what you are after?"

"You must've suspected what I'm really after for some time, and now I'll admit it. I'm no longer workin' on the insurance claim because I don't care if I help the company or not. I'm after personal fulfillment. I want to solve the case everybody else has screwed up and come out top dog in my own eyes. In fact, I no longer care if anybody knows the truth but me. I just want to be right! So here I am today, askin' you to help me out. No, I'm beggin' you."

How egotistical was Beach's lust for satisfaction in private. Here was the art thief who never shows his booty. The anonymous tipster who buys all the papers to gloat about his success in secret. The helper who hides his selfishness under the cloak of the Good Samaritan.

Yet, by admitting the truth at last, he stimulated me to give him more of a chance. Although the stakes would rise, it would be fun to extend the game. I would respond to his need to be right, which I recognized as a fundamental prerequisite for all men to be happy. After tripping him into the mire of his self-love, I would leave him wallowing there—short of his objective. But, in order to safely control the result, I needed to establish certain rules first.

"Very well, Mr. Beach! I am willing to explore this matter with you on a theoretical, intellectual basis. However, you must bear in mind at all times I will not be blaming anyone."

"I understand."

"And you must agree not to incriminate anybody by revealing whatever we talk about from now on."

"I agree."

"And our discussion will, in no way, be used in an attempt to overturn the court's decision. Do you accept these conditions?"

"I accept. I will treat the remainder of this interview as a classified affair not for publication. Like I said, I just want to be right. I am grateful for your consideration."

Failing only to wring his hands and grovel at my feet, Beach dropped his eyes, hung his head, and slumped in his chair. Taking charge from the high-backed Windsor was my next logical move. "Like a grave robber, you have opened the coffin. Let the dissection begin."

"Very well! The first thing I want to sort out is the hanky-panky. Contemplation of the circular accusations from those three has amused me, but failure to pick out the real killer would annoy me."

"Why, in heaven's name, fuss over such absurdly false claims? That is a waste of time."

"Let's put aside the question of whether those accusations were false or not for the moment. That a trapped individual will try any means to extricate himself from a desperate situation is highly predictable."

"Are you talking about an individual turning to murder to solve a problem? Or trumping up charges to escape a murder conviction?"

"The latter, of course. Each man stated he saw one of the others kill Nate. It was easy to see each guy was out to save his butt. Even Luke—the dunce—made up a dodge."

Beach separated three of the folders I had stacked together. "I would've expected two men to agree on the same other one as the guilty party. Somehow, inconceivably as a matter of fact, each pointed to a different man. What are the chances of that?"

Setting them up in a triangle, his hand looped over the folders, round and round. "Roundabout convolution like this actually doesn't connect. Two lied about another, one told the truth about another, but it always pointed to a different man? That doesn't make any darn sense."

A commotion rose up at the barn. Sometimes, when the sun burst out from behind a bank of clouds, our rooster—I had dubbed him Cock Robin—announced a new day, and the chickens argued his mistake. Happily, this crowing and clucking combo never played long.

Once the poultry piped down, Beach invited me back into the game. "Let's check the hand each guy showed and see if we can pick the winner."

The dealer drew a breath. "Harley against the tree witnesses Myles pull the ladder down with Nate huggin' it. Harley sees Myles scoot back to the top of the path and Luke disappear on the roof. The mutt starts to bark, and Harley sees Patience down on the porch. In this instance, Myles becomes Murderer Number One."

What breath Beach had left whistled out, making way for the next. "But Myles at the top of the path witnesses Luke push the ladder down with Nate clingin' to it. Myles sees Luke disappear from the roof and Harley propped against the tree. The mutt barks, and Myles sees Patience down on the porch. Thus, Luke becomes Murderer Number Two."

Beach was sucking air, shallow and rapid, where he could, between words. "But Luke on the roof witnesses Harley pull the ladder down with Nate ridin' on it. Luke sees Harley run back to the tree and Myles at the top of the path. The mutt barks, and Luke sees Patience down on the porch. So, Harley becomes Murderer Number Three."

Beach stood up, strode to the rail, and spun around. "So where does that leave us?" Arms spread, palms up, he raised his hands to the skies. "Nowhere."

Although Beach was playing interlocutor and end man at once, this was not a minstrel show, so I piped right up. "Not at all! What sounds like poppycock explains itself. All you have to do is ignore the falsehoods about someone else handling the ladder. Each man made up his own story about a killer, but the rest of what each said was true."

"But we still have a murder in need of a murderer."

"You do not get it, do you? It is so obvious—the three fabrications cancel each other out. Nobody touched the ladder when it slipped out under my husband. Yet each defendant, terrified of being convicted, invented a criminal and a criminal act to save his own skin."

"Your passion for your family blinds you, Mrs. B. An accidental event is what doesn't fit. A cyclone of lies whirls around an eye of truth."

Eyes shut, deep in thought, Beach slid one finger round and round in a circle on the table as though he would never stop. Finally, abandoning the melodrama, he rephrased the crucial question.

"Who set the ladder in motion? There's but one answer to that, and I think I'm close to comin' up with the lucky pea. It's almost time to turn over the walnut and see if I've found it." Pleased he had not found it—yet—I let the shell game proceed.

"But, first of all, I want to hear your take on the finger-pointin' in court.

Examination of the how and why of all three claims will help pinpoint the real killer. For instance, let's look at what Myles claimed. He pointed at Luke, which seems feasible from a technical point of view. As Myles came up the hill, he was able to witness everything Luke did up on the roof."

"I cannot argue with that fact."

"But why, in your opinion, would Myles pick his own brother as the one to accuse?"

"I boil it down to a long-standing, deep resentment that made Myles jealous of Luke."

"Why would someone as bright as Myles be jealous of a blockhead like Luke? He wasn't any competition."

"Luke took all the attention away from Myles. Caring for and educating Luke took tremendous amounts of time."

"And the poor little fellow required this for a much longer period than most youngsters take to grow up." For a split second, sympathy softened the callous man.

"Indeed, Mr. Beach, even a grown-up Luke needed a lot of attention."

"So Myles couldn't count on you to provide the nectar a hummin'bird requires." Leaning toward the romantic but recognizing his errant ways, Beach pulled up short. "Damnation! I've begun to think and talk like Patience Brewster. Always introducin' some lame comparison in the natural world around us to explain human behavior."

Beach was not only responding as a student of mine, he was admitting to learning from me. These were fresh flowers to add to the dried-up remnants from my teaching days. "I have already educated you about how the farm was a prison to Myles. He realized he might never get free of the mess he was in. Myles ended up viewing Luke as the second person responsible for his misery, Nate being the most responsible one, of course. As a result, one could speculate that when push came to shove, so to speak, Myles killed Nate and then picked Luke to accuse of the crime."

"Sort of like tryin' to kill two birds with one stone?"

A red squirrel chased a gray squirrel down a tree and across the lawn. Sometimes the race went across the lawn first and up a tree after, but it was always the littler fairy diddle driving the bigger bushy tail away.

Beach pressed on in his chase. "Now, let's deal with Harley's claim.

That he singled out Myles is feasible, at least in the physical sense. From his location beside the tree, he was able to observe Myles when he came back up the hill."

"That is a given."

"But, supposedly father and son, why would Harley choose Myles as the one to accuse?"

"Harley was as resentful and jealous of Myles as Myles was of Luke."

"A grown man bested by a mere boy?"

"In particular, Harley foresaw Myles achieving the personal satisfaction and happiness that had eluded him. Harley was envious of his own son."

"Jealous of his prospects for marriage, fatherhood, and so on? But if you consider that Myles was not the sort to—"

"Paternity is not the issue. Harley hated the real prospect that Myles would be gone, sooner or later, leaving him alone to cope with Nate and Luke."

"And cope with you, too. In any case, you think Harley secretly wanted to go to the big city?"

"My brother-in-law was no longer the farm boy contented with simple pleasures he appeared to be."

"So Harley drank because of unhappiness with his lot here on the farm?"

"It was more complicated than that, but Harley never communicated well, so it is hard for me to piece all the psychological factors together. In any case, one could conjecture that, in a moment of truth, Harley killed Nate and then accused Myles."

"Sort of a modern scapegoat he picked out of the New Hampshire woods?"

On the same tree abandoned by the squirrels, a nuthatch on its way down headfirst passed a brown creeper jealously restricted to climbing head-up.

Beach plowed straight ahead. "Now, let's take up what Luke claimed. He pulled Harley out of a hat, which is acceptable in a practical sense. From his position on the roof, he was able to spy on Harley."

"Another valid fact."

"But I can't figure why Luke, even as dumb as he's believed to be, picked his supposed father as the one to accuse."

"There is a hypothesis I can offer for that."

"I'm sick of your complicated psychology. Your nephew acts like a simple primitive. Like one of those Neanderthals people have buzzed about for years."

"Luke is no Neanderthal. He is like the rest of us."

"Of course! You've already taught me the scientists weren't wrong. Humans, gorillas, and chimps are all alike." Unlike a true moron, Beach was not trainable.

"You'd be better off climbing another tree. Seriously, you seem to be forgetting our discussion of Luke's inability to comprehend parenthood. Luke could not grasp who might have been his father or his brother. Let alone what a father or brother actually was."

"I'm not convinced Luke was that defective. Oops, excuse my mistake. We've been callin' him slow."

"You should ignore the paternity issue here, the same way you should have done with Myles, and reconsider what I told you earlier. Luke was mad at both of the adult men for treating him the way they did."

"Are you sure this is not just your imagination? Was Harley as rough on him as Nate?"

"I am imaginative, to be sure, but I am also exacting in my analyses. Suffice it to say, Luke recognized that Harley had never treated him right, even from his very first days. We need not go any deeper than that. Just accept that Luke was mad at Harley. One could postulate he killed Nate in anger and then accused Harley for the same reason."

"So Luke joins the other two as we try to figure out which one did your husband in."

"Not we, it is just you who is working on that. I am not talking about my husband's fate. I am only giving you some explanations for why each suspect picked the individual he accused. Although I believe my projections are closer to theories than hypotheses, do not forget for a minute that they may still be products of what you called my imagination. What you do with them is entirely up to you."

Beach left the seat where he was stymied and sat down on the porch rail where he could regroup. A sparrow hopeful of not having to double scratch for a meal took his place at the table.

"The sun's passed over the barn, Mrs. B, and we should move ahead, too."

The sunshine bouncing off his glasses blocked a chance to read how Beach was adding things up, but I expected he would be changing course. "Since I accepted all three of your conditions a few minutes ago, don't you think it's time to tell me what really happened up there?"

Luke on the roof.

Harley by the tree.

Myles on the path.

Nate hit the ledge.

Molly barked.

"I hate to sound like a Victrola, but I was sound asleep."

"But you woke up! You could see all of the suspects! If you please, without the I-don't-remembers, what happened?"

"I swear to you here, as I swore in court before, I did not see what happened to Nate." Beach's directness increased my desire to prolong our skirmish. "I know what you're looking for, so hear me out, once and for all. I did not witness Harley, Myles, or Luke commit murder."

"Or any combinations thereof?"

"Not one. Not two. Not all three."

Beach attacked my sidestepping head-on. "While you may not have perjured yourself in court, I think you withheld certain critical information and now I expect you to be more candid with me."

"Do I now have some additional obligation to you I am not aware of?"

"Will you continue to thwart my best efforts even now?"

"Perhaps you are destined to battle windmills, Mr. Quixote."

"If you only released a few truths, I could wrap this mystery up into a tidy little package."

"The jury has already tied the knot. Now you expect me to untie it, but I do not get the feeling we are working within the terms of our recent agreement. Are we still in agreement at all?"

"In agreement? I'm just askin' you to clarify a few things—out of fairness—from the goodness of your pure and noble heart."

I could not decide. Ingratiating? Obsequious? Condescending? The person Beach wanted to help was not an innocent convicted wrongly of murder, but Beach himself. He did not care who the culprit was; he only wanted to arrive at the right conclusion. His reward was not the identity of the murderer, but the success of his investigation.

"I have told the story many times."

"I don't want the so-called story. I want what you know to have happened in full and honest detail."

Beach broke from his post on the rail. "Things like whether Myles was comin' up or goin' down."

Beach rushed across the porch. "Whether Harley was lyin' down or standin' up."

Beach took a lap around the table. "Whether Luke was at the edge of the roof or up by the hole in it."

Beach reared up before me. "Facts like that. Those are the details that will determine who is guilty."

The Windsor was suddenly a fortress. As if she was afraid Beach might pick on her, too, Molly hopped onto my lap. How such a long dog could land so compactly always amazed me.

"I gave my testimony on those matters. Why not read your own notes?" Although their content was no longer a mystery, the reason the pachyderm needed notes escaped me.

"In court, you displayed remarkable powers of observation. Given our recent discussions, how can you expect me to believe there's no more for you to report?"

My suggestion was sweet. "I suppose, old and worn like the rest of my body, my eyes were not working well that day."

His retort was sour. "Not workin', like hell. It's called aidin' and abettin' a criminal."

Then Beach shook his fist at me. "Why do you protect the killer? Why don't you help the victims?"

I offered my palms to him. "The Bible says, 'the Lord giveth and the Lord taketh away.' What happened was out of my control."

Speechless, he stared at me, and I smiled at him, in silence.

The man in the wilderness asked me,
"How many strawberries grow in the sea?"
I answered him, as I thought good,
"As many as red herrings grow in the wood."

—Anonymous Nursery Rhyme

DELIBERATIONS

The smack of rain hitting the roof broke down the silence. I had overlooked the wind building up and the cloud coming in. My invocation of the divine Lord had sent the secular bully back to his seat where he was leafing through his paper catechism. His forehead furrowed more and more as he got closer and closer to the bottom of the pile. All of a sudden, he pushed aside the old, useless scraps and tossed me a new bone of contention.

"Okay, it's time to drop the human features and pick up the wooden ladder. So much revolves around that blasted thing."

A masterpiece by Father.

Sharp adze and skillful hand.

Uprights straight and true.

Rungs sturdy and mortised.

Certain under load.

"Father's ladder was more than a farm implement. It was a work of art. I can still remember his look when he came rushing out of the woods, excited about finding the perfect ash tree. It was straight enough to split into uprights that were long enough to reach the top of the barn. If he ever had to do repairs on the roof, he would not have to worm out through the tiny trapdoor up there anymore. The ladder was going to be a great solution."

"I appreciate now how dangerous that roof is, but that doesn't make a stupid ladder great."

"Stupid ladder? It still bugs me how the authorities were so eager

189

to study and discuss the slipperiness of the ledge. Yet, when it came to accepting that the ladder simply slipped out, the matter became unthinkable and absurd. That is what is stupid. Do you not agree?"

"Not at all. What I'd call stupid is how you ascribed an active role to the ladder—like the damn thing was an accomplice to murder."

The ladder shook off its sleep.

From the shed.

Up the hill.

To its target.

A tall reach to the eaves.

Geyser of life up its rungs.

Death plunge to the ledge.

"Only if you, Mr. Beach, are stupid enough to believe it was murder."

"At first pass, your opinion that your husband's death was merely a combination of coincidences was tempting because it seemed logical, but it failed to hold up. When I factored in the evil creatures on the ledge that day, when I added their personalities and actions to the equation, it became untenable to explain the event as a simple act of fate. It had all the earmarks of a preconceived human act."

"Earmarks, my eye! The jury failed to look at or listen to the pivotal evidence."

"Before the jurors made their trip out here, your theories had tempted them, too. Afterwards, the only issue was push or pull. I will admit, however, I enjoyed the wranglin' about the ladder you thought so self-sufficient."

"Never would I have dreamed Concord had a surfeit of ladder experts."

A black ant out on a shopping trip marched along the arm of the Windsor, accepted an airlift on the back of my hand to the table, and struck out for the generator of groceries, Beach.

"The jurors considered the spot where the ladder stood to be secure. They concluded some specially applied force beyond your husband's weight made it crash down."

"The ladder made its own decisions. The jury should have come to that conclusion instead."

"You continue to beat a dead horse. The ladder's stability was proven, time and time again, when the boys carried their loads up it without any slippage. Most important is the fact Myles came down it safely to go to the outhouse, so why would it come down a few minutes later under Nate? The two men were about the same size and both empty-handed."

"But remember there was some roofing gear scattered on the ledge."

"That stuff must've been what was chucked off the roof in anger. There was no reason to think your husband would carry shingles, a hammer, or even a nail. That was definitely not in his character. Besides, since the job was only partway done, there was no reason to carry things down at all. You can't argue a greater load made the ladder slide. I'm certain somebody did something that made it fall down."

"That everybody fancied themselves mechanical engineers and resisted my ideas frustrated me. And I certainly did not welcome the attorney who questioned a female knowing anything about ladders."

"Don't forget the sheriff had traced where the ladder stood and where it later lay on the ground. That really gave the experts things to talk about."

"I do not understand how that big-shot ladder manufacturer could be so cocksure of everything. He came all the way over from Portland to blow his horn."

"It was plain that fellow knew his field inside and out."

"His adversary called him pompous. How apt! Can anyone guarantee the behavior of an inert mass of lifeless struts and rungs, especially when it is lying flat on the ground?"

"Earlier you granted that dead mass humanity, but now you won't permit a live expert his science. You may be an educated woman, but you're really only a dabbler. You should leave matters to the male pros." Beach misinterpreted my silence as acceptance of his critique. "Every ladder has legs and feet, but they don't walk by themselves. They will follow the principles of physical science inevitably. So let us now talk specifics. Was its bottom near or away from the barn?"

"My goodness, I knew ladders had legs and feet, but was not aware they had bottoms. Seriously, Mr. Beach, how do you expect me to be able to tell which end was which? Even if I could, do you think I would have noticed? The thing was lying right beside my dead husband."

"Were you still too sleepy from that perfect nap of yours to be able to tell?"

"The shock scrambled my brain."

"That I can't believe, given that brain of yours. We'd get closer to the truth if you'd only be your usual precise self. Be as accurate as you can be."

I could be precise without being accurate, which would protect the truth.

"You see, Mrs. B, it has to be one way or the other. If the foot of the ladder was near the barn, Luke must've pushed it over from the roof. If the foot was away, then Harley or Myles must've pulled it out from the ledge." Beach was fidgeting under the two hats of prosecutor and defender.

"That is a fallacious concept. A ladder can only have feet when it is standing up. If it's lying on the ground, which it was, the puzzle has no solution. What is more, a fallen ladder cannot tell you if it was pushed or pulled."

"I feel certain you have information nobody else has. So I expect you to clear this question up, but you continue to split hairs, and we get nowhere."

"You are pulling for my precision, but you are pushing too hard on this subject. I ask you to forget which end was which. Why not accept the simple fact the ladder slid out and fell?"

"Reason forces me to reject simple slidin' out as the explanation. Trust me when I say I listened carefully to all the testimony. A good grip on the ledge was the consensus."

A quick inhale produced an inflated addition. "What's more, my examination of the spot yesterday, complete and detailed as it was, confirmed that in spades. Adequate friction between the wood and the rock made mechanical failure extremely unlikely."

His swelling chest almost popped the buttons off his shirt. "And, while we didn't need it, even you, as the strongest proponent of the fluky fall, admitted this in your testimony. That point was so obvious I didn't include it in my nifty little compendium."

But Smart Aleck could not force me to eat humble pie. "You know full well the lawyers forced me to agree with them in court. That demonstrates what I said yesterday about lawyers unfairly controlling witnesses."

"Of course, I remember your speech, but we should focus now on the actual facts, not your perceived whimsies."

"Those of us who lived on Granite Ledge knew how treacherous that rocky surface could be. Regardless of what all those other people said, the rock may have seemed bone-dry, but I insist the ladder was not secure where it stood. The awful proof still haunts me. Bacon slices, bits of cheese, rhubarb chunks—worst of all, blood in a big, wet, slimy puddle."

To make sure Beach paid attention to the point I appended some scientific terms. "Dry ledge or not, given the coefficient of friction between wood and rock, how could you expect a few square inches of contact to handle the load of a large ladder plus a human body?"

"I hope your delicacy in describin' your dear departed husband as a 'body' lightens the load for you. However, I recall yesterday you said you were not a ladder expert—those were your exact words, I can assure you—so clearly now you have stepped on turf where you don't belong. Now, if you can't—or won't—answer where the ends of the ladder were, perhaps an easier question would be whether the ladder was on or under the corpse."

"I would prefer the term 'husband' to 'corpse.' It is now my turn to remind you of what I said a minute ago. The ladder lay beside my husband. You will find that in my courtroom testimony as well, although you did not see reason to include it in your devious little summary."

"Relax, my friend. That was a way to jar your memory and knock some new information free. It was a little trick I used to double-check on things."

"I wish everything I saw that day could be knocked right out of my head." What I really wished was to knock the liar right over the head. "Moreover, we're not anywhere near becoming friends."

"If the ladder had been on top of your husband, that detail would suggest a push from the top. So Luke would be my target again. If it had been under your husband, then, Harley and Myles would be the targets. That would narrow things down a bit, which is why I am curious about the point."

"A detective has to play with the cards dealt."

"But all detectives bank on Lady Luck as well."

Rising to change his luck perhaps, Beach moved over to the porch rail, where he fingered a line of dirt-crusted paw prints not yet washed away by the rain. Most evenings, after we went to bed, the raccoons tidied up. The mother climbed up the balustrade, trekked along the rail, hopped onto the tabletop, and swept dinner down to the children clustered on the floor below. I usually left a few treats out for them, but with care to see that their biggest enemy, my husband, remained unaware. Their black masks predicted house robberies to Nate and forest masquerades to me.

"Okay, Mrs. B, we need to pass on from your reticence about the ladder. Actually, it's been hard not to rush on to the fingerprints. There was plenty of evidence there to help the jurors pick their man."

"Help pluck him like a rabbit out of a hat expresses it better. Sensible folk would not have turned to such legerdemain."

"Admittedly, identification by fingerprints is relatively new—the FBI only began to collect them a few years ago—but it's a true science. Think how some good prints would've helped pin down those greasy anarchists, Sacco and his crony, Vanzetti."

"That fiasco proves my argument about this trial."

Chubby face beaming with glee, Beach began to sing. "Ah yes, those fingerprints! Talk about works of art. Those close-up photos were spectacular—hidden images that swirl like magic in special dust and ultraviolet light."

"You are putting butter on bacon. Such exaggeration renews another hot debate. Is photography art or merely science?"

"We're talkin' about geometric patterns, not brush marks."

"Well, what was a ladder leaning against a barn became an easel in the courtroom. You should be thankful the wood sanded by Father's hands made a sketch pad for the men's fingers."

"I thought of it as a police blotter. What their fingers wrote on his ladder must've turned your father in his grave."

"But were those writings graffiti or hieroglyphics?"

"The ability to define and separate the ridge patterns of each man's fingertips was quite impressive—even if the graphics did go over your head."

The male songbird was listening to his own song. I needed to squelch Beach's attempt to dazzle me with his command of the new technology. "Actually, I did comprehend the fingerprint specialist, but the analysis was not conclusive at all. The only thing it proved was that each suspect had handled the ladder at some point. We did not need fingerprint magic to know that."

"On the contrary. The study was accurate down to the tiniest of traces—even when, at first, the results seemed to defy logic."

Dampening this ardor was worth another try. "The excessive minutiae only bored me."

"The process depended on the smallest details. Recognition of specific characteristics permitted the identification of each suspect. It was really quite instructive in the end."

The rain was now intense enough to wash the raccoon trial away and chase Beach back from the rail. Because the Windsor was still unavailable, he took a lesser chair. Sitting upright, he squared his shoulders and set his chin, which made him look tough, except for the dewlap of skin drooping under his jaw. At least, this image was more pleasant than the forward thrust of hostility I was used to seeing.

By this time, my new friend, the black ant, had discovered some golden eggs at the foot of the bulky bean stock. Lofting one overhead, she started the journey back to her nest to report her find. When Beach's thumb squashed the scout in one squish, I realized a single conclusive fingerprint would have brought him satisfaction, too.

"For example, look at what we learned about your nephew, Myles. While his fingerprints were on the ladder, the deficiency of prints near its lower end tended to clear him of the crime. I admit I struggled to explain their absence for a while." Such an admission I never expected from my self-ordained tutor.

"Well, I submit my nephew only handled one end. I recall he was the leader as he and Luke carried the ladder past me on the porch. The end he held logically went up to the roof."

An alarm rang out. "Hold on a second! A few minutes ago you carped about ladder ends, but now you use the damn things to support your argument. Well, the end of interest for this discussion was on the ground." The clanging kept on. "Remember we had testimony that Myles pulled the ladder out with his hands on the bottom. So why were there no prints there? In fact, I will be more specific. Harley stated that Myles had grabbed the lowest rung, but it was completely clean. However, I found the clue I needed to explain that discrepancy, thanks to you." Forced to share the bell rope, Beach tolled more gently. "You described how the day had started out cold. Ergo! When Myles went to work, he must've put on gloves." The final pealing tailed off in an echo. "Myles would've taken 'em off in the outhouse, of course, but he could've pulled 'em back on—when he decided to stop Nate's little work project, once and for all."

"You are getting hung up on a pair of gloves nobody could seem to recall seeing."

"You testified in court that you couldn't remember if Myles had gloves on or not. It would be helpful if your memory got better now."

Myles passed with the ladder.

Brown hands on blond ash.

Veins full in his struggle.

"When you work as hard as we did, grime and gloves can look the same. It is hard to be sure what I saw. I have to say I just do not remember."

"For some reason, Patience Brewster, the eagle eye who could tell us his straps were goin' up and not down, can't remember whether she saw gloves or not." Not waiting for defense or rebuttal, the inventive Beach floated an alternative. "Now, if for some reason Myles chose not to wear gloves, he still could have wiped his prints off on purpose. After all, no one ever did adequately explain those peculiar smudges found at the very bottom of the uprights, the ones around the ladder's feet—the ones that did suggest wipin' off."

"Why, in Heaven's name, would he ever think of wiping them off?"

"Easy. Like yourself, Myles spent his free time with his nose in a book."

"A most rewarding endeavor I can assure you. Maybe you should try it sometime."

"Your nephew had to have read about fingerprints somewhere."

"That is easy to explain. We did not restrict ourselves to reading classics. We liked mysteries, too. Indeed, two of Mark Twain's books involve fingerprints, but—"

"I'm talkin' about how Myles talked about Galton's details and the files the FBI keeps when he testified in court. That's pretty damned sophisticated. Maybe he got fired up as he thought about how to pull off the perfect crime."

"Because my nephew preferred to study rather than to till or milk does not make him a criminal."

"To wipe away fingerprints would be precocious for a teenager stuck on a farm, but appropriate for a criminal determined to get away. The ladder was covered with his prints everywhere but at its foot."

"The absence of prints cannot prove him guilty."

"Well, it couldn't be mere coincidence, I'm sure."

"My prints were nowhere on that ladder. Does that make me guilty?" Dropping that rock on Beach's foot stopped him dead in his tracks. Extending my hands, palms up, fingers spread, toward him expressed how eager the aunt was to protect her firstborn nephew from scrutiny.

In my rush to rescue Myles, I turned the spotlight on Luke. "Let me play the devil's advocate for a minute. In fairness to Myles, the experts made a similar fuss about Luke's fingerprints at the other end of the ladder."

"Luke's prints were all over the ladder. However, as you say, it was shown at one end that his fingers had been on the outer face of the uprights and his thumbs on the inner side. That end must have been the one up at the eaves."

My stint as prosecutor was over, for Beach rolled out more facts. "His fingers pointed both front and back. One direction showed he had climbed the ladder, but the other proved he had grabbed the ladder when he stood on the roof. The set of digits at the very top of the uprights pointed away from the roof, not towards it. That would be the optimal way to push his uncle down to his death."

Beach's ice cube lenses gleamed, excitement streaming from the hot eyes behind. "We heard Luke wanted to get down off the roof, but your husband wouldn't let him. Can't you just see the poor lad at the roof's edge? He shakes that ladder in rage? He gives it one big shove? As a matter of fact, did you see him do it?"

Hole halfway up.

Ladder at the eaves.

Luke drifting.

Up and down.

Back and forth.

"I could only see part of the roof and Luke only part of the time. I would have had to guess where he was."

"And I have to guess whether you're tellin' the whole truth or not."

"We know Luke left the roof through the hole into the loft. I wonder if he ever even saw what happened to my husband."

"But I wonder if, before he left, he was up to more than just bein' the clod he seemed to be in court."

Up on the barn, the open mouth in the roof yelled down to me that Luke had not done it. The rain splattering around the hole added exclamation points.

My effort to protect Myles had made my other nephew vulnerable to inspection. To rescue Luke from the backwash of guilt I had released meant it was Harley's turn to be in the limelight. "In fairness to Luke, and Myles as well, my brother-in-law's fingerprints were found on only one end of the ladder, too. You have to consider that fact the same way."

"You've got that right. They were on the other end from Luke's prints—at the end where there was a problem finding any trace from Myles. That, by the way, was further proof of which end was the bottom of the ladder because we know Harley never left the ground. His thumbprints were on the outside, pointing up plus they were on one upright only. That was the upright nearest to the apple tree unless, of course, the ladder danced a pirouette on the way down."

After laughing himself breathless, Beach bit off some air. "What does that suggest about Harley's role in this to you?" Pursed lips, he hissed the real question. "Are you sure you didn't see him sink back down on the tree?"

Tree swaying.
Apples bobbing.
Red hat moving.
Harley erect.

"I still cannot be sure. Maybe he was getting up. I really do not know."

"You understand, don't you, that the presence of his prints limited to one side of the ladder—remember he was never really involved in the repair project—suggests Harley got up from his nap and pulled the ladder down?"

"Is that your convoluted way of saying he was guilty of murder?"

"It's a little tricky because your brother-in-law swore he'd helped the boys drag the ladder out from the shed. That could explain the thumbs up and outside configuration. Myles did admit Harley was in the shed when the two brothers went to get the ladder. Harley was probably out there in search of one of his bottles, so it is possible he put his mitts on the ladder then."

"Even if you do not believe Harley handled the ladder in the shed, by the time he got to the top of the hill he could not have handled anything. He was really drunk."

"Only if he was really drunk. I don't mean really drunk like very drunk. I mean really drunk as in truly drunk."

"Well, he smelled like it."

"He's no fool, nor are you. Who would know better than a drinker to cover himself and his breath with booze if he wanted to appear drunk?" The moralizing shifted far afield. "I trust you noticed your brother-in-law never once referred to those boys as his sons throughout the trial. I was curious to see if a sober Harley would show any affection." Perhaps a drunken dad or a father who did not care lurked in Beach's closet.

Stimulated to defend the brother-in-law I had exposed, I turned the spotlight of suspicion back onto Myles and Luke. "Understand that blaming Harley depends on believing Luke and denying Myles."

Prosecutor or defender? Who was who? Beach and I were arguing the way the attorneys had brawled in court. Fighting to save their respective clients, they attacked the opposing counsels and clients with cruelty.

"Round and round we go, flogging the same horse. The prints do not tell the whole tale. I'm sure of that, Mr. Beach."

"Maybe not the whole tale, but enough to help me cut right to the heart of the matter."

"It will take a lot more honing to let you open it up. If I were you, I would consider tempering your approach with some common sense."

"I figure I've got all I will get from reviewing the print evidence with you, so we can move on."

"Well, before we do, I need to serve up one final fingerprint fact. There was irrefutable proof my husband was instrumental in his own demise. His prints were on the ladder."

I had thrown one of my best pitches.

I left the mound and headed for my dugout.

La passion fait souvent un fou du plus habile homme,
et rend souvent les plus sots habiles.

Passion often makes a madman of the cleverest man,
and often renders the greatest of fools clever.

—La Rochefoucauld
Maximes

FINAL ARGUMENTS

Returning to the porch with some lemonade, which I had ready in the fridge, I anticipated reviving my opponent after whiffing him on the fingerprint analysis. But I found my curve ball had not retired the side, for Beach rejected the refreshment and stepped up to bat again.

"The competition in the courtroom seemed to do a number on you, Mrs. B. I could tell the back-and-forth about the ladder made you uncomfortable, and the fingerprint business doubled your distress."

"It was more tedious than uncomfortable. In the beginning, I struggled a bit because I did not have the background to understand many parts of it. But, as I got more and more educated, I liked the challenge of sorting things out."

"Much of the evidence was circumstantial in this case, so it was very important that the details be handled by experts. No wonder some of the discussion went right by you."

"It was simple jargon. No, that is unfair. It was very scientific jargon. However, I felt it was wrong to stubbornly focus on material fact and discount human psychology. Of course, the court never allowed me to get my opinion on that subject into the record."

"You shouldn't be so critical. After all, you are quite stubborn yourself. One could even say opinionated."

"Testifying is based on personal experience. Opinions come from that. Expression of those opinions should not be denied."

"Alright then, in your opinion, what should the court have considered?"

"The personalities of those involved, which I daresay would have defined each as innocent."

"And I daresay the inner workin's of each did get examined."

"People, however, are not clocks."

"Clocks tick and tock. People do, too. What they say reflects what drives 'em. The defendants were listened to."

"Listened to, yes, but not heeded. More attention should have been paid to the psychological components—both conscious and unconscious—that determined their behavior. The analysis was superficial from the beginning, and things only got worse. For example, the three men should never have been accused, let alone tried."

"How so?"

"I accept that each of the men had increasing anger directed toward my husband. And I will agree that, on the day in question, the cauldron was at a rapid boil. But I do not believe any one of them had sufficient cause to commit murder."

"What about a combination that gave them the strength for a cooperative effort?"

"That would have been impossible, too. There was never a hint of sufficient cohesion among them to act collectively."

"I tend to agree with you on the solidarity issue. Three may keep a secret, if two of 'em are dead—that's what Poor Richard taught us." Surprisingly, this Franklin fan skipped his chance to direct more humor toward the Poor family.

"Bear in mind, Mr. Beach, I was the one who lived together with these individuals for years, so I was—and am—in the best position to judge them."

"On the other hand, if you had teamed up with 'em, well, then, that makes any interpretation you offered—or offer—suspect."

A slow inhale prefaced a quick outburst. "Actually, it's impossible for me to imagine you workin' with any one of 'em to do your husband in. First of all, I noticed you, as bereaved widow and distraught family member, didn't really do much to support your kin in court. Now, since I have managed to wade through your palaver, I question your commitment to your family even more."

"It is correct to say I did not team up with any of those men, but it is wrong to say I have not committed to the family. My mind and heart told me those three men did not kill my husband. I believe I best served the family by staying neutral and not lying to protect anyone. That was too likely to backfire, and, even more important, I have always acted with integrity. My statements in court and comments to you over the past few days attest to that. Has it been a waste of time for you to learn that Granite Ledge was not a bed of roses? That's hardly palaver."

"You may have taken the high road, and maybe there was no team, but we do know all three men agreed Nate was the Devil."

"You mean they tried to agree. As I implied before, that was one of the most infuriating things about the trial."

"What? That they all agreed?"

"No. That the lawyers can force any witness to give the answers they seek."

"Interrogation is what lawyers do."

"But they do not do it fairly. If they do not hear what they want, they rephrase the questions until the answers come out the way they want."

"It's only in a legitimate effort to be accurate."

"If the answers do not come out the way they want, they change the line of questioning. If, by some miracle, the witness beats them, they have that part struck from the record."

"Yet you, Mrs. B, you were joustin' with the lawyers like it was some great game. Now that I know you, I realize you positively enjoyed the fracas. That's my—impartial—opinion."

"Enjoyed being accused of conveniently forgetting? Happy to hear I was defending a bunch of brutes? I think you missed the poison in their questions and the antidote of my replies."

"Come now, you invited those darts." Could he see through my pupils into the depths of my brain?

"I resented the implication I was a helpless female at the hest of a bunch of conniving males."

"Is your reference to the lawyers or your kinsmen?"

"Both—all of them—I was not about to let any man get the better of me."

"You acted like your confounded integrity was at stake. Indeed, your performance was topnotch."

"I was not play-acting."

"Did you feel safe because you weren't on trial yourself? That is, you did not have a thing to lose?"

"Was I supposed to let them distort and misinterpret the evidence?"

"Each of the men was on the defensive. Your approach was offensive." Beach was either punning or pummeling.

"They were underdogs who needed my help."

"Did that extend to perjury?"

"Each man had a private set of truths."

"My question referred to your testimony, not theirs. Anyway, it was clear to me truth went out the window of that courtroom."

"Are we on trial again? You are like those other buzzards circling to pick someone clean. Everyone—be it prosecutor, lawyer, or judge—was out to find a scapegoat."

"My goodness, do you really mean to call your relatives goats? The court procedure was fundamentally sound to my view." While it meant a spanking for me, I had redirected Beach's aim.

"I disagree with you, Mr. Beach. The process was flawed. It did not matter whether the person chosen was guilty or not, so long as they picked someone."

"Any—one?"

"No. Anyone."

"And your first choice was?"

"The fall guy could just as well have been Harley, Myles, or Luke. Or Molly. Or the rooster on the ridgepole."

Luke on the roof.

Harley by the tree.

Myles on the path.

Fluid and free before the moment.

Later frozen in time and space.

Wound up now, I did not yield the podium to Beach. "The jury's decision bewilders me. Those jurors folded under pressure to make a choice. Some choice. Any choice."

"A hung jury benefits no one."

"How they picked even one perpetrator is beyond my comprehension."

"Yet I remind you the vote was unanimous."

"The jury's choice was an arbitrary guess. Like a shot in the dark."

Luke hollering.

Harley swearing.

Myles shouting.

A trio of accusations.

"Enough of this, Mrs. B. This is just an attempt to sidetrack me. We've covered the ladder and the prints. Given what we know about who grabbed where, we must look at the fall itself. There are three possible reasons why the ladder went down."

Despite my obvious choice, Beach chose to rerun the list. "The first would be that your husband killed himself, but I've eliminated suicide. Nobody of any intelligence would've pushed himself down on a ladder. A swan dive from the roof would've been infinitely more effective and, I might add, dramatic."

Leaning toward his audience, back of his hand by his lips, the lecturer whispered a quip. "But a halfwit might've pushed someone else down."

Such denigration disgusted me. "I hoped you would have done better than that by now, but I can see that was too much to expect. Yet you are right about suicide. Over many years of hard luck, Nate displayed a capacity to cope with the biggest calamities. He rode right over the toughest obstacles. Self-destruction was simply not in his bag of tricks."

"It gives me pleasure to uncover one thing at last that we both agree on."

"What is more, my husband took extreme pleasure in his position as our leader. He was a Caesar. He delighted in watching others squirm under his foot. He never would have cashed in his kingdom for a horse."

"How well stated. The psychologist speaks, and I accept your formulation, and now I wonder if you'll go along with mine. It is a bit more basic. Will you concur your husband was a true bastard?" Beach hit hard again to crack me, but that possibility had crashed with the ladder. "The term is not a reference to his lineage."

"Speaking of bastards, the typical insurance agent would jump through hoops if he thought he could prove suicide. In your case, your company would not have to pay a red cent, and you would win that fancy award. Of course, we can bury that sham now, for we know how little you actually care about your job and those rewards."

"I'm not the one under examination, so let's get back on track."

"Certainly. Let us take up the idea of an accident again. It is easy to see how a few small mistakes by my husband could have knocked the ladder down. Maybe he twisted it getting on. Maybe his foot slipped going down. I hate to get anywhere near your fashionable fingerprinting again, but perhaps his hands jolted the ladder, causing it to give out."

"Your husband was much too smart and too much in control to let that happen. I sense your emotions have pushed you to grab and hang onto that frantic explanation because it makes you feel better. You're waxin' hysterical." If Beach hoped to knock me out of kilter, he was misdiagnosing. The psychologist in me knew I was, most definitely, not a hysteric.

"You need not be nervous. I don't mind a return to the prints for more help. The photographs were quite clear. They showcased your husband's fingers as though they were frozen to the ladder uprights in terror."

"Still photographs of a few fingertips cannot reveal the live action of a full pair of hands. I suspect Nate let go of the ladder. Remember he landed on his head. We need an explanation for that because most people falling from a height try to land feet first."

"In fact, I would have expected him to hang on to the ladder for safekeepin'—like a wooden parachute."

"Not Nate! He was a very, very confident man. He probably thought he could beat fate with what you just called a swan dive."

"Well, I can see how he wouldn't have wanted to be a skipper who went down with his ship. That would have made him seem as if he had succumbed to an upshot he couldn't command." Though it was a mixed-up comparison, it did fit Nate.

"So why not accept the accident as an accident?"

"You're such a dreamer. Your theory's baloney no matter how thin you try to slice it." The prosecutor continued loud and clear. "The fact is, it was a deliberate act. The final force was human. It was plain old murder."

Clouds had stolen all the light. The birds had taken to the trees. The wind had stopped. The rain was but a drizzle. The farm was still and silent.

"My husband is dead and buried. What good comes from pointing fingers, from fixing blame? Convicting a murderer does not help anyone."

"Just who do you hope to help?"

"I would like to help them all. It is tragic that, whoever may have been guilty, the fate of all of them—"

"We've touched on this before. In spite of what you'd like me to believe, there is a responsibility to identify the killer. The legal system—"

"There is another level of interpretation, and a much higher one at that. Even without the trial and the conviction, each man was on a preordained track."

"Do I and the rest of us heathens need to listen to your religious mumbo jumbo again?"

"Absolutely! You need to understand it, so I will lead you through it one more time. Not one of those men was going to return to Granite Ledge Farm."

Searching for illumination in the darkness of the porch, Beach leaned toward me.

"It was easy to predict the future, Mr. Beach, even before the jury's verdict. Driven Myles was on track to break away from this place for good. Disabled Luke was destined to be a lifelong ward of the State. Deteriorating Harley would never leave the hospital except in a pine box. Those truths were established truths. My husband's death was merely incidental. Do you not understand that by now?"

"You're in fantasy land. Do you actually believe each man was placed on a special path by some omniscient creature?"

"You just do not get it!"

"I get that you seem to think it was divine providence. Why, I'd rather accept what has happened to you as tough luck."

"I am not talking about what has happened to me."

"Nor should you be. The reason we have a corpse to talk about is because some unhappy person crept around this farm for years until he decided Nathaniel Brewster's time had come."

The darkness and drizzle had joined in laying a blanket of gloom. A cold, condensing mist shrouded the barn, its red walls and gray shingles reverting to black.

"I am sorry now that earlier I agreed to help you explore the issues theoretically. My husband was the only one creeping around on Granite Ledge Farm. However, I contend his behavior was not sufficient to ignite a murderous impulse in any one of the other men. Even if a fuse was smoldering, which I do not believe was the case, not one of them had the gumption necessary to kill another man."

"I disagree with you on that. There were loads of examples throughout the trial that showed how each had the capacity to take a life."

"But none of those anecdotes—those mindless exaggerations by people obviously unfamiliar with our life—involved putting a human to death. I argue for a greater power, for the work of a superior being."

"That's bull. You can forget God, and bad luck, too, for that matter. I'm certain a killer was behind this. That's the only logical explanation."

"But, even if one of them might have done it, there was too much chance of being seen by the others. Why, one would have to be crazy—"

"That's just it! To use your own term, crazy is the point." The famous forefinger tapped his temple twice. "Whoever was the monster was crazy. Absolutely crazy."

"Stop right there! Damn it, Beach. Stop right there."

"The killer was nuts, Mrs. B. That's spelled N—U—T—S."

This explosion proved a human time bomb had been ticking the whole time Beach had been grilling me. Those four letters, that single word, spelled the end because I was ready for his outburst.

This proclamation was a self-protective smoke screen. Unable to complete a suitable schema by interrogating me, Beach had settled on a weak way to excuse himself. If the killer was insane, Beach could not expect or be expected to find the answers to his questions and achieve his goal.

Having run into the brick wall of his own inability, he was trying to exonerate his crack-up by blaming the irrationality of a crazy being. Making craziness the linchpin was a ploy to try to stop the wheels on his self-image from coming off. The absurdity of forgiving himself showed how unrealistic the ordinarily practical man had become.

Beach, the egotistical self, could not think like the rational person he sought—the same one he now called nuts. Instead of unraveling and reweaving the particulars into a meaningful mesh, he had only twisted a rope of sand. In fact, when Beach invoked craziness, he had pointed to his head, not mine, and thus signaled his helplessness and hopelessness before the dilemma of identifying the culprit.

But, in one sense, I had failed as well. As I led Beach through the fog enveloping Granite Ledge Farm, I had given him the chance to see what life under the thumb of Nathaniel Brewster was really like. He should have recognized that wherever there is evil in the world, there is a human responsibility to correct it. Eradication of the source of evil is desirable, necessary, and just. Plainly, I had not succeeded in impregnating this justification in his brain or seeding this rightness in his heart. Since he was unable to perceive the problem, he could not visualize the solution. That was my failure.

I was dissatisfied with my effort, but still felt secure.

I was disappointed in my student, but was mainly mad at him.

To view the solution to our troubles as an act of insanity insulted me. To visualize the impetus as madness was a slap in my face. The sting from a man was there again and instantly predictive. I was not going to wilt under his accusation of craziness. By standing strong, I knew I could force him to retreat while still ignorant. The secret would remain intact.

No longer sneaking along under a smug hat of suspicion, Benjamin B. Beach was now sporting a cocky cap of conviction. It was time to knock it off. I would drive this most recent tormentor away to join the others. He was done for.

Exploiting my height, I rose to my feet. "I will not put up with your nonsense another minute. I refuse to participate in this travesty any longer. The interview is over."

Shrinking before my stare, the man fled down from the porch into the yard, so I sat down, satisfied.

A flock of sparrows and a pair of chipmunks stepped aside, but did not flee. Right at Beach's feet, one tolerant robin kept on pulling an earthworm into an elastic band and, once dinner popped out of the lawn, she lingered to eat.

Not only was the loser ignored, he was trapped in an inferior position—a liability in any battle—and he had run out of ammunition.

Back towards me to shut me out, Beach stared up at the barn.

The barn stared back.

How soon I was cut down,
When innocent at play,
The wind it blew a scaffold down
And took my LIFE away.

—Tombstone epitaph for Henry Brown
In Baldock, Hertfordshire, 1861

SENTENCING

Rain stopped, clouds gone, and sun out, Cock Robin made his customary mistake. The purple martins flew out of their gourds. A pileated woodpecker drummed deep in the woods. Life was starting up again.

Unmoving for many minutes, Beach first pawed, then stamped and, all of a sudden, charged the porch. Quick to dodge the bull's rush, the robin hopped to one side, the chipmunk couple scampered off, and the sparrows fluttered away.

At the top of the stairs, Beach snorted and stopped. Eyes flashing to his opened hands, he begged the arches, loops, and whorls for a final clue. Finding no answer, he clenched his fists and dropped his arms to his sides.

Stomping over to the table, Beach scooped up his paper piles. Stuffing the trash into his briefcase, he slammed it onto the chair.

Snatching up his pipe, he stormed to the edge of the porch. Smacking the bowl on the rail, as dead ashes showered to the ground, Beach launched a fiery attack.

"This damned place still hides an unnamed killer."

Steam sputtered from the crater within his molten face.

"An innocent man rots away, never to return."

Sparks crackled from the caverns of his fuming eyes.

"Two sorry relics live on, a woman and her dog."

209

A thunderbolt of declaration shot forth from a cloud of desperation.

"Be warned I will keep on digging."

But Molly and I blinked away his nagging finger.

"Benjamin Beach will unearth the guilty creature."

I knew the battle was over and it was time to end the war. "Should you choose to continue wasting your time, Ben, you can be sure it will not be back here on Granite Ledge Farm. I thought by now you would have recognized that you can never square a circle."

As I hiked my skirt and crossed one leg over the other in a closing flourish, Beach misread me one last time by believing his raised hand stopped me from getting up to escort him to the door. "I can see myself out, madam. I don't need the help of any woman."

"Well, mister, there is just one more thing before you go. You should acknowledge what you have learned from one. The gray mare proved to be the better horse."

The briefcase just about fell apart. The screen door all but broke off its hinges. The front door may have cracked, but its knocker countered with a brassy send-off.

The rooster, woodpecker, and martins were applauding.

I settled back in my rocker.

Molly curled up on my lap.

I'll have my brains ta'en out, and butter'd,
and give them to a dog for a new-year's gift.

—William Shakespeare
The Merry Wives of Windsor, Act III, Scene 5

FINAL JUSTICE

The sun had buried itself behind the mountain. Night was closing the hole in the barn's roof when the stack of shingles, which had parked there all winter, slid off in silence. I heard a thud and pictured a heap of splinters and chips. The scene was gloomy, but I felt happy. The last of my antagonists was gone. Savoring my freedom, I replayed the primal sequence:

Nate blasted Luke on the roof.

Harley snored against the tree.

Myles fled down the hill.

Patience lurked on the ledge.

"Well, Molly, I can say that nasty man was right about one thing, if nothing else." The tip of her tail fluttered at my voice. She was eager to hear more.

Quick to the basket.

Lid up. Pot open.

Slick yellow fingers.

Greasy ladder ends.

Hot sun. Slippery stone.

Seeping butter melt.

"Just as Beach said, it was a perfect day." A barred owl hooted her greeting to nightfall, and a mockingbird repeated the call.

Rocker still.

Eyelids shut.

Slip.

Splat.

Silence

"But he was wrong about my focus. It was a perfect day to act, not to snooze." My rocker creaked in approval, the song of its joints restored by the warmth of spring.

Scanning ears.

Sound of passing feet.

Squinting eyes.

Shadow on the path.

Time to wake the world.

"And there was that timely speech from a very good dog." Thanks flew to her ears and coursed through my arms as I cuddled Molly's head to my breast.

The barking broke the news.

An announcement of the kill.

An alibi for the killer.

"Yes, indeed, it was a fitting farewell for a very bad man." This conclusion I whispered through lips pressed into the soft hair on my ally's brow.

Luke drew Myles to the barn.

Harley fled by himself to the bushes.

Patience led Molly to the ladder.

"You've earned butter treats every day, my dear, as a reward for helping me get free." As Molly lifted her head to study me, my love dove into her deep brown eyes.

Buttery wood.

Hungry dog.

Lapping tongue.

Kisses to the savior's feet.

"But it will not be served on ladder ends again."

Out in the pitch-black before us, the trees were not cracking, the leaves not rustling, and the spring peepers not calling. Basking in this peace and quiet, I should have remained happy.

Nate was behind me. The Poors were out of my hands. I had driven

Beach away. Molly was beside me, and I was looking ahead to Cleve. With everything so perfect, the show should have been over.

My husband's end had brought me some remorse, of course, but I could live with that. Right now, however, after smoldering for many months, pangs of guilt churned in my stomach, chest, and brain.

Abandoning the Poors was gnawing at my gut. One hopeless, one helpless, and one hyperactive, they were still my responsibilities. They always had been. I had not abandoned them before. I could not do so now.

Deceiving Cleve was breaking my heart. So trusting and loyal, he deserved the truth. If the facts destroyed his love, that would be my forfeit. If I could earn his respect and preserve his friendship, it would be worth it.

Not being Patience was poisoning my soul. Dire situations did not justify devious means. Underhanded methods ensured later disasters. Dedication to integrity had sustained me in the past. It could rescue me now.

In defeating Beach, I thought I had choreographed a finale, but it was crystal clear now there was going to be an encore. Faced with losing everything and everybody, I had one more step to take. As I had gambled to get rid of my husband, I had to gamble to retain the others.

Sleeping on it is the common advice given to someone faced with making an important decision, so I headed off to bed with Molly. I was unsure if I would sleep at all, but we could always talk things over some more.

Breakfast was reheated coffee and cold beans, so I could get to the day's work faster. A little ironing finished up the laundry for the week. Cleaning out the icebox was easy, for a woman and a dog barely use one shelf. I only needed to smooth a few wrinkles out of the bedcovers since I had wanted nothing between Molly and me throughout the night. Sweeping the house was the last tidy-up, and it ended in the living room by plan. After I wrote out instructions for dog care at the rolltop desk beside Mother's memorial couch, I placed them on the curly maple table under the Wimple family pipe stand. Harley and Luke were never coming back to see that heirloom, Myles would shun it after the court rescinded his conviction, but Cleve might enjoy it as a reminder of us all.

Coming to rest in my rocker, I took Molly onto my lap in the same way our life together had started.

Before she curled up in a ball, I gave her a hug.

"Well, old girl, I have to tell the judge what happened."

She raised her head and looked at me.

"It's time to send a call to Mr. Parsons. I'm sure he'll drive us into town."

As I gave her a final kiss, she licked my wet cheek.

"Talk, Molly! Talk!"